What Gina Did

Jacqueline Bowman

Cover design by Holly Matthews

ISBN: 978-0-244-45340-4

PublishNation
www.publishnation.co.uk

For Alan

1

Gina knew that she would have to deal with Zak, at the moment he kissed her in front of their friends and family, on the steps of the registry. On other occasions, moisture had not been a problem, indeed it had been a lubricious delight, but this…was different. How could she have failed to notice that he actually dribbled from one corner of his mouth. And his hot sweaty hand on the shoulder of her grey silk suit, was not welcome. She flung her bouquet, right at Issy, and tried to put the kiss out of her mind.

For a second wedding, it was rather lavish, especially following the tragedy which had marked the end of the previous one. Obviously Zak bankrolled it, or rather his rich Saudi father did. His parents, looking as wealthy as in fact they were, smiled up at them from the small crowd and led the way to the waiting cars.

Gina looked wonderful. Naturally beautiful, tall, slim and dark eyed, with thick, brown, slightly curly hair, which had been piled on top for this occasion, she looked like a sultry, Arabian princess. Not having known her father, she had only her mother's scanty information about him. He was mixed race and had been a 'good-looking bastard' according to Louise.

Gina seriously thought that she and Zak should lead the group, but you can't argue with the very rich. They always seem to know who's in charge!

The party was fun despite the fact that alcohol was not a big player. They went on to a club to get drunk and dance and generally make fools of themselves. Back at Zak's flat, they all carried on carrying on and the following day, the couple was barely in a fit state to make the flight to St Kitts, for a brief honeymoon.

At Heathrow, Zak's mother cried, his father embraced him, Gina's mother just looked miserable despite the fact that she was to be treated to lunch at a smart restaurant to talk about the newly weds, obviously, once they had left.

Eight years earlier, Gina had married Ed, following a brief liaison after which she believed herself pregnant, ironic in retrospect. It was easy to encourage Ed to ask her to marry him, which, despite her mother's protests, Ed's seniority and her own youth, she'd agreed to with enthusiasm. As it happened, Ed adored Gina, and though he was 17 years older, she, at 18, was happy with her sugar daddy.

A week after the wedding and before she had the chance to tell him of her interesting condition, it turned out that it wasn't - interesting, that is. What's more, she couldn't. Or rather, she felt, Ed couldn't. Not that they didn't try. Ed was a lusty 35 year old and she was even lustier, so they had plenty of opportunities to procreate.

What was odd was that she knew Ed had two sons from a former marriage. Apparently, according to Maggie and Isobel, her two pals from schooldays, they were blond, blue-eyed giants whereas Ed was quite dark and barely 5'10". It was commonly assumed that Caroline, his first wife, and his senior by a couple of years, had been carrying the older one when she married him, and according to the gossips, went on having the affair for years until Ed 'found out', and divorced her. She got a huge settlement as well as her two gorgeous boys, the younger one presumably by her long-term lover also, whom she had since married.

Of course, perhaps Gina should have paid more attention, but she was young, besotted with Ed's good looks, his wealth and the possibility that she was pregnant!

But nothing happened. They did not conceive, and apart from this they were reasonably happy for a few years. Ed earned big money having inherited his father's butchery business, and had recently opened three more shops and a meat warehouse in the Midlands, with several supermarket contracts and he'd cornered the market on the fancy and expensive restaurants in the centre of England. He had also recently set up a link overseas, and he had the organic demographic well sorted.

So when he married Gina, he was quite a wealthy businessman and was able to provide very well for his new, adorable young wife. Together, they were a handsome couple, Ed, though a little short, extremely good looking, with thick, dark hair, deep-set eyes and a smooth, solidly angled jaw, always slightly unshaven. They had a grand house, fast cars, enjoyed overseas travel and Gina had a great wardrobe full of fabulous clothes, shoes and handbags. Their friends weren't altogether Gina's favourite kind of people; some of the women were so much older than her. Ed's business partners were of course more his age, and she failed to make many intimate friends, but they went to dinners and met people in smart bars, saw shows, and now and again she and Ed went to a club, but in all truth that wasn't really Ed's scene, so they asked acquaintances round occasionally, and lived a relatively quiet life.

2

Sometimes Gina felt cheated, bored, hard done by, or all three on a bad day, but on the whole, life trundled on. 8 years went by, she, still hoping for a child, fending off her mother's insistent questioning, and trying to be forbearing. She went to the local radio studio four mornings a week to do some clerical work. This was despite Ed's objections, believing that his wife didn't need a job. Financially, this was true, but she felt happier doing something, and enjoyed her time there. Largely, she was in charge of her own area - barely a cubbyhole of space, and she didn't need to answer to anyone, as long as she got on with the fairly dull tasks she had been assigned. At lunchtimes, she enjoyed the company of others and was admired by her colleagues.

Gina sometimes wondered if her calm and happy childhood had spoiled her somewhat. She remembered a very cherishing atmosphere at home with her mother. Louise, who had married young, had Gina relatively late, considering her early marriage. Once, when she was about six, her mum had asked her if she remembered her sister. She had said no, she didn't, and in fact at the time did wonder what her mother meant. But something in her tone suggested to Gina that she should never question her mother about this again. In truth she had barely remembered this exchange in later years and assumed that she had at best imagined it, at worst just forgotten. As an only child therefore, she was somewhat indulged. Her mother gave her a great deal of attention and organized her nursing career to be with Gina as much as she possibly could, arranging shifts and days off to coincide with school times and holidays. Her grandmother was helpful in caring for her too, and she and Gina had a very loving relationship, though she recalls her Gran and her mother occasionally disagreeing about the way Gina was being brought up.

'You're too easy with her - give in too much. She needs a firmer hand.'

'Oh mum, you're just so old-fashioned. She has her own views...'

'Too many of them if you ask me...'

'I didn't...'

'Maybe you should...'

'Mum! She's very precious to me. You know that and you know why.'

'I do, but you shouldn't let it spoil her.'

Such were the random exchanges that Gina overheard between her mum and her Gran and Gina was sure that her father's disappearance meant that her mother doted on her so much more than might be thought of as her entitlement. In an odd sort of way, Gina recognized this and tried not to take advantage. Unselfish by nature, but quick tempered, and sometimes headstrong, she often acted precipitately, and she knew that it upset her mother. She also knew that her mother tried her hardest not to be too critical. When she was an early teenager, and her friends came to their house, they experimented with cigarettes and alcohol. Her mum was indulgent; Gina heard her on the phone to Maggie's mum:

'Oh, Sue, they're just kids, they just want to try things...........well, I don't suppose banning them from the house when they do this will stop them.........No. I don't.........So. But Sue! No! We can do that......well, then they'll experiment somewhere else and we won't know where they are or who they're...........Sue, listen, no, I can't do that, I trust Gina to do the right thing.........oh, don't say that, they are such good friends. Maggie will be more upset than.............' And Gina had deliberately walked into the room so that her mother could see her and she rang off hastily. For some weeks, Gina did not see Maggie and she knew that she had been forbidden to meet with her for a while. Gina was distressed and put out by this. Maggie was almost the exact opposite of her own physical self. Very tall, big-bodied and very red-headed, her creamy skin was sown with many freckles which multiplied in abundance whenever she was in the sun. But unusually for someone of this colouring, she was calm and kind and did not respond to the usual taunts which seem to follow redheads universally. In fact she was given to pensive contemplation, and her opinion was always speculative. She was a wonderful friend for

Gina, getting her to see reason where Gina would answer hotly and immediately. She had called Gina impetuous from an age when she didn't even really know what it meant, but she was right! Maggie used words in that way, even as a teenager, and Gina teased her often sometimes laughing at her and asking the meaning of a word that she was sure Maggie did not know and causing her some embarrassment!

Maggie did complain about her bulk and often tried an outlandish new diet, which sometimes she was able to persuade Gina to share. As teenagers they consulted not only on diets but on every subject imaginable. They discussed everything from skin care to contraception, from hair products to boyfriends and personal issues that they were certain would make their mothers blush, so Gina was especially troubled and cross about their forced separation and was angry with Maggie for not resisting what Gina felt was Sue's ruling. When they began to get together again a couple of months later, Gina told Maggie how she had felt at the time, but Maggie had just shrugged.

'Well, here we are - still OK aren't we?' This was characteristic of Maggie - taking things as they came, not making a fuss, and using her favourite phrase - 'It'll be fine - you'll see.'

'Yes, we are still OK,' and Gina hugged her friend.

But such instances of dissent with her mother were relatively rare and as Gina went through her teenage years, she experienced little distress or sadness, she was a normal girl who was kind and generous even if she was somewhat impetuous. She could recall spending all her savings on a gift for her mum's special birthday. Her Grandma had told her that being 40 was very important so Gina had gone into the West End and bought expensive perfume, soaps and other fancy toiletries with all the money that she had saved over a year, and when she gave the package to her mum, Louise had burst into tears and hugged Gina until she could barely breathe.

'Why did you spend all your money on me?'

'Just wanted to - I love you Mum.'

'You're a bit impulsive Gina.'

'No, I'm not, it's not impulsive, it's mmm, it's spontaneous. That's what Amy says I am.'

Amy was one of her newest and now closest school friends. She was a talkative, bubbly blonde. Although she hated her uncontrollable curls, she was indisputably pretty, very popular, a constant chatterbox, also something of a gossip.

'What does Amy know?'

'I gave her my blue jacket and she said that...'

'You did what?' Lou sounded outraged.

'Gave it her. My blue jacket.' Gina had shrugged unconcernedly.

'Gina, get it back. I love that jacket.'

'No mum, just because you bought it for me, doesn't mean you can have an opinion about it. It didn't really suit me. Looks great on Amy...'

'But she's three inches shorter than you and a bit wider, too!'

'That's why it works better on her.'

Gina and her mum exchanged many such conversations, and often enough Louise would end up biting her lip, giving in, not discussing the topic any more - knowing that Gina could always find a logical response, that in the end Gina would have the last word. That in truth, Gina was probably right.

During those years she occasionally wondered at her mother's remark about a sister, did she really ask that? Of course she never referred to it. Sometimes, her mother would become pensive and Gina could not get her attention but she just needed to keep nagging and eventually her mother would respond. Once, Gina found her mother in tears. She asked her why.

'Just feel a bit down.'

'What's bothering you?'

Lou laughed and pulled the back of her hand across her eyes,

'Just getting old and wondering what will become of me.'

'Whatever do you mean?'

'Oh it's just hormones Gina.'

'Yeah, well, I have those, I'm fifteen.'

'Right. Well. I'm nearly 40. It can be tough.'

At forty, Louise still looked great. Slim enough, her darkish hair now peppered with grey, suited her very well, though she mostly tied it back in a rough bunch. At about 5'4" Gina was already the same height as her mum and clearly had some further growing still to do.

7

Gina decided that it was because her mum realised that she couldn't have any more babies now she was 40 and when she talked to her gran about it, she agreed.

'That'll be why darling,' her gran had said.

'Why didn't mum get married again gran?'

'Nobody good enough for her!' Her grandma had laughed and hugged Gina.

Gina never caught her mum crying again.

Her father had left when she was a baby so of course Gina could not have known him. Sometimes she wished she did have a sister, who would obviously have been older and then she could have asked her what dad was like. Asking mum was out of the question. Louise called him a complete shit and a bastard, but offered no details. In fact she seldom mentioned him at all.

3

Thus, her childhood was largely untroubled and her schooldays pleasant; as a teenager she was very popular. She could always afford to be choosy about her friends. Issy, Amy and Maggie were very close to her then and she still thought of them as her best friends. Of course there were boys; Gina was always the pretty one, and she wasn't averse to allowing a hand on her breast or along her thigh, indeed, she was 'far too interested,' Lou insisted.

'You've got to get your A-levels - and then get some more qualifications. Go to college. Leave the boys alone.'

Issy was not a good influence in those days, although she and Gina were similar in many ways. Issy, dark and petite, and a real flirt, with what she lacked in beauty, made up for in a chatty, engaging personality. Issy was also very smart, although neither she nor the rest of the world realised it at this time.

When they were out together, Issy would be the first to strike up a conversation with the best looking boys in the place, whether it was at the local disco or in later years, in the pub, but often enough, it was Gina that became the focus of their attention.

And Gina did protest that it was the boys that wouldn't leave her alone, and she had plenty of short-lived friendships with some of them. She complained that they were childish and only interested in sticking their hands up her skirt, but it didn't stop her going out on plenty of dates, even though her mother was keen for her to study and was set on her further education.

But at the end of the summer, a year before she took her A-levels, she left school. Her friends were astonished because she was really clever according to any test or exam she had ever taken. She was clearly capable of taking exams and gaining entrance into university, but suddenly, precipitately, she just made up her mind to leave.

Her form teacher called her in for 'a chat' and Gina kept the appointment, but apparently, according to Miss Seymour, she got very angry, shouted at her, and then stormed out. Miss Seymour asked Maggie if she could throw light on this uncharacteristic behaviour but Maggie couldn't. She was as shocked and surprised as anyone, and when she asked Gina, was hurt by the dismissive response she got. It was so unlike Gina to be short with her.

'Just don't ask about it. It's nothing to do with you!' had been her response.

'But Gina, we were going to be together at uni, we were ...'

'No,' Gina interrupted her sharply, 'I've changed my mind.'

'You're weird and pretty dumb too,' Maggie said hoping a cruel remark might provoke her friend, but it didn't. She tried 'This is not like you at all Gina, is there something wrong?' But that got no response either.

Gina was just not interested in talking about her decision. At that time, she did not want to further her education. She wanted a job. She wanted some money so that she could 'go out and have fun' in her words.

Maggie said 'Even Issy is going to Uni. You could do that and you could have fun too ...'

'Too much work to do at college. I can't do all that. I want to enjoy myself.'

'There's plenty of time for that,' Lou remonstrated, echoing Maggie.

'I want it now,' Gina argued, 'while I'm young.'

It was the only time that she and her mother had had a serious disagreement over something significant. They almost came to blows. Gina had thrown her school bag forcefully across the table in the direction of her mother, and Lou was clearly very distressed that her bright and able daughter was about to embark on a wasted life, which is how she saw it, rather than 'bettering herself'. Gina was impatient and dismissive and had to do a lot of talking and even then she could not convince her mother that she was making the right decision.

'Where will you get a job?'

'Somewhere.' Gina was hot and shouting. She banged her fist on the table and turned her back on Lou.

'Do you have any idea at all?'

'No, but I'm not stupid...' Now she grabbed her bag from where it had landed and swung it so that, again, it almost hit her mother.

'No, that's the problem, you're not, not in any way...'

10

'...and I'll find something.' And with no apology for almost whacking Lou she banged out of the door.

The job she had secured for herself was in a local travel agency. She was quick to learn and soon got the hang of identifying the right kind of ideas for various people. Turned out that she was good at it. In those days, the use of the internet was not common with most people, and her new expertise proved invaluable. He manner was engaging and her looks and figure were charming - clients enjoyed chatting with her. She was personable, seemed to have the right, light touch with customers, and was on their wavelength with great ease. The rather blowsy woman in charge did not like her much. Alice was 40-ish and rather large, though she made the most of her ample bosom and wore her skirts sufficiently short to demand at least a second look. She had a habit of bending over the filing drawers which stretched her skirt over her bottom, and she leaned deeply over the brochures, revealing a stunning cleavage. Even Gina had to admit that. The sad young man who also worked there was a milksop. Frank had an awkward manner and though he spent ages ogling Gina, she found him both tiresome and rather odd. At just 17, she was the youngest in the office and a bit naïve; she found it difficult to discourage him. Indeed, in her usual friendly way, seemed to have encouraged him, though this had not been her intention. He must have been in his late 20s and Gina wondered if he had ever even been on a date. Alice, more worldly-wise, showed amusement, if not disparagement. She didn't like Frank either, and displayed it by largely ignoring him. Gina was kinder, but she would have liked to stop his unwanted attentions.

Most people who came to the agency steered straight towards Gina, greatly to Alice's annoyance. And one day, in walked Ed.

At the moment when he had entered the office, Frank was again trying to make some sort of conversation with Gina. He had become bolder. He was asking where she lived, and of course Gina had no plans to tell him. She was, however, finding it hard to give him the brush-off. Ed waited for a moment, before Gina, who had already seen him, as he had entered the shop, turned brightly and asked if she could help. Ed leaned forward and said very quietly:

'Looks like it's you who needs the help,' and he raised his brows and inclined his head in Frank's direction.

Gina giggled.

'I think I do,' she said in a low voice.

'What are you doing for lunch?' he asked, quietly.

This was so surprising that Gina lost her usual composure and said:

'God! I've no idea!'

'Can I rescue you? Come to Carlo's - nice salads…'

Without giving it much more thought she said yes, but explained that she wasn't due to take lunch for 15 minutes.

'…and Alice would not approve,' she explained in a mock serious tone.

'No problem,' he said, 'I've got a great many questions to ask you about Malta as a holiday place.' He stroked his chin. 'I need a really good hotel.'

'Oh, I have loads of those.'

'Well, let's not go too fast, take your time,' he said, smiling.

She glanced up. He was a gorgeous looking guy and she liked the twinkle in his lovely dark eyes. She understood, and felt a bit foolish.

'Ah. Yes. OK. Those requirements might take some time to identify,' she said more loudly. 'I'll see what I can do.'

The fifteen minutes passed, and then she had announced that she was going to lunch.

'Bring me a tuna mayo wrap, will you?' called Alice.

'Can't,' she had said briefly, 'I'm going to a restaurant.'

She'd sounded a little more lofty than she had intended, but she was out of the door before Alice could offer a response.

As they left, they were both laughing.

'She's quite a woman, isn't she?' Ed said.

'And she displays most of it too,' Gina agreed, rather cattily.

'Not your best friend then?'

'Absolutely not.'

'What about that sad young man - I'd say he had the hots for you…'

Gina coloured. 'I think he's keen, but he's not my type.'

'What is your type?'

Again Gina felt the heat in her cheeks and was unable to look directly at him. Instead she said:

'We haven't even been introduced and you're asking personal questions!'

'Sorry. You're quite right. Please. Allow me!'

And he extended a hand and shook Gina's in a ridiculously formal and overdone manner, so that Gina was laughing as she told him her name and didn't stop laughing all through lunch. He was totally charming and Gina was quite captivated.

And Ed Mackenzie was no less enraptured and quickly dated her.

In the next few weeks he took her to clubs, restaurants and theatres she could only previously have dreamed of. He was mature, rich and experienced. After three months Gina believed herself truly in love and in the front seat of his amazing vintage Lotus Élan, she had the best sex ever (heaven knows how) and her first fully penetrative experience - unprotected as it happens - but feeling truly in love, it hardly mattered.

She had frequently talked with Maggie who repeatedly told her she was mad. Her mother told her this also, as did her other friends, but she was sure they were wrong, jealous or didn't understand. And then came the pregnancy scare...and maybe yes, Gina had encouraged Ed to ask her to marry him. At the time, saying yes had been easy, even if her mum had protested strongly and made a fuss. It made no difference. Less than three weeks after that, they were married.

And they had a quick, quiet wedding for what seemed like obvious reasons, with only her mum, Maggie and Amy present, Issy being away for what she called a gap year.

4

Ed had a beautiful old house, at the posh end of Charlotte Road in Edgbaston and Gina was happy to move away from the dingy streets of her London childhood to begin their married, childless life together in a lovely part of Birmingham. Her mother was sad to lose her even though Gina promised her lots of visits and said she would return often.

'It's only Birmingham, mum, not Australia!'

Issy returned, Maggie came to stay quite frequently and Gina tried to make friends, though it was not easy and truth be told, she missed her lively youthful life in London. A year passed, and then another and then eight years had gone by and still she had not conceived. Occasionally her mother broached the subject. Only once did she allow her daughter to know that she was anxious about it.

'Do you think it's you, or him?'

'Oh for God's sake mum, that's just nothing to do with you. I don't know how you can ask.'

'You sound quite upset about it anyway.'

'Yes,' Gina was angry and tearful. 'I am. Very, but just leave it, will you...I do not want to discuss it.'

'But darling...'

'Oh shut up, please. Just stop will you? What can I do? No. Don't tell me. I don't need to get advice from you about babies.'

This was cruel, but she was truly angry and adopted an unusually icy manner; there was a strange distaste in her voice. It had been many years since Lou had heard her daughter lose her temper, and it frightened her a little.

Louise didn't bring up the subject again.

One afternoon Gina had just returned from the garage having taken Ed's car there for service, when the phone rang. Ed had decided he needed to visit the warehouse and cold store with his foreman, Mike, who had driven him there, but he needed a lift back home. She sighed. She said OK. She drove to Halesowen.

In the 20 minutes it took to get to the cold store where Ed would be waiting, she did a lot of thinking.

'Hello darling.'

'Hello dear.' They greeted each other and shared a kiss.

'Mikey said the thermostat was giving trouble…I'm just checking.'

He went into the cold store.

'Drop the thermo,' he called to Gina. 'I'll see if it's registering now.'

She pushed it right down.

She waited. She glanced idly around the office - there was a message on his mobile phone, it read:

'watch for the fail-safe mech - on the blink.' It had arrived just a moment ago.

Quietly she moved towards the massive door that closed on the freezer store, she could see Ed's back as he fiddled with the control panel. She moved round the bulk of the door and gently, very gently, pushed it. When it was fastened closed, she backed away, heard nothing, and went out to the car. She got in, paused briefly and drove home.

On the way back, along Hagley Road, using the in-car connection to her phone, she called her mum. They had a little chat, quite normal for a Tuesday evening. Gina told her she wanted to watch a favourite tv programme, which was on in a few minutes, so they ended their conversation. She did, in fact, miss the start of the programme, since she was on the road for another 15 minutes, but when she got in, she accessed it on catch up, poured herself a glass of wine, enjoyed it, deleted all the messages on her phone and went to bed.

She awoke rather late. Normally Ed would disturb her early, but not today. She immediately called Mike. 'Did Ed spend the night at your place?' she asked. It had happened before, so she controlled her voice to an unconcerned calm.

'No - I took him to the store…he said he would call you for a ride back. Said I'd wait, but he said it was crazy, I live so close to the store - just go home, he said, no problem, Gina would come…'

She still remained calm.

'Huh, typical! But, you know, I never heard from him - he didn't call me at all! So the question is, where is he now - any idea?'

Several minutes of conversation finally established the need for the rising panic, which she duly displayed, ending by screaming at Mike and urging him to go to the store, and within the hour the ghastly truth was revealed.

The coroner described it as a tragic accident, particularly as Ed had clearly left his mobile phone outside the freezer and was thus unable to call for help.

5

Almost at once, Gina had a call and then a visit from the family solicitor. She had met him once before, but she did know that Ed had left more or less everything to her, capital - a not inconsiderable amount - and of course the house. So, except for a fairly generous annuity to his sister, she inherited a large fortune, not to mention the ownership of the business and a privileged position on the board. For his mother, provision had already been made, for the rest of her life, from capital set aside for this purpose from Ed's father's estate when he had died several years before.

What Gina did not know, and the solicitor was quite clear about this when discreetly questioned shortly after, was that a large insurance policy had also been in place.

Of this, Gina knew nothing and again the solicitor was equally sure that it was true. He made that quite clear. Gina had no knowledge of this at all.

Gina was to be the sole beneficiary. This of course now came into effect and to her great surprise, Gina was indeed an exceedingly wealthy woman.

Gina spared nothing in planning the funeral, but allowed all the agents of support to just go ahead. The Funeral Parlour took care of nearly everything, though she instructed them to go over the top with flowers. She retained the best restaurant in the city, and several of its staff, to provide fantastic finger food and on site staff for several hours in their home when everyone came back after the cremation.

The lady - a humanist chaplain - who had come a few days before to discuss the service was encouraged to go the full distance with the ceremony. The eulogy was long and detailed, there were several readings and songs - music carefully chosen with the help of Ed's mother and his sister Jennifer, who came immediately from Canada to help with the proceedings. At the ceremony, there were some non-denominational prayers and a protracted candle lighting ceremony with many participants. There was much sadness and copious tears. But there was plenty of transport back to the house where everything was in place and perfectly organized.

The wake was agreed to have been the best bash Ed never went to. In a moment of genuine kindness, Gina had invited Caroline and the two blond gods to come along, and they accepted. Indeed they said they had enjoyed it, as these things go, and were grateful that they had been asked and had had a chance to say goodbye to their father. Gina made no observations to this, despite a quiet snigger from Maggie, but continued to play the perfect bereaved widow with grace, dignity and charm, and by the end of the day, found herself accepting an invitation to visit them at their grand house near Northampton. Caroline, having achieved the healthy settlement she had hoped for, had thoughtfully moved out of the area and settled down to live with her painter/decorator and two charming boys, who, by the way, were growing into very attractive young men.

Gina appeared inconsolable, and moved her mother in for some weeks to help her recover. Her mother was most understanding, and nursed her back to a normal state rather more quickly than might have been expected if she had been on her own. There were times when mum reported to her friends that Gina was 'near suicidal' but she pulled her through and during this time, she went to stay with Caroline, where they were able to reminisce about Ed and remember what a lovely bloke he was. She swam, played tennis with the boys, went for walks with Caro and Dave and their big yellow dogs, and she told them how beneficial her stay had been. An insight into fulfilled family life got her feeling all the more broody and it was probably partly instrumental in getting her back to normal.

That, and a long stay at an expensive lodge in Switzerland, which helped both Gina and her mother through some very difficult times. Her mother described it as a sanatorium for the rich and lazy, and Gina did not demur.

Sometimes, during this stay, Gina had gone through a mental agony, and had been very tempted, but resisted. It was useful too, not being with her friends, because while she was close to her Mum, she wasn't that close. Instead, she scribbled a few cryptic thoughts into a notebook. Sometimes she surprised herself, because she cried and wrote down rather emotional feelings, which included an uncalculated declaration of love for 'my Ed' She looked at it after she'd written it, a few days later and wondered what it was all about. But she admitted no culpability and she felt a great therapy in what she wrote. Indeed on one occasion when Louise came upon her as she was writing, she asked her what she was doing.

'A few thoughts mum. The therapist said it was useful.'

'Can I look?'

'Well. I'd rather you didn't. Oh. Just this page then?'

Lou had looked at it and then put a comforting arm round her daughter's shoulders.

'Don't blame yourself love,' she had said.

Gina drew the notebook back quickly. She looked at what she had written and what her mother had read. She turned the page quickly.

'No. I don't, it's just silly. I mean, maybe if...'

'Oh, don't start that,' Lou said, 'it doesn't help. But I think it's probably a good idea to write it down. I'm sure that Dr. Trescothick is right. It's healing.'

Gina did wonder how her mum had suddenly become an expert amateur psychotherapist, but she was happy to go along with the exercise. She continued to write in a sketchy way from time to time, although once back home she more or less forgot all about it.'

It was helpful too, while she was away, to meet other people, and inevitably she met a few guys. Almost more surprisingly, her mother met and became close friends with a rather attractive 54 year old. Her mother was herself a very presentable over-50 year old and since Gina's dad had walked out when Gina was 7 months old, and she had never known him, she had no thoughts of resentment or any other censorious feelings, about this blossoming relationship. In fact she was quite pleased for her mother. On one occasion, Jim clearly wanted a bit of time alone with Louise, so Gina went to the local restaurant by herself.

She was known there and made welcome. She was sharing a cocktail with one of the regulars and enjoying a conversation with him and eventually he bought her dinner. It was a surprise to Gina that she could enjoy the company of this young man, and though she was not particularly attracted to him, she began to find herself again, which was welcome and she felt her confidence returning.

As Jim and Lou became good pals, Gina went often to the tavern. Meeting a few men was helpful and gave her a feeling for a new relationship, which previously she had vaunted as 'highly unlikely'. Gina was sure that she had not contrived this approach to meeting new people. She felt it came naturally, but it served to support the view of her friends back in the UK that she was re-habilitating well and at 27 might be considerably better and ready for a new relationship. One evening, close to a time that she had more or less decided would be the end of their stay, she met Zak.

6

He was so handsome and again it was the dark, good looks that attracted her. They met several times; she extended her stay. Fortunately, Louise and Jim were happy with that, and of course money was not a problem. Zak's wealthy family owned a huge 10-million euro villa outside Geneva, and she had been to swim, to stay, to eat and to eventually fall into bed, or rather onto the couch in the living room, with a hotly passionate Zak. He didn't even dare to come into the room she stayed in, a bedroom of massive proportions, for fear of being found by his mother or father, or even one of his sisters. Once, when he was 11 he had been caught spying on Lylla, his older sister by two years, as she changed in the poolroom. His father had actually thrashed him, despite his protests that he hadn't been spying, just going for a swim himself. His father wasn't interested in his reasons for being there and punished him anyway.

So any love-making was to be fast and seriously clandestine. Gina always wore attractive and provocative clothing, low backed, if not low fronted, and very short skirts. On this day, she moved to the sofa. She sat with her back to him. She knew he would dare to do very little without serious encouragement. She slid her lovely bottom close to, and then onto his thigh, with her back to him. He touched the top button at the back of her top - one of three. His slowness, fuelled faster only by terror of his parents return, was so exciting, that Gina could barely control herself. Eventually, all three buttons were unfastened and she slid the top forward. With a skilled one-handed movement, she undid her lacy, barely concealing bra, and pulled that forward and onto the floor. She was imagining his face - probably eyes closed, head pulled back, and she could already feel his erection as she moved happily against him. Eventually, his hands crept forward and cupped her breasts from behind and finally, she rolled over to him, expertly dragging her skirt up and out of the way in doing so. Her tiny pants proved no obstacle, in fact their presence heightened the experience and they both quickly climaxed without any protection or indeed any fear.

This act was, to Gina, a kind of statement. It said I don't care if you get pregnant, I want you in a serious way, and she was surprisingly happy with that. And to be fair, apart from a slightly crooked and large nose ('Rugby - very dangerous game' Zak had explained), he was the embodiment of charm; tall and terrifically handsome, with dark glowing eyes which had clearly bewitched Gina. All that and a big fat bank account. Who could ask for more?

In fact, when she later told Issy of the event, Issy agreed, and thoroughly sympathised with what might otherwise have been described as a rather hasty decision about a second marriage.

Maggie was a bit more cautious, and she and Amy talked about 'Gina's recovery' as though it were supposed to be a longer process. And it was typical of Amy, a caring and thoughtful rather sensitive young woman, to openly advise Gina against what seemed a rash and perhaps poorly-thought through move.

'You're still getting over Ed,' she said in a kindly way.

'Oh God, I've not been ill,' Gina assured them.

'No? You lost your husband in tragic circumstances. So yes. In a way you have been ill. Emotionally, you have.'

'I'm lonely,' Gina had said, softly and sadly, 'and I want a family.'

In a surge of sympathetic emotion, Maggie hugged her and decided to offer no further advice or resistance. Amy remained uncertain of the wisdom of Gina's behaviour but listened to Maggie.

That night, Gina found the notebook in which she had written what she had thought to be healing thoughts, and she added a few more about her attraction to Zak. Then she hid the book in the bottom of an infrequently used closet, under several shoe boxes.

7

As it happened, she did not conceive on that occasion, and Zak asked her to marry him very soon after. She said the wedding had to be in the UK. All his family and friends could afford the trip and in any case many of his friends lived in London. His family agreed that it could be in London. Birmingham just wasn't posh enough they felt...and although Gina could easily have afforded to pay for a wedding, she made it clear that she would not. She had kept her wealth fairly secret, while at the same time, she indicated her admiration of expensive clothes and the luxuries of an extravagant lifestyle.

Zak waved all thoughts of wedding plans airily to one side - 'Just decide - of course my father will pay!'

Thus they came to be standing on the steps of Camden Town Hall, after enjoying the pleasures of the Camden Council Chamber with its art deco chandeliers, gorgeous wood panelling and with a million additional flowers. And of course the catering was amazing which despite the lack of serious booze, was hugely enjoyed. And there was champagne, 'for those who wanted it', so largely, it was a success.

That was the year of weddings and babies. Issy got wed, Maggie set up house in North London with a business partner, claiming it was just a platonic and convenient arrangement and then she announced she was pregnant! At almost the same time, Gina discovered she was too, and they had baby boys in the same week. They called him Shafiq Edward, and Maggie and Simon called their little boy Thomas. Zak was jubilant and his parents came over at once, though Lou wasn't entirely delighted with that initiative, especially as Soraya announced she was moving in for a while 'to help out'. She and Yousef did stay for what seemed to be rather a long time, but eventually the situation was handled diplomatically, and Gina got on with being a happy mummy. She and Maggie would meet either in London or Birmingham to escape from time to time, to discuss deeply serious issues, like the cost of nappies, the failings of their men, their disconcerting and annoying habits, and what they would like to do next week.

Maggie was almost at the end of her maternity leave and her little Thomas would go to nursery. Issy was also pregnant now, and while this would keep Gina entertained for a while, as they shared baby stories and experiences, it would not last. She had given up the work in the radio station when she had become pregnant, and although her nanny was very helpful and cared for Shafiq particularly well, Gina had very little to occupy her.

Zak was working for his father in the conveniently close jewellery quarter in Birmingham, where his import-export business could be furthered, and the gold, silver and diamond trade could flourish. He usually came home on time and they enjoyed pleasant enough evenings together. Zak, who had been educated at excellent schools in the UK and in Switzerland, was completely at home. Once, Gina brought up the subject of further education. She explained that she had not been able to take advantage of a university training and wondered if she might do that now. Not surprisingly, Zak was quite against this, and despite several discussions she made no progress. She even got the prospectus for courses she was interested in, but it cut no ice. She got pregnant again, had a little boy again, Hanif, and then got pregnant once more. This time it was a girl, Thana - immediately known as Tanni, and five years had passed.

She recorded the birth of the three children in her notebook - she had come to think of it as her necessary therapy - and frequently added a few thoughts about the way she felt her life was going, particularly her sadness that Zak was unwilling to entertain the idea of her further education. It was a real disappointment to her and the wish to study never really left her. She wrote what turned out to be a deeply emotional essay about the gap she felt in her heart, how she missed the chance to study, and to work, and how she looked back with great regret at the decision she had made concerning her early chances in higher education. Re-reading this a few weeks later, she found herself crying. And, incidentally, she realised she had some considerable ability to write clearly, and in this case, movingly.

Her marvellous nanny Rayna took most of the burden of childcare, and Gina was free to do as she pleased, but not to study.

Zak was always adamant about that. Forceful as she was by nature, Gina felt unable to fight him on this subject. Indeed she felt weakened by his fierce and rather angry insistence that she should maintain her place in the home and not make life difficult. Indeed, his flashing dark eyes, originally such a powerful attraction, now became fearsome and almost threatening. On one occasion she had remonstrated with him that she was not trying to make trouble, that on the contrary she was simply trying to use some of her excess spare time and to exercise her brain. 'It's becoming enfeebled,' she had complained. But he had been harsh in response.

'Gina, I don't want to hear any of this ever again. Enough of this nonsense! You are a mother and a homemaker, that's what you do.'

One day, in September, Zak announced 'I need to go to Saudi for, well, a few days, some problems - the exporters, it's - you know - it's a bit tricky.'

'Are we in trouble?' she dared to ask, although it was clear that her interest was not usually welcomed.

'No, it'll be fine. I just need to be asking some questions, face to face with some of those guys.'

Accordingly, Zak went off for a few days and Gina just hoped that he could sort out whatever issues had arisen. On the whole, she trusted him to run the business with the acute shrewdness he had always displayed and she knew that their wealth had accrued from his acumen. True, his father's money had helped to set up the original venture many years ago, but Zak had the charm and the education and a very European approach. It had taken him far and he had a large group of confederates, all similarly wealthy, whom she occasionally met socially. On these occasions she felt oddly out of place. Conversation did not normally present problems for Gina - she was a happy chatter - however, in this company she felt moved to reticence and was oddly silenced. The women were worldly and elegant, but in Gina's view, they were also given to vapid and sometimes politically incorrect opinions. Although without the formal further education she wished for, she was smart, thoughtful and critical of political changes in the name of progress but which she was not afraid to describe as regressive. Such views did not always meet with approval. It was clear that several of Zak's colleagues really thought she should not express her opinions at all.

And It seemed a good opportunity for a bit of grandparental bonding so she took Shafi, Han and Tanni, who was still a small baby, to her mother's in Buckingham, to where she had moved a couple of years before with a bit of discreet financial help from Gina. It was here too, where Jim had moved in, since he had just retired, and they all had an enjoyable visit together.

She couldn't quite understand why it all suddenly felt so different from what seemed to be a rather artificial existence in a Georgian mansion in Edgbaston. Seeing Jim and Lou together gave her a new perspective on family life. This was, after all, something she had not previously experienced and hardly knew what was normal. But both Lou and Jim had had an ordinary childhood in traditional homes, leaving to get married routinely and fairly early, and maintaining a good relationship with their parents. In fact, Gina's Grandmother had died over 10 years ago. She had been a dear lady and Gina had loved her hugely. Her grandfather she barely knew - he had died when she was very young. That, therefore had constituted Gina's family experiences before she had had children of her own. And now, much of the care was up to Rayna, the devoted and very helpful Polish woman who worked for them and looked after most of the children's needs, so even now, it was hardly the kind of family experience that most people had.

Gina had a truly lovely time with her mum and Jim; by contrast she would have to admit that when she was at home, for quite a lot of the time she was somewhat bored.

8

Returning home at the end of her stay, she found Zak anxious.

She attempted to ask a few questions but he was dismissive. Gina was sure that he was very close to saying something along the lines of 'Don't you worry your pretty little head...' but since he didn't actually say that, she couldn't take issue with him. And the truth was she was actually quite afraid of him, especially when his tone became bullying and harsh. Certainly she felt discontented, couldn't quite say why, but did try to indicate to Zak, as diplomatically as she could, that she would like to know more of what was troubling him, to know more of the business, to perhaps be able to play some part in it herself. She certainly knew she needed more to do, but as usual, Zak impatiently brushed aside her queries.

She searched out her journal and scribbled down some angry thoughts; to be sure, it did help her mood a bit but not enough to dampen her hopes regarding her college ideas completely.

Then, suddenly, out of the blue, he suggested getting a motorboat.

Gina was astonished. 'But we live miles from the coast and I don't know anything about boats.'

'We'll all learn together, the boys are nearly old enough. There's one for sale in a bay off the Hampshire coast. Let's go at the weekend.'

'Where on the Hampshire coast? That's quite a long way.'

'Not sure. We'll Google it.'

'How did you hear about it?'

'A friend.'

'Who?'

'You don't know them. Don't you trust me?

Gina pulled her lips into a grim smile. 'Course,' she said.

* * *

At the weekend, and with Lou and Jim, who had been invited along, they all piled into the 4x4 and set off.

'Put this into the satnav,' Zak said, and passed her an address.

'You need to learn to use this yourself,' Gina observed.

'Why would I when you're so good at it?'

'Do you know that we have to climb down 102 steps?' she asked him after a few moments checking the device, and also staring at some extra information on her phone.

'No. I didn't. How do you know? Are we up to it, I mean. We'll have to climb back up...'

The children groaned. Lou announced she was fine with it. Zak raised his eyes skyward and shrugged. 'What's the choice? Can we drive any further?'

'Long. 2 mile, slow, winding road, bit of a rough track I think. But it gets down to the beach eventually.'

'OK - I'll give it a try.'

Quietly, Lou said she'd rather climb than be sick on the bends.

'You will drive slowly won't you Zak?' she asked, 'I'm not great on twisty roads.'

'Are you going to be sick Granny?' asked Shaf.

'Hope not! If your dad is careful.'

'If you're sick, will you lean out of your window?'

'Shaf, just stop that. Be quiet,' Gina scolded. But Lou looked apprehensive and gripped the back of the seat in front of her.

It was a longish journey not helped by Zak's rapid driving and Lou's anxiety. It was a fairly bumpy and awkward ride at the end, along an unmade road as they approached the coast. Zak seemed to have no awareness of the poor road surface, nor did he seem to have any regard at all for the safety and comfort of his passengers. Lou was really unhappy until they crunched onto the back beach where the gravelly sand was heaped up from earlier spring tides. Here, she couldn't get out fast enough announcing that later, she would climb the steps to get back, and meet them on the road. The children fell out of the 4x4 and dived after her. They chased off along the beach. Jim followed more slowly. Gina was hit by an outrageous thought.

'Zak - you're not into some sort of smuggling are you?' Suddenly, Gina wondered if she had made a discovery, but Zak just shouted out loud and laughed -

'Don't be ridiculous - are you crazy?'

'No, but I hope you're not.'

'What, crazy?'

'Well, I'm hoping you're not mad and not doing something wrong either.'

Zak continued to chuckle at what he saw as a preposterous idea. Gina was not sure that her idea was entirely ridiculous, but hoped that bringing it to attention like this, Zak might realise that she was on to him, if there were to be anything in it. But she couldn't help but join in the smiling about what was, she saw, an outrageous suggestion.

The boat was anchored off the coast, opposite a rather decent beach house a couple of hundred yards up the beach, just where the steps and footpath came steeply down to the shore. They opened up with the keys that Zak had been lent and found the dinghy that would allow them to reach the motorboat.

'Wow!' Shafi yelled pointing to the launch - 'it's big.'

'30 foot cabin cruiser,' Zak told him, as if he knew all there was to know about boats.

'Do you know how to drive it?' Shafi asked.

'You don't drive a boat,' said Han.

'What do you then?'

'You steer it.'

'What's steering?' asked Tanni

No-one paid much attention except Jim, who attempted to give them some rudimentary mariners' vocabulary. He had done some sailing and would be useful.

'We need a navigator,' said Zak. Gina agreed and was pleased that there was a good reason to have Lou and Jim along.

Gina and Jim found lifejackets in the beach hut and handed them round, despite objections from the boys, but Gina insisted. Zak flung his carelessly round his neck, not really wearing it at all.

With an effort, they managed to get into the dinghy, First Gina, Lou and Tanni who all went with Jim. He seemed to know how to pull on the outboard motor and it barked into life. In just a few moments, they were in the deep water alongside the boat, and Gina was pleased to note that Jim hopped up a conveniently sloped set of steps. She handed Tanni up to him, and she and Lou followed, with no great difficulty.

Jim returned to the shore and the others piled in. The dinghy rocked dangerously as Shafi bounded into it, with his usual powerful, over-enthusiasm, and Gina, watching anxiously, put a hand to her mouth.

Jim and Zak and the two boys dashed to climb up the side ladder. Everyone was getting splashed and laughing a lot, while Zak was pulling up the anchor with a relaxed unconcern which worried Gina - surely he didn't know what he was doing - somehow it left her feeling nervous!

'This is going to be fun,' Zak announced and at that moment it was hard for anyone to disagree.

They explored the boat, Gina worrying about the dampness of the linens and the duvets, though impressed at the way it was kitted out.

Lou was inspecting the galley.

'This is the kitchen,' she explained to Han, 'look, there are pans and dishes and all sorts, even some tins and things.'

'Can we cook stuff?' Shafi asked.

'We can but not today,' Gina said, and then they all jumped as the engine started with a deep, low rumble.

'Hey, we're moving,' yelled Han, and the children skittered up to the deck and the helm where Jim and Zak were fiddling with controls. 'We can't really move into deep water - too many on board - not legal,' Zak said, 'and you kids, just watch out - not everyone is wearing a lifejacket!'

'Why not?' Gina shouted. 'I think you should wear one all the time - I mean you Zak,' because she had seen that he had flung his to the deck floor.

'Aw, mum, don't be so wussy,' Shaf said, and Han, usually polite to his mum, chose to ignore her on this occasion.

'Can we help?' 'I want to steer.' 'Let me have a go.' They were all shouting at once and they all got to try various buttons and controls, and motored round the small bay - shouting and waving to other boats as they went. Finally, after an hour or so, Zak ordered them to stop and collect their things.

'Can we come again?'

'Sure, we'll come again. As soon as I've mastered the theory.'

'You should go on a course,' Gina suggested.

'Well, maybe I will.'

Going home, Lou did indeed climb up, and beat them to the top of the shore cliff by several minutes. She was waiting patiently for them as Zak rounded the bend, at such speed that he almost drove right past her.

'We'll all walk down next time,' Gina said.

But she wondered when that would be, because Zak was so very occupied for many days and the following weekend he was off to London.

'Business conference,' he said, vaguely. 'Be back Monday night - I'll go straight to work on Monday. Be good all of you.'

And he was gone.

Gina called Maggie.

'I'm suspicious of him.'

'Oh come on, what makes you think that?'

'Hey, I thought you'd be on my side!'

'I am on your side - why would I want him to be having an affair with someone?'

'Well, I didn't mean that, it's just - I'm worried - I feel anxious. He doesn't do this. Go away. And he's been to Saudi and now he's off again. And was he in Saudi? How do I know...'

'Oh, for god's sake, just stop this, you can't be serious.'

She sighed; they talked of other things.

She called her mother, and she talked it through as she had with Maggie. Her mother responded in the same sort of way.

'You don't know when you've got it good, girl. Lovely home, lots of help, great kids who'll go to posh schools, as many clothes as you want, lovely car...'

'But mum,' Gina interrupted 'I just feel it in my bones. What if I'm right?'

'Don't cross bridges,' Lou warned.

Zak came home. He seemed gloomy.

'How did it go?'

'Fine, some people made idiots of themselves...'

'What do you mean?'

'Spoke badly, said silly things about trade movements, don't seem to know what a recession is. What are we eating?'

Gina let it go.

31

9

'Let's have a party,' said Zak suddenly, 'we should enjoy this Indian summer - I'll book a marquee, and we'll use those great caterers everyone talks about. What are they called? Summerlicious - they do a fantastic barbecue, and we'll have loads of bubbly, a band - fireworks - it'll cheer everyone up.'

'Are you very miserable?' Gina asked.

'No, I mean it'll cheer you up.'

'I'm not miserable.'

'You look it. You've been sulky since I came home - what's the matter with you? Tell you what, we'll make this a boat-buying celebratory party - I've more or less fixed all that up this weekend. How about it?'

'Yes, OK,' she said without much enthusiasm, 'I'm up for it. Let's do it.'

She tried to sound cheerful and excited, and they began to plan. By the end of dinner and as the children went to bed, everyone was genuinely fired up. Zak had been persuaded to have a bouncy castle and a chocolate fountain (though he drew the line at a carousel) and the guest list was huge. Gina confessed that she didn't know most of them, but Zak said they were important clients. Within a few days the great autumn party was in place and invitations were sent.

And fortunately, the Indian summer continued, so as October began, the weather was balmy and the skies clear. Since darkness would fall at 7, they had decided to start at what would be a late lunch. People started to arrive at 2, to the amazing smells from the barbecue, the music from the jazz band and the sound of corks popping.

All was going swimmingly and there was a great atmosphere. The marquee had been charmingly erected over a large section of lawn and shrubs and the garden pond, and under a separate awning, the swimming pool had been heated up, so that everyone could enjoy a dip or a paddle, and several leggy lovelies were strewn down the Roman steps, drinking and spilling champagne, and laughing a lot. It looked absolutely tremendous. There was a photographer, and she snapped all afternoon; even Gina was having fun. As the day wore on, the jazz band played for dancing, and the more energetic jumped around on the specially constructed wooden floor. The very young exhausted themselves on the bouncy castle and no doubt dipped far too much from the chocolate fountain. Some of the older ones probably drank far too much of other things, but it was all very good-natured and people seemed to be having a great time.

Gina wandered around chatting to this one and the other, not seeing Zak, wondering where he was, when she came across Amy sitting on the stone balustrade outside the side door of the kitchen. She looked miserable, chin in hands, staring down.

'What's up?'

'Josh. Of course.'

'Ach, get him out of your life.'

'I should, but he's such a flirt, so I don't know when he's serious. When I suggest we finish, he gets mad and says it's just a bit of fun, and can't I be more understanding.'

'Can you?'

'No, I'm sick of it. Every time we're out, he finds someone else to schmooze and for all I know, to screw. I've had enough.'

'How do you know he's up to his tricks now?'

'Seen him.'

Amy, small and slightly chubby, and cherubically pretty under normal circumstances, looked rather frail and vulnerable just now. Her big blue eyes were moist with tears and red-rimmed, her pretty blonde bob, dishevelled. Gina was surprised to see that she looked unkempt and messy. She felt a surge of warm emotion for her friend and took her arm as she helped her stand.

Amy led the way along the side of the house and to the far end of the garden. Here, out of the way of the rest of the party, there were sheds, scrubby land, very weedy and with several compost bins and a pile of wood that they would burn later in the year. By peering through the windows of one of the sheds they could see, beyond that, a broken bench. Seated there were Josh and someone so exposed that Gina feared for her health.

'Definitely going to catch a chill, dressed, or rather undressed like that,' she said grimly.

'There's a lot going on there, best if we go…' she added and they moved away, Amy weeping and searching for tissues.

The light was fading now, and as they picked their way through the weedy, unkempt ground, a light came on in the house, and Gina looked up. Astonished, she realised that it was from an upper room, at the side of the house, rarely used. To her further amazement she saw a young woman, unclothed at least to the waist, which was as far as was visible, and then, unmistakably, Zak! They moved from view almost at once and the light went out. Certainly this particular window would be completely obscured from the lawns and terraces below, since it was far to the side and the room was towards the front of the house. It would be necessary to walk into a particularly nasty part of the garden to get this view. Of course, this is exactly what they had done. In shock, Gina steered Amy, still sobbing, back to the side door and into the kitchen, where the caterers were preparing the evening delicacies, and deposited her in there with a box of tissues. Gina had drunk very little throughout the afternoon but now she grabbed a glass and tipped champagne into it. It overflowed, but she filled it again and downed it at once. Then she did it again. And again. And again.

* * *

Angry and confused, eyes full of tears, she walked through the kitchen and then stepped once more into the garden. She walked to the bouncy castle. She found Shafi, Han and Tanni and ordered them to bed. They protested. She was unreasonably and uncharacteristically harsh and they were baffled by her severity. She called to Rayna 'Get these kids in, they need to go to bed.'

'What about the fireworks?' Shafi shouted at her.

'Oh for god's sake,' she yelled back, 'I don't care. Do what you like.'

This was particularly out of character for Gina, and she was so near tears herself, that she really didn't care, and taking her anger out on her children, while not justified, might be considered understandable.

Deliberately, she went over to the little dance floor, elbowed her way in, and started to dance. She threw her arms about and around

34

anyone who was willing to be embraced. She sang and shouted and generally behaved as loudly and as badly as she could. Male friends, pleasantly drunk, danced along with her, embraced her, even kissed her. She vaguely recalled later, a warm, exploratory tongue, a hand on her breast and even between her thighs. She didn't care. On the contrary, she was fully engaged in various forms of licentious behaviour for quite a time. She drank a lot of wine from other people's glasses.

Darkness began to fall, lights came on, candles were lit, more champagne was poured. The music seemed to get louder. Soup, snacks and other delectations were served. She carried on dancing, drinking and singing. People came, people went; she barely noticed. The fireworks began. They were lavish. There were the usual ooohs and aaahs and there was an arm round her waist, it was Zak.

Gina controlled herself with difficulty, as she knew she must. Give nothing away, she told herself.

'There's cake,' he said, 'want some?'

'Sure, let's eat cake,' she said screaming above the noise, 'why not?'

10

The last time Gina was sick from eating cake, she was 10 and she had been to Danny Moran's 12th birthday party where Mrs Moran had shown herself to be the perfect mother and hostess.

'Eat all you like, what you like and when you like,' she had instructed carelessly.

Gina had tried a sausage roll, two egg-and-cress sandwiches, then a slice of cream jelly cake, which she particularly enjoyed, followed by a chocolate brownie, and then a second one. This was followed by two slices of pizza, loads of crisps, several handfuls of smarties and finally another sausage roll. All fantastic, she'd decided, and she'd rinsed through with cola, lemonade, and a particularly sweet, sticky green drink, followed by more cake. Perhaps it wasn't just cake, then, that had made her sick, but sick she had been. Very.

Within ten minutes of eating the party cake in her own garden she had felt extremely ill. Obviously, it might have been the excess of champagne that augmented these feelings, but she didn't feel inclined to analysis and gave into being very, very sick. In her own bathroom - yes, she had shown just enough presence of mind to know that she should get away from the guests - she had sat on the floor and wept and vomited by turns, into the welcoming porcelain.

Shuddering, cold and miserable she crawled into a bed in the guest room where she slept deeply for a couple of hours, waking in tears and thinking about her life. She found herself thinking particularly about Danny Moran. At twelve she had thought him gorgeous but had told no-one of her girlish desires. At fifteen she had manoeuvred her way to getting him to ask her out. He had discovered her very satisfactory teenage breasts and they had enjoyed several exploratory encounters in the park, in the back of his dad's van and in the prep room at the back of the chemistry lab. But after a hot and breathy autumn, Gina suddenly found him dull, clumsy, awkward and lacking any interesting conversation at all. She dropped him. In fact, she had decided that schoolboys were pathetic and that she wanted to meet older people who were familiar with the ways of the world. Not that she had any idea what those ways were, but it was the reason why, despite the fact that her form teacher had called her 'a bright intellect' and her English teacher spoke of her as 'an outstanding thinker' that she had left school with no intention of any further education, after her A-levels.

11

Before the cleaning crew came in the next day, Gina, with a bit of a headache, hauled back the heavy drapes in her own bedroom and stared out at the havoc and ravages of the party. She stumbled downstairs and made tea. The children wandered in, one by one, and draped themselves over the breakfast bar. Rayna had made toast, and served cereal. The children splashed milk and scattered crispy rice cereal all over the counter. They bickered endlessly. Zak walked into the kitchen looking glum.

'Coffee?' Gina offered.

'Hmm?'

'Do you want coffee?'

'Oh. Yes. OK.'

'What's on your mind?' she asked disingenuously.

'Nothing. Why?' He sounded pre-occupied.

She busied herself with getting through the children's breakfast and nudging them to get dressed. She trailed them upstairs, pulled on her clothes and wandered down and out into the garden. It was cool and fresh out there, but the sky was blue, the grass dewy. Hanif was there already, assiduously draining the chocolate fountain. She ignored him, pulled a dead head off a rose, threw it onto the soil, and found Tanni at her side leaning into her knee. She bent to her, embraced her, wept silently into her thick curls. She drew her hand across her nose and eyes and then wiped it across her jeans, and turned to catch Shafi as he ran towards her.

'Dad bought the boat!' he yelled, 'he bought it...'

'Yes I know, he told me he was going to.' Gina sighed and scraped her hand through Shafi's hair. 'Where is it?'

'Don't know. In the sea I suppose.'

'Oh Shafi, you don't imagine that I thought he'd brought it home and parked it in the drive, did you?'

'No, but we can go and see it again next week, he says.'

'Yes, I'm sure we'll do that. Get dressed Shaf. Come on, we're going to the pool party - remember?'

38

She tried to sound cheery and upbeat. 'You all need to get dressed, no, not in your bikini just yet Tanni, we'll pack it and take it with us. Give it to Rayna and go find a pretty dress to wear.'

Returning indoors in an attempt to encourage the kids to get ready, Gina asked herself, what kind of mother am I? I barely see my children, and when I do, if they fight, I rely on Rayna - not even a family member, to sort them out. I don't even ask my mother over very often, to visit and to help, and I think she'd like to. But then, she thought, more angrily, what sort of father are you? Zak was not in the room, but she addressed him, nonetheless. Money - that's all you offer, she hissed quietly. Extravagant parties, expensive schools, expensive clothes and ridiculous cars; but why did they need three? And why did he get that Morgan? In yellow? It was all a substitute for care and proper fatherly attention, especially latterly, when he had been away so much. Thinking this, she felt sad all over again though something else was troubling her which she couldn't explain or even put her finger on. A kind of odd anxiety, a disquiet, something quite separate from the massive anger she had felt last night when she had seen those images in the window at the top of the house. As Zak walked in she stopped the nagging thoughts and turned to speak to him.

'Are you nearly ready? Sunday traffic on the motorway might be slow - we're expected by 11.'

'I'm not coming,' he stated flatly. 'Will you be OK driving by yourself?'

'What do you mean? Will and Dee are expecting all of us - it's Will's 40th - you know they are...'

Zak interrupted her sharply.

'I'm going to sort this boat transaction out. Have to do this man-to-man. On the spot. You know.'

'There's no fuel in the Morgan.'

'How would you know that?'

'I drove it Tuesday.'

'Why?'

'Hard to park the Range Rover in the spaces near the Farmer's Market. Why are you quizzing me? Aren't I allowed to drive it?'

'No,' Zak snapped. He slammed upstairs and into the bathroom.

Gina sighed, followed him up, and went into the children's room. Here, rather miserably, she collected the children's things into a large canvas bag. Rayna had finally got Tanni into a dress and wiped her clean. Shaf and Han were still only half dressed. Gina wandered listlessly into her room. She dropped heavily onto the bed. She could hear her mother: 'Don't cross bridges.' She held back from saying something she might regret. But she knew what she had seen. She was sure that Zak was having an affair, but just how serious it was she didn't know. Nor did she know if it was one of several, or even why he had embarked on such an escapade. Zak was, she realised, something of a control freak, and as such he would not contemplate any further education for Gina, nor would he permit her to think of any kind of employment. She knew that he found any thoughts of his wife 'dirtying her hands' as he put it, distasteful. Gina found herself becoming more and more resentful and restless, and had recently joined a group of women, not all of whom would Zak have approved, to make cultural trips to galleries, museums and gardens and especially to take in the various blockbuster exhibitions that abounded in every major art centre. The organizing committee did all the work. Gina would not have had the courage to do this on her own. The truth was that she felt that she would not really have known how, but the group approach had made it easy and to her astonishment, she was actually enjoying the visits. Going to London was especially good. They nearly always ate out together on the return trip and it was a revelation to her how rewarding life could be. There was so much that interested her, though she felt she knew nothing. But she was fascinated and she was learning fast - enjoying it too. So far, she had barely made close acquaintance with three or four of the members. However, she was a regular monthly attendee and she was hoping it would lead to closer and better friendships. She had been to coffee with a couple of the women and certainly her knowledge of art and art history was improving.

Aroused from this reverie by Zak crashing out of the bathroom, smooth-chinned and sweet-smelling, and complaining anew about the lack of gas in the car, she roused herself to join Rayna and the children, and prepared to drive to the party.

Zak offered her the opinion that it would be too cold to swim, anyway, so why bother. She pointed out that the pool was partly covered and that it was heated, and that the actual party would be indoors, and anyway it was more about going for Will's birthday and just being there... but by that point Zak had lost interest and was talking on his phone.

As Rayna loaded up the Range Rover and as she finally rounded up the children, they clamoured to say goodbye to him. Zak paid them scant attention, barely checked to see if Gina had put the address into the satnav and when she said she was fine, he returned to his conversation on his mobile.

Gina slammed into the driving seat. In reverse, she crunched noisily over the thickly gravelled drive, swung round forward, stones spraying, and was gone.

12

Suffering from the hangover and a headache that had been gently throbbing since she awoke, Gina was not great company at the party. Fortunately, she knew few people so was able to cruise more or less anonymously, a vague smile on her face, while the children lost themselves in the crowd and were generally happy to behave like animals, throwing themselves variously into the pool or the flower beds and onto the trampoline. Rayna was supervising them and Gina indulged her miserable mood by soulfully examining the flower borders and making occasional conversation with guests. The food was dull, but at least plentiful and the lunch did accommodate everyone in seats. She sat next to a charming chap - not someone she knew, and his wife was across the table. He was somewhat flirtatious, and Gina was rather embarrassed by his attention, though had to admit that she was agreeably moved and somewhat flattered by his approaches. His wife seemed indifferent, or maybe she was unable to hear, but in any case, he stayed by Gina's side, even when they were all invited to return to the garden where the cake was unveiled.

The cake ceremony was as expected; toasts and speeches were made and Will was as boring as he always was. Gina silently reflected that the friendship with Dee and Will had lapsed somewhat, and she wasn't very surprised, but Shaf and their older son Billy, were great buddies and appeared to get on famously, so they kept in contact for their sake.

She tried to shake off her new admirer and went to talk to a couple of people that she knew who had moved out to country properties but hardly saw now. Richard (for he had introduced himself properly, by now) followed her and finally she made her excuses and went into the house to find a toilet. In there she stared at herself in the mirror. She saw a very beautiful woman. Her long, thick hair she knew, was in part inherited from her father. Her mother had told her that he was of mixed race, and extremely handsome. Gina also had his darkish skin - honey coloured, that tanned well in her case, and yet she had large blue eyes - an odd combination but which resulted in very striking good looks. She had her hair cared for well, and it was lightened to a dark gold, fashionably streaked. Tall, slim and elegant, she did not wonder that she could turn heads, but it was not something she had really thought about much in recent years, until now. And she surprised herself as she experienced the old frisson of sensuality and desire, which had not been evident of late.

She sighed, pulled herself up to full height, smoothed her dress, picked a long hair from off her shoulder and returned to the living room. Here she dropped onto a sofa next to Chris, someone that she had known since before either had married, and they had actually been to the same school. They swopped histories, spoke of their children, and the afternoon passed agreeably enough. Indeed, Gina cheered up considerably until her headache returned and she remembered why she had felt so gloomy. As she stood up, Richard spotted her again and waylaid her once more. She wasn't in the least bit attracted to him, but she had to admit that she found his interest in her most flattering and it made her feel good. With a guilty jolt, she stopped herself from scrutinizing the room too seriously, for what might be a better catch out there!

She sought out Rayna and instructed her to get the children ready to go. Rayna seemed surprised.

'Yes, I know, it's early. I've got a headache. Yesterday was all a bit much...' Rayna smiled sympathetically - and began the near-impossible task of rounding them up. 'I heard somebody say there was an accident on the motorway,' she told Gina.

'No problem. I'll just use the satnav. There's a B road,' she said, consulting the machine she had kept in her handbag 'The B1090. We'll use that or something.'

Once on the road, Gina felt sure that if she just avoided the motorway, the satellite navigation would kick in with a new route. As they approached the motorway junction, Gina took an impulsive left turn and drove slowly until the system finished plotting a new route, and sure enough, they were quite soon instructed 'in 400 yards, turn right.' It was almost dark now, and the road was unlit.

'This doesn't look a likely route,' she murmured to herself. She half expected a response from Rayna but she was busy trying to get

Tanni to sit in the child seat. Somehow she had escaped being strapped in correctly and had wriggled her way out. Now Rayna was trying to be patient as the self-willed Tanni fought her efforts. In the rear also, the boys were squabbling, which didn't help anybody's concentration.

'In 100 yards, turn left.' The gentle Irish voice was calm and reassuring, but the turn was blocked by a four-gate barrier reinforced by red and white adhesive tape. Gina swore softly.

'You shouldn't swear, mummy,' said Shafi from behind. She tightened her lips in a grim smile. Funny how they can hear you when they want to, even in the midst of other noise, even when they're arguing. Naturally when they want to ignore you, they just don't hear! She slewed the 4x4 round with no difficulty in the narrow roadway, and crossly accelerated away. In an attempt to re-set the satnav, for she had no idea where she was or where she was going, she pressed a button on the machine. In the short moment that this action took, she failed to see a bend in the road and driving fast, went straight into the ditch. Everybody, including Gina, screamed or yelled and there was prolonged wailing from Hanif, then all went still and quiet. With remarkable presence of mind, Gina shouted:

'Get out - everyone get out. Now!' She unbuckled herself and dashed round to let the boys out of the back, at the same time shouting at Rayna.

'Get Tanni out – get out yourself.'

The boys tumbled out of the dangerously leaning vehicle.

Rayna was crying. 'Tanni. She bad hurt. She is banged her head.'

Gina dialed 999 and asked for help, unable to say exactly where she was but giving some useful details from the satnav which she retrieved from the car. The boys sat on the verge, dazed and shocked. In shock herself, and feeling sick, she lifted Tanni carefully into her arms and put her face close to hers. She hoped that she could sense a tiny breath. She whispered fiercely into her ear, 'Don't go Tanni. No. No. No.' From under her little canvas sunhat that Tanni had worn all afternoon and not removed, she saw a thin trickle of blood.

'Oh my god…' She held her closer and bit her lip. 'Tanni, Tanni. Can you hear mummy?'

It seemed to be hours before the ambulance and the police arrived but when they came it was just a few moments before they had everyone into the ambulance and after a few brief questions to Gina, took them all to the hospital. Gina was treated for shock, as were the boys who were also checked over for any physical injuries. Hanif complained of a pain in his arm, which seemed to have been trapped against the car door, but it was decided that it was badly bruised and nothing more. Tanni, unstrapped at the moment of impact, had been flung against the metallic frame of the car and was still unconscious on arrival at the hospital.

Gina texted Zak. He called her to find out more and began angrily, until Gina explained that Tanni was unconscious, when he responded to say that he was on his way.

After a first emotional exchange, they didn't say much to each other, but he grasped her hand and they sat in the waiting area, desperately anxious. The boys were restless and tired and eventually, on hearing that Tanni was stable for the moment, it was agreed that Rayna should take the boys home, Gina called a taxi and hugged the boys, asking them to be good.

'How will we know if Tanni's OK?' asked Shafi.

'I'll call you.'

'We might be asleep.'

'Rayna will wake you and tell you - won't you Rayna?'

'Of course,' she promised, but understood a look from Gina.

A long night's vigil began.

13

Gina stared at the grey stone floor between her knees as she dropped her head into her hands. The nurses came and went. Zak brought her strong tea which she could not drink. She looked up pleadingly at a nurse who walked by, but who gave no sign that she might go again to see Tanni. Soon she stood and walked along the corridor. At the nurses station she asked if she might see Tanni. She used her full name: Thana Sayeed, and the nurse said 'Who are you?'

'I'm her mother.'

'Oh. Right. I'll just see.'

She went away for several minutes. Gina paced despondently backwards and forwards along the corridor, looking at photos of recovered children and their thank you letters and drawings to the nurses. She barely registered them. The nurse returned.

'You can go in if you want to...'

In a moment, Gina was looking at Tanni and tears were soaking her cheeks. She knelt by the bedside and whispered 'Don't leave us Tanni, don't go, don't, don't... you are my treasure, the apple of my eye, my darling darling darling,' and held her small limp hand, feeling helpless and despairing. All the time a strong sense of guilt filled her being and she could scarcely breathe. It was a bit like a panic attack and she had to steel herself. 'I need to stay strong for you,' she whispered to herself, 'I need to be here for you...' A nurse was opposite, suddenly.

'You *should* talk to her...it's good.'

'Can she hear me?'

'Perhaps. All her vital signs are good, but she is in a coma. We can't say how long it might last.'

'Hours?' said Gina hopefully.

'Mmm. Maybe. Could be days...you know...'

'Can I stay?'

'Oh yes. Talk. Sing. Bring music.'

At once, Gina moved more purposefully. She returned to Zak. She explained the need for music, for familiar things, for her favourite doll that she treasured at bedtime.

Despite his protests, he was sent on this errand and also in order to reassure the boys.

Gina returned to Tanni's bedside. There was no change. She sat and waited.

* * *

Some time later, Zak returned. They placed the familiar objects around the bed and put the doll in her unclenching arm. After midnight, when the hospital had become much quieter, Gina sang songs to her, nursery rhymes mostly, and told her stories. She and Zak took it in turns to walk around a little and Gina went into the hospital grounds for a while. As promised, she called her mother again.

'No,' she said in response to her mother's questioning, 'there's been no change. I can't believe it mum, she just looks asleep, you wouldn't know...it's like...she ...she doesn't move a muscle. It's like, she's, she, I keep thinking, she...' and then Gina stopped, unable to carry on talking, her voice trapped in her throat, her sentence drowned in tears, her heart full of pain.

Back by her daughter's side, she said 'Grandma Lou sends you a big kiss and says you're to get well soon and Jim sends you a hug too. Please come back to us Tanni, please. We love you darling.' And she wept again.

Zak was gently stroking Tanni's hair which curled darkly onto the pillow. Helpless, hopeless, Gina leaned back in her rather uncomfortable chair and closed her eyes. Her mother had said she would come over in the morning. Gina was glad. She felt she needed that comfort, and Zak had said very little to her since his arrival. At first he had been angry, 'What happened?' he had shouted. But after an initial shocked outburst, followed by warning looks from Gina, he had calmed down and soothed the boys before sending them off with Rayna. Following this, he had become somewhat taciturn and Gina also had resorted to quiet consideration and thought, turning her mind inwards and towards keeping herself controlled.

Only half awake she pondered her life and her family responsibilities, and tears again rolled across her face. Short of food, short of sleep, she had little resistance and fell into a doze, from which she did not fully emerge until Zak shook her gently and offered her again, the dark strong tea. This time she felt she had to take it, along with a biscuit bar and the two chewed silently as dawn lightened the little room to grey, and their daughter lay still and silent in the big hospital bed.

Eventually, they had to go home and the days that followed were tortured, dark and gloomy, with little sleep for either of them, fretfulness from the boys and occasional outbursts of anger and frustration from either Gina or Zak, and much crying. They visited the hospital either together or by turns and Gina decided to let the boys go back with Louise, at least for a few days. Their friends were kind and solicitous, came with books, food, whatever they felt would help them to cope. Night ran into day; Gina barely knew if it was Wednesday or Saturday and did not care. Her mum brought the boys back and told her it was Sunday - again!

'What do you mean?'

'It's been a week darling.'

'Oh. Is Zak back from the hospital yet?'

'No, but you can go if you want. Jim isn't expecting me back too early. I'll stay a while.'

14

The phone rang. By now, Gina had stopped dashing to answer. Rayna put her head round the door.

'I should get it?'

'Sure.'

Gina and Lou heard Rayna's startled shout

'When? What? Who is talking please?'

Suddenly Rayna was waving and calling to Gina.

'You go now to hospital. She is being moving...'

Gina and Louise made a joint dash for the door and the car.

'I'll drive.' Lou was firm. Gina stumbled into the car. Lou drove rapidly, ignoring a red light, hurtling round corners, and tried to talk with Gina.

'Did she say she was being moved or that she was moving?'

'Hard to know - but something is happening...hurry up.'

Lou turned the car into a staff parking spot, careless of any possible consequences, and they both dived out and ran into the hospital.

When they got to Tanni's room, Zak was kneeling by her bed.

'Tanni. Tanni, it's me, Daddy. Can you hear me? And here's Bonnie...'

He waggled her dolly in front of her and Gina bent down and squeezed in front of him kneeling on the floor, reaching up to her daughter.

'Darling, can you hear me? It's Mummy.' She took Tanni's hand. 'Can you hold my hand?'

To her huge relief and joy she felt some tiny pressure on her fingers.

The nurse pointed to the response graphs which clearly indicated some increased brain activity and a quickening of the pulse.

'We noticed a sudden change about an hour ago. She hasn't opened her eyes yet.'

Zak took Gina's arm and turned her to face him.

'She seems to be pulling through - I am going to phone mum and dad.'

The nurse was cautious.

'It's early days. This is just a start, please don't … you know- we can't say it's all over...we need to be patient.'

But Zak had gone, and Gina and Lou bent over the gently breathing form, Gina especially determined to stay with her little girl until she opened her eyes.

As it turned out, this didn't happen for another three hours, during which time, Zak brought the boys back.

When her eyelids finally fluttered open, she saw her family smiling at her. She offered the faintest of smiles back. Everyone cried except Tanni!

Gina could barely speak, barely breathe. 'Hello darling,' she said, bit her lip and buried her head in the pillow next to Tanni. The boys were more excited and needed restraint. Zak warned them to be calm and not to be too noisy, but they were difficult to control. As soon as it was clear to Louise that Tanni was not going to relapse or have any kind of setback at this stage, she felt she could leave and take the boys back home, leaving Gina and Zak with their precious baby.

In the following weeks there was much time for reflection and thought. Lou stayed for a while and she and Gina spent hours talking together. They were all exhausted after the effort of driving backwards and forwards to the hospital, the emotional stress of waiting, and the sheer torment of not knowing if Tanni would be well. Tanni herself quickly improved after the initial recovery and within a week was back home under careful supervision and constant care. She became stronger and quite soon had resumed a more or less normal life. The boys, who had rallied so well round their stricken sister, soon relaxed into their usual behaviour patterns, returned to school and lived off their adventures for weeks. Gina heard Han telling his friend Luke how 'the car nearly exploded, we only just got out in time…' In truth, this had initially, been one of Gina's main worries, but at the moment that she had seen Tanni a limp ragdoll figure, everything else went from her thoughts.

Now, she watched her carefully and spent a good deal more time with her than she had before the accident. Sometimes Gina thought she detected a difference in Tanni's behaviour, but surely it was just that she was growing up. Maggie, now again very pregnant with her second child came to stay for a weekend and assured Gina that Tanni had not changed, had simply got a little bit older. But there were days when she had to work hard to convince herself of that. Each time she saw her climb onto the trampoline or sit on the swing, or even just run ahead a short way on the road, her stomach clenched and her heart beat faster. It took weeks before she felt she could leave her with Rayna alone. Even then, she thought about her constantly. It was tremendously difficult for her to let Tanni go and to release the emotional hold on her that the accident seemed to have engendered.

15

Lou helped. She visited a good deal during those weeks and spent time with Tanni. Gina trusted her mother like no-one else and the tension began to ease. During this time, Gina had the chance to ask Lou about her father again and apart from hearing 'That shit just walked out on us when...' she paused, 'you were 7 months old.' Gina got little else. But she did notice the pause in the brief bit of information that her mother gave. Why did you hesitate, she wondered but knew better than to ask.

It was at about this time that she decided, finally, to get in touch with her cousin Lily, the daughter of her father's brother. She had first thought to do this when Tanni had just become conscious; after all, Tanni was her father's granddaughter and maybe he should see her. Access, she knew could only be through Lily. At the time, she had not mentioned this idea to Louise, but although she had done nothing about it then, and now she felt she would, she decided that she would not mention it to her mum now, either.

Naturally, the relationship with Lily had lapsed somewhat, Lou being generally averse to contact with her ex's side of the family, but Gina made a real effort to reconnect. It was a bit of a paper chase, and not altogether straightforward. There were a couple of dead ends and a few false turns, but finally she succeeded. Within a week, she arranged to meet up with Lily, and though it was easy for Gina to leave her brood behind, Lily could not, and brought her 3 year old with her. She also had 2 older children, both teens, Lily being several years older than Gina. The boys were in school, but even so, time was limited. Lily needed to be back for their return later that afternoon.

They had lunch in a pleasant cafe in Dulwich. Gina had agreed to make the longer trip, as she was not encumbered by children nor was there any urgency for her about returning. Lily lived quite close to the cafe, and the moment Gina saw her, she recognized her; tanned-looking skin, pretty, dark brown hair - very like her own. Boy, those brothers must have been good-looking - both of them!

They both smiled in instant recognition and somehow liked each other instantly. At once, they began chatting. They seemed to be making up for the lost time of adolescence and they quickly gathered information about their families and their husbands - they had both had 2 each, Lily had left the first one, why, Gina had not yet discovered, but intended to find out, and if not this time, then soon. Clearly they would meet again. Little Holly had finally settled to do some crayoning and was being reasonably well behaved.

Finally, Gina dared to ask about her father.

'Did you know him?'

'Yes. I did.' Lily spoke sharply and looked severe. Gina wondered why.

'What was he like?'

'He was my uncle,' Lily responded as if that answered Gina's question.

'No. What was he, you know, like?'

'A bastard. A mad bastard. That was the only excuse.'

Gina frowned.

'Excuse for what?'

Lily looked up, a shocked expression on her face.

'You don't know do you?' Lily appeared startled. 'Aunty Lou, your mum, she - she never said? Anything?'

Gina became agitated.

'Anything about what? What don't I know? Tell me what you're trying to say.'

She became angry and hot-faced.

'You're talking about my father. He may have walked out on my mother, but he's still my dad and I know Louise calls him terrible names, but maybe I don't have to feel that way about him. Maybe we could meet and there could be a reconciliation...'

She stopped, seeing Lily's face. It was a mixture of incredulity and shock.

'Reconciliation? How can you think of such a thing? After what he did? I can't believe what you're saying.'

'But I don't know what you mean. What do you mean "what he did"? Lou has never told me anything - please tell me what it is that's so awful'

'Seriously, she's never said anything?'

'No. Tell me. Tell me now.'

'It's difficult - don't know where to start. Did you know you had a sister?'

Gina breathed in hard and held the breath. She closed her eyes and then slowly opened them. She looked hard at Lily, frowning.

'No. Well. Yes, I thought I did. Mum once asked me when I was just a little kid, if I remembered her. I had said I didn't. To be truthful, I've been a bit scared to explore what she meant by asking me that and it was ages ago. She sort of sidestepped it at the time. Obviously she didn't want to talk about it though something made her ask. I think she immediately wished she hadn't. Please Lily, tell me what happened.'

'She died,' Lily said simply. 'Victor smacked her - or that's what he said. More likely he thumped her.'

There was a long pause. Gina sat back in shock. She took in her breath sharply and opened her mouth to speak but for some seconds she could not. Her eyes had filled with tears.

'Victor? Was that his name? I didn't even know that.' Even as she said these words she was aware that surely this was the wrong response. Surely the expected reaction should be concern for the child, for the dreadful deed that had been inflicted on her sister, the sister she had never known, or at least could not remember. She tried to correct this inappropriate response by asking about her lost sister at once.

'What was her name?'

'Cristina. Your mum liked your 2 names together - Cristina, Georgina - that's why she called you that. But when Victor was left alone with the two of you when your mum did a night shift, he just lost his temper with Cristina. She was doing what 5 year olds did, do, she was just being annoying; defying him. She did it all the time, she was a bit wayward and did a lot of shouting, but she was a darling, gorgeous child, and I adored her. She was a few years younger than me and always fighting for attention. You had just come along and she must have felt a bit threatened. When you're five, you don't realise that your parents can still love both of you. She just tried it on, you know, probably wanting to get reassurance. Aunty Lou - your mum - could handle her, but Vic couldn't. He was a bad tempered git anyway, but this was terrible. Nobody thought he wanted to really hurt her but he just lost it that night. Hit her hard it seems, on the head. She fell on the fender round the fire, banged her head really badly on the metal bit at the end. It seems she died at once. He did time of course. Manslaughter.'

Gina could not say anything. She just sat there staring at her cousin, letting her talk and not even able to cry. She felt so sad and so hurt, though why she felt hurt she could not say. Naturally she was thinking of Tanni and how near to death she had come and, weirdly, how it would have been her fault and maybe she too would now be in prison if her darling had not survived. Suddenly she felt a huge wave of sympathy for her unknown father. Wisely she did not mention this to Lily. Instead, all she found to say at last, was:

'It's horrendous. I couldn't have imagined anything like this. I don't know what to say.' And at that, she felt the tears fill her eyes and drop silently onto her hands folded on the table.

Lily looked gloomy. 'I'm sorry I had to bring you the news, and after all these years of our not knowing each other. I'm sorry,' she said again.

They ordered another coffee and were relatively quiet for the next half hour, chatting, filling in family details, though Gina refrained from telling of the events that put Tanni in the hospital. Under the circumstances, it might have seemed, at best odd and at worst - well, who might guess how Lily would interpret the situation. Gina did not want to alienate her and she clearly had little time or sympathy for Victor. Gina tried to assure herself that the two situations were not comparable, but she couldn't quite convince herself.

She did ask Lily if her father had indeed 'walked out on' the family, but Lily said he had not, though they did eventually divorce. Lou clearly had not been of a mind to reveal the truth and had used this phrase as an explanation for his absence. Gina decided that she would never speak of what she now knew to be the truth to her mother, but she hoped that Lou might eventually mention it.

Soon it was time for Lily to get back for her boys. The three year old, after a period of chasing round the café, had dropped off in her pushchair and they had had a peaceful last hour. Now, as she was awake, it was clearly time to go.

Gina drove back thoughtfully. Later that evening, she wrote of her feelings and of her sadness, except that it was distant and elusive. She had not known her sister, after all. As she loaded the shoeboxes back on top of the now rather battered journal, she reflected about her father. Was he still alive, she wondered. Where might he be?

16

ZAK

Zak held his head in his hands and stared at the rug between his feet. His thoughts wandered to the day he had bought it. He had been early for a meeting with a business contact and he had emerged at Green Park tube station planning to walk to the lunch venue. This was partly to kill time and partly to think through what he was going to propose to the wealthy Russian he was about to meet. In a shop window near Burlington Arcade he spotted this fine Afghan rug, notable particularly for its great size. The polished ancient boards in this living room where he now sat demanded a huge elegant carpet and the one he had seen that day had been perfect. Moreover, the pale creams, bronzes, the dull yellows and greens would be glorious in this lofty old room. When it arrived and was carefully laid on the dark burnished planks, when the grand piano was restored to its position and when the rest of the furniture had been set in its proper place, the transformation was astonishing. The room simply glowed and when Gina was finally allowed in to look she had actually gasped. She had been pregnant with Hanif at the time and had dropped heavily into an armchair in what Zak had assumed to be amazed silence. In truth, she was just a bit breathless, but nevertheless, she had certainly been impressed. Zak had good taste, of that there was no doubt.

Now, he continued to stare at the floor, his thoughts running to other matters. He was meeting with his Russian colleague Yeshevsky tomorrow and it would involve the exchange of a large sum of money. He was wondering how best to effect this transaction. It was not the first time he had done this type of business. Previously, it had been at a very personal level but now, the widening network required a different approach. In his jewellery business it had been relatively easy to engage in gold trading. He knew the ropes and he had friends in the right places. He had got to know dealers and the trading had been very carefully monitored and supervised for legitimacy. His father had played a key role in the initial stages and had in fact instigated the moves that had led to setting up the consortium in which Zak himself was now a key player. It was risky, they all knew that. But when it was successful, and just now it was, then it was also very lucrative and the money piled in. Careful accounting and tax planning ensured that funds were safely stowed. Zak was comfortable with all this and while the retail jewellery outlets provided an excellent cover for the wider trading that this venture represented and it was small beer in comparison. Now, however, there were other plans, which Ivan Yeshevsky was exploring with Zak.

Zak had been to Bucharest, a fact not known to Gina, and had worked out the basic plans some time ago. With his father's help, he had laid out a large amount of money to establish his interest and commitment to the project. Yeshevsky was the key player. He instructed Zak in the major moves; he would arrange the details. It was Yeshevsky who had decided that a high-powered motor boat was essential.

'I can't handle a boat like that,' Zak had said.

'You will learn.' Zak was uncertain whether this was an assurance or an injunction, but he had agreed and the boat was bought and kept on the south coast for many months before Zak revealed its arrival. He also took instruction in its handling, although he was persuaded that there would be an experienced crew to pilot and navigate the craft.

Gina knew none of this. Of course she had noticed that Zak had been impatient, offhand and not always in tune with her moods and then there had been the party. When Gina had seen the figure of the young woman in the window she had felt a bitterness and rising anger, which she had not felt before. Zak was aware that Gina had shown some resentment and distress in the previous few months but he had decided that it was the anxiety and concern incurred after Tanni's time in hospital. He did not ascribe it to any of his own behaviour. Zak assumed that Gina would continue to efficiently direct the running of the household and to concur with his plans whatever they might be. He didn't expect any discussion, far less objection from Gina, and largely, she offered none. He seemed quite unaware of her growing rancour, dismissive of her interest in returning to study, and expected her to be only grateful for the wealth he brought to their marriage. He saw her occasional objections to his plans and behaviour as a minor nuisance, a way of displaying her disquiet and probably a wily way to get something she wanted.

'What might it be this time?' he would think, 'a new outfit, a trip abroad, a new car?'

'Have what you like,' he would say dismissively. And hadn't he suggested the big autumn party? Why - he had suggested it purely with the intention of cheering her up and having some fun with their friends. He knew the kids would love it and that would meet with Gina's approval. Zak thought it odd, the way she was so devoted to them. Why she didn't use the services of Rayna more, he didn't know. And the fussing over Tanni when she was in hospital and then when she came home, well, it seemed so unnecessary.

17

Once the party had been arranged, the date had turned out to be rather inconvenient, as it happened. It had been arranged for the second group of young women to arrive on that weekend and Zak could do nothing about it.

The day before, he had travelled to London, where the boat crew had taken the girls and had supervised their placements. Three went directly to Glasgow and one to a massage parlour in Ealing. The fifth girl could not be placed immediately and it was agreed that she would return with Zak. It was a risk, he knew, but he decided it was worth taking. She would be lodged briefly in the top floor of their house, behind a locked door. Zak would be the only one who had access and he would personally supervise her and her meals until a location could be found for her. It was quite a trick to get past Rayna, although Gina was less of a problem. There had been a sticky moment when he had brought her in. Gina had been out, a fact known to Zak, since he had spoken to her on his mobile half an hour before. This had made the decision to bring the girl, very much easier.

'I'm having a colour put on my hair,' she had said 'but do try to hurry home, Rayna is struggling with the kids.' And indeed he had made every effort to get home in the fastest possible time. He certainly didn't want to arrive when Gina was back.

When he arrived, the children were in the process of having supper and getting ready for bed. Rayna had heard him drive up, although he had been careful to park in the garage, and she went to the door to greet him. She had been a bit upset about Gina going out so late, and Zak not being home, but Gina had decided that she wanted to get her hair done for the party and she had taken the only slot they had - a cancellation as it turned out, so she had been lucky. Fridays were always busy, of course, so she had made hasty excuses and apologies to Rayna and dashed off a couple of hours before.

Zak was usually home by now and Rayna was troubled, because the children were upset. On hearing him arrive, she was keen to get him to take Tanni to bed and read her the story that she always expected. At the door, Zak was put out by her welcoming attention.

'Yes. Yes. I'll be in soon, just need to get my brief case - I left it.' He put a finger to his temple, indicating forgetfulness. He waved in the direction of the car and motioned for Rayna to go back in. Back at the garage he indicated to the girl cowering on the floor of the rear of the SUV that she should be quiet and wait there until he returned. He locked the car, and went in. Now he turned his attention to Tanni, and with rather unfatherly haste, ended her favourite story somewhat abruptly, He waved away her complaints about mummy not being home, tucked her in bed in a hurry and returned to the garage.

He knew that Rayna was bathing the boys and as usual they were creating watery mayhem and making huge demands on her. This gave him the opportunity he needed and he ushered the girl rapidly and quietly into the house, upstairs past the havoc in the bathroom, up the second flight and into the upper dusty attic room. She barely protested and he indicated the bed and the chair. She sat mutely as he tidied the room a little, opening a window and turning on a sad little light. He checked the tiny toilet in the little closet in the room, not brilliantly clean, but functional. The single tap on the crusted, green-stained basin was jammed fast, but he decided that didn't matter. In an old wardrobe that they had long ago stored in the attic, he found some clothes: a jacket, a sweater, a blanket and some old cushions that would double as pillows. Again, he indicated that she might want to use them, but within a few moments, he left the room, when the turn of the key in the lock must have been audible to her. Again, she made no protest. He went quietly down the top flight of stairs and wandered into the boys' bathroom, as casually as he could. The chaos had barely been controlled and he knew that Rayna would have to clean up the flood on the floor and get the boys to bed. Shaf would demand to be allowed to stay up longer than Han. She would let him play on his DS or whatever he was currently addicted to just now. She would insist that he stayed in his room, which he was happy to do provided that no-one stopped his playing.

He greeted the boys. 'How's it going?' he asked.

'Yeah, great dad!' Han shouted and flicked water over Shafi. Most of it missed him, but splashed dangerously near Zak. 'I think

61

I'd better go,' he said as he dodged to avoid the soaking. 'You OK Rayna?' he asked without expecting any denial, and of course there was none. 'Han, call me when you are in bed. I'll read you a story.' This was fairly unusual for Zak, but he needed to ingratiate himself with Rayna. She did look relieved, he noticed, and he slipped away quickly to the kitchen. Here he grabbed a few slices of bread, a piece of cheese, a plate, a mug into which he carelessly tipped some milk, found a knife and a couple of apples, all of which he put on a small tray. He hopped at speed up the stairs, keeping his selection well out of sight and up the second flight where he hastily opened the door and put the tray on the table. He said nothing, but left, locking the door behind him again. Now he went down to Han's room and started a story. Within a few moments, he heard Gina call from the hall. 'Where is everyone?' Somewhat disingenuously, Zak called back, 'In Han's room - reading a story.'

Gina did not come up the stairs.

'OK - see you soon,' she sang.

She sounded happy, Zak thought. With the party on the next day and the marquee already up, the caterers due tomorrow morning along with the florists, all was in place and Zak assumed that she was pleased with her hair and looking forward to the event.

The boys were excited too, no doubt the reason for the extra level of high spirits he had just been witnessing. He assured Han that there'd be no party for him if he didn't settle down quickly and he went to the bathroom to deliver a similar sort of injunction to Shaf. With relative calm established, he went to speak to Gina.

He remembered to compliment her on the hairstyle. He even noticed that the colour was different. 'You look good,' he observed appreciatively.

Gina smiled - a faux-coy smile, but she seemed pleased.

'Is everything all sorted?' he asked.

'Fine,' she replied, 'the firework people came, they've set that up, the floor came this afternoon, and Summerlicious have delivered all the plates and glasses and the heaters and so on. They'll be here at 8 tomorrow. I think this will be a great event Zak, don't you?'

18

The day of the party was bright and as the band arrived and began to practice in the crisp autumnal morning air, Zak began to feel that he might enjoy this day. The caterers came, furniture was set up, linen was flung high across tables, landing with practiced professional accuracy, and flowers were put in place. The interior of the marquee was transformed into a grand and elegant setting for their guests. Outside, The barbecues were lit and meats placed ready.

But it would not be easy to deal with the young Russian girl. Zak would need to choose his chances carefully. Fortunately Rayna had taken the two boys to the park in the morning, and Gina was very occupied with outfits for Tanni and herself. They were both trying on dresses and skirts, tops and shoes and other varieties of ensembles in the big bedroom. Of course it was mainly about Gina, but Tanni was doing copycat stuff and enjoying it. While they were preoccupied he'd darted up to the attic with more food and drink. The girl was startled by his arrival, but apart from a mumbled phrase or two, which Zak took to be 'thank you' she said nothing.

At noon, Gina was out supervising the erection of the trampoline and Tanni was eager to try it out, so they were occupied for quite a time. The jazz band was setting up kit and speakers. Gina would be diverted for quite even longer. Again Zak visited the girl, and seeing that she was relatively comfortable, simply pointed to his watch to indicate that he would return later on - and as it turned out it was not until some hours towards evening, when he could manage to do so.

Suddenly it seemed, their guests began to arrive. The garden was suddenly alive with people, children skipping everywhere. The sun shone and the barbecues were busy, the music floated through the garden and the chocolate fountain flowed. People filled their plates as canapés were offered, and there were ample places to sit, though some chose to stroll. The children had been very adequately catered for: sausages and pan pizza done on the grill - Gina had never heard

63

of that before - all went down well. Later, the adults murmured their approval of sophisticated meats, fish and vegetables and salads. The drink flowed and was served with unobtrusive grace by numerous charming men and women, dressed stylishly in red and black outfits. The bar too, was busy.

As the afternoon light began to fade, and at a time when Gina seemed involved with a group, Zak darted quietly and quickly inside the house and up to the top. He took too, a plate of canapés and some juice. He thought he had almost been spotted by Amy, but she was miserably lost in her own thoughts at the other side of the kitchen and he was able to pass by without her seeing him. Once in the upper room, he set down the plate and glass, and asked Olga if she was OK. She seemed to understand that and nodded, although clearly her knowledge of English was very limited. She indicated by gesture that she felt cold and indeed the evening had become chilly. He mimed removing and changing her thin dress, and dashed down to their bedroom from where, in a closet, he extracted a sweater and an old skirt of Gina's, that he had not seen her wear for a long time. He knew that its next journey would be to the box for the charity shop, something that Rayna would deal with in any case.

On returning to the upper room, he was astonished to see that the girl had removed her dress and was more or less naked. Quickly, and averting his head, he passed her the clothes and returned to the door where he turned out the light. There was just enough light from the party outside to dimly illuminate the room and he pointed to the switch, waving his forefinger from side to side and firmly shaking his head. She nodded slowly, understanding his meaning and he placed a finger on his lips, a gesture she also understood and she sat down, now clothed and quiet. He left her to the crepuscular safety of the oncoming evening while he returned to the fun in the garden. It seemed he had not been missed and although he'd noticed Amy again, now standing at the kitchen door, dabbing her eyes and looking solemn and miserable, he slipped by unnoticed and passed into the garden where the caterers were bringing in the massive cake, now all cut and ready for the guests.

19

The day following the party, Zak knew that he had work to do. Somewhat hungover, he had decided almost at once that he would need to find an excuse for missing Will's party. Will was probably his oldest friend and he wasn't going to like it. Dee would give him a mouthful, he realised that, whereas Will would be quietly resentful. Zak was sorry, but there was nothing to be done. He had to get Olga sorted and delivered. He made a couple of telephone calls and then announced to Gina that he was not going to Dee and Will's. She was understandably upset, but she couldn't do anything about his decision. He knew she couldn't argue with him, not really, and he was particularly cross with Gina since she had borrowed his sports car without telling him, and failed to fill it with petrol. Now he would need to stop to fill up, and that would cut his timing to a worrying minimum, but it had to be done. Gina was angry too and drove away in undue haste, the children and Rayna shaken about when she reversed rapidly, spraying gravel up from the wheels of the SUV to race out of the drive.

With the house now empty and the caterers busy clearing in the garden, he raced up to the top of the house. In a closet he found several bags marked for the charity shops. Gina did not keep clothes very long and she dispatched them as soon as she had enough to fill the boot. He dragged a couple into the room where Olga sat, staring gloomily out of the window.

'Here,' he said, gesturing to the bags, 'choose some clothes.'

She understood this well enough and began to look through the bags. Zak returned to the small dark space where he now discovered an old canvas bag, once used for his sports gear and dragged that in also. He banged off the worst of the dust and indicated that she should pack some clothes and shoes into it.

Zak went down to gather the few things he needed, and as soon as he felt she had had enough time to get herself organized, he dashed up to usher Olga, with all speed, into his car. He noticed that she was wearing a pair of Gina's old boots, and he nodded at her choice approvingly. She had on a decent light raincoat and carried a handbag.

She lifted this item towards Zak and raised an interrogative eyebrow. Zak nodded and with a small upward wave of the hand indicated that he was happy with the choice, and for her to take it.

Zak had raced along the motorway, stopping only to fill the car with petrol, visit the ATM and to arrive at King's Cross in time for the 11 a.m. train to Edinburgh. He searched the crowded forecourt for Luke, and recognizing him, pushed his way towards him with all haste.

'You OK with all this?' he asked.

'Sure. I got her ticket here. I'm only going one stop. Settle her in for the journey, then I'm off. Here !' He thrust the ticket towards Olga and she frowned but took it. She opened the newly acquired bag and put the ticket into the little wallet inside.

'Luke, can you do enough Russian to explain?...'

'Yeah, I'll tell her where she's going and who to look for in Edinburgh. You got some cash for her?'

'Oh, yes,' he remembered. 'Here Olga,' he said pushing a small wad of notes into her hand, 'put it in your bag. Now.' He stabbed at her handbag with an urgent forefinger. She took the money with a downward pull of her mouth and a small pout. She eyed Zak darkly from beneath heavy brows but said nothing. She stowed it into the wallet.

She stepped away from both men, and stood alone in the hugeness of the station, setting the old canvas bag at her feet.

'OK Luke, you phone Dmitri - yes -? Explain that there was no room at the London House for Olga.'

'Will do. No worries.'

'Have you got that photo of Dmitri? The one I sent?'

'Sure, I'll show her. She can check before they meet, but Dmitri has a pic of her too, so it'll be fine!'

Zak moved a pace towards Olga. He put a hand lightly on her slim shoulder, said 'Good luck' and moved away. She did not smile. She did not speak but lifted the handles of the canvas bag onto that same narrow shoulder and walked towards Luke, who, with a tilt of his head, indicated that she should follow him towards the platform where the train was waiting. Zak watched for a moment and then returned to his car which had been badged with a familiar black and yellow ticket. 'Shit,' said Zak, as he pocketed the document, smiled grimly and drove off.

20

When Zak received the text from Gina to say that they were in the hospital and that the car had been damaged, his first reaction was anger, but Gina continued to explain that Tanni was unconscious and he went at top speed to the hospital. He'd had a long, hard day and had barely returned from London when the text came. Although angry with Gina for what he supposed was careless driving, he forced himself to think only of Tanni.

His anxieties were not assuaged as he regarded the still form of his tiny daughter. She looked so vulnerable in the large hospital bed and he was inclined to get angry with Gina again. But he attempted to remain calm and walked to the drinks machine where rather unpleasant tea was dispensed. The boys had gone home with Rayna, and he waited with Gina by the bedside. Neither of them could drink or eat and the night passed painfully and slowly.

In the days that followed, Zak and Gina spoke little to each other, interacting only through the boys and attending to their needs in rather distracted ways. Much of what was required was dealt with by Rayna. Lou was there often and was always helpful. Zak and Gina were at the hospital by turns, Maggie and Amy both came to support them, Amy gloomy, Maggie upbeat and due any day by the look of her. Gina was jumpy whenever the phone rang at home. She was dark-eyed and exhausted. Louise took care of the boys and coped with them lovingly, allaying their fears and offering jolly outings which were diverting. They asked about their sister often and she simply said that 'Tanni is getting better'.

It was fortuitous that Lou was in the house when the call came – Zak, with Tanni at the time, recognized that - and Lou and Gina dashed to the hospital to see Tanni emerge from her dark days and see her gently returned to life and to the family.

Zak noticed that Gina was obsessed with caring for Tanni in the weeks that followed, in what he felt was an unnatural way. But for him, it was useful as by then his mind was on other things.

The previous group of girls that had come to the UK had been succeeded by yet another set, and they too had been settled at various addresses and places of work. Olga had arrived in Edinburgh; Luke had returned to London. Zak was aware of the increase in the balance in one of his many accounts of which Gina knew nothing. He was also clear that a degree of money laundering had occurred and he had been asked for another large amount of investment by Yeshevsky. Zak's approach was to ask as few questions as possible. Ask nothing, know nothing - surely that was the safest way?

Yeshevsky and Dmitri had then asked for another meeting.

Zak decided, given the level of nagging from the boys, and given that spring was on the way, that they would organize another trip to the boat. He had put this off many times, using Tanni's accident and subsequent recovery as an excuse, and then the cold winter weather, but now it was inevitable. Gina asked him repeatedly, and finally he gave in.

It occurred to him that he might combine the trip with a meeting of Dmitri, Yeshevsky and himself. Suddenly it seemed a really good plan and he began to put a strategy together.

It seemed a good idea for Yeshevsky to meet him at the boat. How exactly he would do this, Zak did not know nor did he ask. He knew he had his contacts and he knew he had ways of getting things done. In truth, Yeshevsky was a bit of a thug. He nearly always got his own way. Zak was sure he would make the meeting which is why Zak acceded to Gina's suggestions and she began to make plans.

21

GINA

Gina wanted Lou and Jim to accompany them on the trip, but they had gone on a European tour and a Rhine cruise.

'Gina, I've never had such a chance before, Jim is very keen to give me a "special birthday" present,' Lou told Gina, weeks before.

'Mum, don't sound so apologetic,' Gina had told her when she had heard the plans. 'Why on earth shouldn't you go on this holiday? It sounds great and it's about time you had a real break with Jim. You were amazing when Tanni was in hospital and I couldn't have done without you.'

'Oh, you'd have managed.'

'No, I couldn't have, and you're probably exhausted from all the running about and driving you did, and looking after the boys too - you're not as young as you were mum.'

'Well, thanks for reminding me.'

'You were brilliant. Don't know where you get the energy.'

'Oh shut up Gina, really, I was so glad to be useful.'

Gina had taken Lou on a shopping trip and treated her to a whole new wardrobe, especially for the holiday, plus shoes, bags and accessories until Lou had yelled 'Stop this now - I've got enough...' and they had collapsed laughing at the ridiculous free-spending luxury of it all and drunk coffee in Costa and then went for a mediocre glass of champagne in a truly terrible bar nearby.

Returning home, Gina called Maggie to tell her. She had never really got over the charm of being able to spend what she liked, when she liked. It was also true that she loved spending on others, although such ostentatious generosity would not always have been welcome. Now she was sure that it was entirely justified as a thank-you to her mum. She felt high after her spree, and especially as her mum had loved it too, and they had had such a great time.

'Imagine, "I, I who had nothing",' she sang.

'And you're not Shirley Bassey now,' Maggie said, 'nor Tom Jones.'

'Do you know they're both Welsh?'

'Yes, course I do, what's that got to do with anything?'

'Nothing! Oh, Mag, I do love you and it's so good to just talk rubbish and laugh with you - I miss you - come and stay, we've got lots to talk about and the phone's not enough.'

It was barely an hour away from Maggie's home in North London, and she came over on Saturday morning.

Maggie came with her new little girl ('How clever was that Gina - one of each - the full set?' she had said when she was born.) She had called her Polly because, she said, she looked like a Polly. 'You had to have a third to get a girl…'

'But I managed it.'

'Not as clever as me and Simon.'

'It's not clever, it's just chance.'

' 'Tis clever.'

' 'Tisn't.'

' 'Tis.'

' 'Tisn't.'

' 'Tis.'

'How old are you? We?' she asked, laughing at their girlish silliness.

'Oh Gina, we're both nuts, you know.'

They were standing in the kitchen in Gina's gorgeous house and Gina turned to her, hugged her and said in the most melodramatic way:

'Oh Mags, don't ever leave me!'

Maggie pushed her away laughing.

'Of course not, you're my best fwend,' she lisped, and then: 'Tell me more about Lily.'

For Gina had been relating the story of visiting her cousin, although she hadn't got to the bad bit yet, indeed, she wasn't sure she would do so at all, best friend or not. And during this visit Gina did not quite have the courage to do so. Indeed she steered the conversation to the more trivial matter of buying Lou's new clothes and they discussed the nonsense of the prices charged for fashion goods, Maggie a bit more vociferous on the subject than Gina.

'The bad thing is I wanted them to come on our boat trip next week - and now, with this cruise, they can't. You're not free are you?' she asked, smiling.

'Oh, sure, me and the baby, she'd be a real asset on a motor launch! - Mind you, she is clever - probably get her navigating.'

They both laughed.

In truth, Gina really did love Maggie and wished she lived closer.

'Do you see anything of Issy?'

'I do. We meet often, they come to dinner - we do the occasional shopping trip together at the weekend. Si would rather look after the kids than go into a store! Wish you lived nearer Gina!'

'I was just thinking that,' she replied, 'but it's only an hour away.'

'Yeah, glad we bought in North London when we did - couldn't afford it now.'

And Zak agreed to the boat trip and was unconcerned that Louise and Jim would not be with them.

'Jim's no great sailor,' he said, 'we can manage without him.'

'He does know about boats,' Gina responded and sotto voce 'more than you do.'

22

But Gina was determined to discuss the trip with Zak and she asked him if he was home the following evening.

'Yes. I guess. Around 6, maybe.'

'Well, can you? Be here by then?'

'Why? What's going on?'

'Zak, I just want to talk about our trip next weekend.'

'Well. Sure. We'll talk over dinner.'

'Will you promise to be here, Zak?'

'Mmmm.' Zak was walking away as he replied, and tapping into his phone. Gina sighed.

Around 5, Gina was beginning to prepare the dinner, Tanni helping, standing high on a stool leaning over the island counter as she stirred, and splashed, a marinade. When the phone rang, Rayna came into the kitchen - 'For you - is Zak,' she said.

Gina wiped her hands and picked up the phone.

'Hi - what's happening?'

'I'll be late - sorry, I am negotiating with - oh well, - can't leave yet. I'll be as soon as I can - maybe 7?'

'OK.' Gina shook her head but was resigned. She continued to prepare the dinner for a few minutes, but then put it to one side and Rayna and she together assembled food for the children. She called them in. Tired, cross and depressed, she snapped at them simply because they didn't sit down promptly and Tanni started wailing which didn't help Gina's mood. She left the kitchen, knowing that her being there was not helpful.

In her bedroom she pondered her situation and tried to understand why she felt so low.

She knew that her marriage was far from perfect. Zak was no longer always kind to her, he didn't spend the time with the children that she would have liked him to. She missed his gentle intimacy that had been part of their relationship when they had first met. She felt alone. Despondent, she returned to the sitting room and listened anxiously to the raucousness of her kids, apparently at war round the kitchen table. After a few minutes, she moved into the kitchen and poked at the meat marinating in the fridge.

'Mum,' Shaf shouted, 'Han spilled the grated cheese over the table.'

'It's OK,' Rayna interrupted 'it was just a little bit.'

'I did not - and anyway you pushed me.'

'Because you wouldn't give it me.'

'Tanni wanted it.'

'She didn't, she just said that because I asked for it. She's a copycat.'

'Oh children, just stop this shouting at each other - what's it matter? And Han, give your brother the cheese - now!'

'But mum he's...'

'I said now - so just do it and if anyone shouts out again, you will go to your room without your Nintendos.'

'You're shouting,' Shaf said very quietly.

Gina ignored him deciding this to be the best response and, unnecessarily turned the meat once more.

Then she pulled a bottle of Sauvignon Blanc from the bottle rack in the fridge and cracked the screw top open. She poured a modest glass and took it with her as she wandered into the garden. The evening was mild and scented; many of her shrubs had beautiful perfume and at the end of a sunny day it was particularly pleasant to walk along the paths and breathe in the benign air. A slow walk round would take her fifteen minutes, especially if she stopped to examine and enjoy the borders. It calmed her. It was after 6 when she returned, the light fading, although it still felt warm for the time of year. She entered by the hall door and stood by the stairs.

'Tanni, you come up now, you're going to have a bath,' Gina called.

'Boys, get yourself to your rooms - do you have some homework? Please do it now.' She spoke quietly and gently. Shaf came up and put his arm round her waist.

'Are you better now mum?' Gina was startled. She realised that her mood was transparently conveyed to her children, and she was distressed by that.

'Oh, I'm fine Shaf - go on now - get that story finished.'

'I've nearly done it, it's only got to be 3 pages and I've done over 2...'

'Ah, but what about the quality, Shaf?'

'What? What do you mean?'

'Nothing. Nothing, just being silly - sorry - go on, get it done.' She gave him a squeezy hug and laughed him on his way with a little push.

Shaf chased Han up the stairs, barging by Tanni who was weary and drowsing on the bannisters.

'Come on little girl, you're tired aren't you?' Gina hooked her hands under her armpits and helped her up.

It was half an hour later when Gina came back down. Rayna had cleared up, made some salad, set the table for two and had left a pan of water simmering for rice.

Gina could hear the TV in Rayna's room, and finding her glass, which was now empty, refilled it and perched at the breakfast bar to skim the papers, which she had not looked at since the morning.

Gina heard Zak crash in through the back door. He threw his coat on the stand in the boot room, she heard his briefcase thud to the floor. Once, she would have rushed out to greet him, but now she simply waited for him to enter the kitchen.

'Hello, did you have a good day?'

'Yeah, good. OK. I have to take this call,' and Zak walked by her as he answered the phone. She heard his imperious response 'Yes?'

He went into the sitting room. Gina pulled the marinade from the fridge and set up a sauté pan on the stove-top. Zak re-entered the kitchen.

'Yes. I can. Maybe I could - just a minute,' he pulled the phone away from his face 'I have to...' he stopped then returned to the phone listening briefly before adding 'Yeah, I'll do that - yeah - I'll be with you by 10.' He rang off. Turning to Gina, he offered the barest of apologies and left to change, returning a few minutes later in casual clothes.

'What are we eating?'

'Stir fry - chicken - rice, OK?'

'Sure - can we be through by 9? I need to go out.'

'Again - why Zak?' Gina tried not to sound too grouchy but there was disappointment in her tone.

'Just do - sorry. Something came up.'

They both sat at the table. There was an awkward silence and Gina poured wine for Zak. She pushed a small bowl of salad towards him. They stabbed the greens with forks in a desultory fashion. Gina stood and walked to the stove. At once Zak was on his phone again and walked onto the patio as he talked. Gina continued to prepare the stir-fry, and drain the rice. She brought the dinner to the table, cleared the salad bowls and called Zak. He ate in a disinterested manner - making no comment and chewing deliberately and slowly. He clearly had his own thoughts and any idea that Gina might have had of pursuing a conversation about their boat trip was pointless.

'Can't you tell me what it is - what you have to go out for? Surely it could wait until...'

'No,' he interrupted firmly and loudly, 'I have to arrange something and I need to consult with people - it takes time. You don't understand, but,' and he smiled in an artificially sweet manner, softening his voice 'we'll have coffee and we can relax a while and talk - about the visit to the boat this weekend?' His tone was conciliatory. Gina had to comply and made no further objections. She hated herself for feeling grateful for this small gesture of appeasement.

When he had left, she retrieved her journal, which was becoming a more regular feature of her life, she wrote of the pleasure she derived from the visits she made with her group of friends. She wrote of her increasing dismay at the way Zak barely noticed her and was so frequently away or just out. She wrote of her loneliness, her sadness, and the sorrow she felt at her own bad temper, which she ascribed to the way Zak treated her.

She read what she had written. 'Of course I could do a degree, I can write perfectly well,' she murmured to herself.

23

The following weekend, they piled into the Land Rover and drove to the south coast. Gina navigated, and although she did refer to the satnav, she directed Zak onto the twisty road, as no-one minded and she was wearing flimsy flip-flops, not well suited to slithering down the crumbling cliff. Zak of course, drove in his usual speedy and reckless manner and Shaf complained that he had bitten his tongue. 'Dad, you're bouncing us, and I've got blood in my mouth.'

'Oh Yeucchh,' Tanni shouted. But Zak just laughed and slewed them round bend after bend, to negotiate the time-consuming, long, twisty road at the end of the trip. Eventually, they crunched onto the back beach and the boys ran towards the boathouse. Gina kept Tanni close to her, and Zak walked ahead jingling the keys in his hand. Zak had arranged for Yeshevsky and Dmitri to meet them. Dmitri was an experienced mariner and navigator and would help with their outing.

He was waiting at the boathouse, a round, somewhat overweight sandy and grey haired Georgian with a pinkish, stubbled face, and wild, grey eyebrows. He had a financial interest in the building of the major oil pipe, the Baku-Tbilisi-Ceyhan pipeline.

Zak knew this and was also clear that much of his investment in the other business that they shared, went directly into the building of the pipe. He had asked Dmitri why it was important and he had explained that Russia and Georgia had operated sanctions against one another and Georgia needed to be independent in oil production and distribution.

'Where is Yeshevsky?' Zak asked quietly.

'We see soon,' Dmitri assured him.

It was bright and sunny when they launched the dinghy to get to the boat, but as the day moved on, the weather changed from bright and sunny, to first more blustery, and then to cloudy with quite a cool wind blowing. As they neared the little island towards which they were headed, the sky was quite grey overhead, though they all pointed out the blue bits with an optimism that was perhaps unwarranted.

'Maybe this isn't such a good idea?' Zak suggested.

'Oh dad! Please - we have to go for a proper trip now,' said Shafi, 'we've got a picnic and everything.'

Reluctantly Zak agreed. On board, it was clear that Zak's navigational skills had improved somewhat since he had bought the boat, but they were not outstanding, especially in this increasingly unpleasant weather and they relied on Dmitri to get them under way.

'There is small island - over there,' Dmitri gestured vaguely with his hand. 'Yeshevsky is waiting. There is a hut.'

They had all seen the island - a low grey lump, minutes before, and they were peering excitedly towards the new shore. The children were not interested in Dmitri or Yeshevsky. Gina was.

'Who's this Yeshevsky?' Gina asked.

'He's the other sailor - we need him to help.'

'But we aren't going to be sailing, are we - not today? It must be too windy - it wouldn't be safe Zak...surely we can manage the motor on our own?'

'No. We will need him.' Zak's tone had the air of finality.

Gina, as usual, stopped discussing. What was the point?

For half an hour or so, the boat bounced rapidly through the choppy water, the boys shouting and yelling, loving the wind in their faces and the spray from the sea. Zak was talking with Dmitri and Gina was holding Tanni close to her. They had tried the cabin below, but Gina had felt slightly sick and needed the air. She was not really enjoying the journey.

'Are we almost at the island?' Gina asked, 'I don't feel too great.'

'Won't be long,' Zak assured her and in a few more minutes, they grounded on a stony shore, which, had the weather been even as good as it had been a couple of hours ago, would have been tempting. Now, as Zak jumped down and dragged on the rope, heading for the jetty, the boys were slow to follow. Zak urged them to help and unwillingly and half-heartedly, they pulled on the ropes. They seemed to have lost some of their early bounce and enthusiasm.

When the launch was secured, Dmitri urged them to unload the picnic basket and the drinks bags. He included Gina in his general dictatorial approach, something that Gina did not like and was inclined to ignore, but it had to be agreed that this was a sensible thing to do. Dmitri himself stood on the deck above them and lit a small black cigarette, which smelled vile and which he kept clamped between his teeth most of the time.

'You go to hut, you can eat picnic. Take basket,' he instructed the boys.

Zak helped them lift the basket to the small hut. There was no sign of Yeshevsky. Once inside the boys opened the basket and discovered the picnic treats within. While they were setting them out, Dmitri and Zak climbed back into the boat and began to talk. Gina could not hear them clearly.

She called out 'What's going on Zak? Why don't you come and join us, play with the kids. This is supposed to be a day out for us all.'

Zak dragged himself to standing and climbed off the boat to walk to the hut. Dmitri announced that he would go to find Yeshevsky. He came down from the boat and ambled off, smoking yet another of his nasty little black cigarettes, crunching over shelly sand towards the headland.

Zak pinched a handful of crisps and stuffed them into his mouth. Spraying little crisp particles, he shouted,

'OK boys, where's the Frisbee?'

They played for some time, even Tanni and Gina throwing themselves uselessly in efforts to get the plastic disc. Eventually, exhausted, they collapsed on the sand, grit in their shoes and in their hair. They were all laughing and asking if they could eat now.

'Of course you can - come and get a plate - load up. Don't just eat crisps Han, take some sandwiches, or a mini quiche... would you like a drink?'

'Yeucchh,' Han responded, 'I hate eggs.'

'You don't,' Shafi said, 'you eat plenty. I've seen you.'

'Do not. Only boiled.'

'Well that's eggs.'

'Boys,' Gina remonstrated, 'do stop bickering.'

'What's bickering?' asked Shaf.

'Arguing,' Han told him.

'I'm not,' Shaf replied.

'You are!' Han was triumphant, but Shaf was unimpressed. Gina raised her eyebrows and left them to it, scanning the horizon for signs of a change in the weather. It did not look good. Clouds were piling up to the west and the wind was whipping up the water.

Zak moved away and went towards the boat. Dmitri had disappeared around the little headland.

Zak climbed onto the boat and went to the helm station. He idly turned the starter. Apart from a strange grating coughing noise, there was nothing. Zak attempted to start the motor again. After a few moments of repeatedly trying, Dmitri, running from the other side of the headland shouted:

'Stop. You are flooding - it will wreck it.'

Zak stopped. 'I can't do it. It won't start.'

Dmitri came aft and tried to get the motor to kick in. It would not. After several attempts, he swore in Russian and announced that he couldn't work out what the problem might be.

'Is there enough fuel?'

'Yes, I checked.'

'How about the kill-switch?'

'Disengaged.'

'And the clip?'

'It's in. I have checked everything.'

'What about the battery?'

'Maybe, I don't know. If it's died, we need help.'

'Where is Yeshevsky?'

'There. There he is.'

The two men called rapidly to each other in Russian, and there was much pointing at the boat.

Yeshevsky looked grave.

'We will call the coastal rescue.'

'You mean coastguard rescue?'

'Yes, that one.'

Which they then tried to do while Gina and the children huddled in the little hut, out of the increasingly squally wind, picking in a perfunctory manner at the sandwiches, crisps, fruit and biscuits. Two of their mobile phones had no signal but eventually, Yeshevsky found that his was OK and they managed to get through.

'Why are we waiting in here?' Han asked

'It's OK darling,' Gina fluffed his hair as she spoke, 'the boat engine won't start.'

'Why do we need the engine - we could put up the sail?'

'They don't want to do that. Well, they can't - they think it could be dangerous in this weather. Don't worry, we'll wait for the coastguards to come and get us. It'll be exciting.' She hoped she sounded more convincing than she felt.

It had begun to rain a little harder, and it had become distinctly colder. As the wind increased, they stayed under cover. Tanni hung round Gina's neck, Han and Shafi leaned in the doorway, kicking idly at the pebbles, looking out for the motor launch.

24

It took a while but after almost an hour, the sound of a small power boat announced the arrival of the coastguard and they were relieved to see the vessel come in close. It chugged quietly toward the little headland to secure the launch to the jetty where two men jumped on to the sharp, chalky shingle. One of them immediately climbed up the sloping steps, carrying a large canvas bag and got to work on the boat. The other walked to where Zak, the two Russians and Gina waited with the children.

'Hi. I'm James, Dan is going to try to fix the boat. How are you all doing?'

'I'm cold,' Shafi announced crossly, 'and getting wet.'

Zak turned to James 'How soon can we go?'

'How soon do you need to go?'

'As soon as possible, Dmitri here -' he waved an arm towards the Georgian 'has to make a meeting and we really need to be there too. We didn't think we would be this long...'

Gina looked surprised.

'What meeting?' she asked, 'I didn't know you had arranged anything.' She could not hide her indignation.

'Yes. Well. Just a business arrangement we had set up... for later today, back in Birmingham.'

'I can't believe you arranged something for today, Zak. We're supposed to be having a family day out.'

'Yes. Well. Day... that leaves the evening and if we'd been back in time, if the boat hadn't played up, it would not have been a problem.'

'And how did Yeshevsky get here - to this island - where did he come from?' Gina asked, frowning.

Zak affected not to have heard, in any case he did not answer.

Tanni clung to Gina's legs.

'I'm tired mummy,' she said and Gina was sure she must be.

'Really tired.' She was close to tears. She had not had a nap and one of the characteristics following her accident had been an inclination to sleepiness, possibly more than previously.

'Darling, I'm going to take you to the little bunk down below on the boat - OK?'

'Mmmm yes,' Tanni said wearily, and Gina lifted her into her arms and took her to the boat. Gina scrambled up with difficulty, Zak handed Tanni up after her. Gina descended below decks and laid Tanni, eyes already closing, in the neat little bunk, covering her with a duvet and smoothing her hair before leaving her to rest. Gina could see that she was asleep before she had even left the room, and she was certain that she would sleep for the night if allowed to.

Up on deck, she observed and heard tools being used as the problem was addressed. She passed by and returned to the boys.

'Give me a hand, Zak,' she called.

But it was James who helped her down to the stony beach. Zak was in deep conversation with Yeshevsky and Dmitri. Heads together, they looked like a wicked trio plotting together in a panto or an opera. Gina turned from them angrily.

'Boys, come here, quickly. Get your things together.'

She entered the beach hut and hastily began to gather the picnic things together, knocking over cans and spilling coke as she did so. She carelessly wrapped up leftover sandwiches and pushed them, along with cake and biscuits, fruit and empty wrappers all into the hamper.

Outside the hut, the boys had put on their jackets and were kicking a small ball around in the shingle. She looked at them for a few moments and sighed, turned away and felt inexplicably sad.

Suddenly, Zak turned and shouted, 'We are just gonna have to go.'

'OK,' Gina responded wearily, 'I'll get Tanni.'

'No, there's no room, Dmitri, me, Yeshevsky, we need to get back and James will take us, the boys can come too. I'll call Rayna, she can get them in a taxi from town and then we can go to our meeting. Anyway,' he added meaningfully glancing at the person working on the boat, 'someone needs to keep an eye on things - and the boat!'

'How will I get back?' Gina asked panickily, 'Tanni and me.'

'Well, Tanni is asleep and she obviously needs to stay that way, surely it's better not to disturb her? Best she has a chance to stay rested.'

For a moment Gina almost believed that Zak was showing some compassion for his little girl, but he followed up quickly and impatiently with 'James, will you be long?' showing little further concern for either Gina or Tanni.

James replied that they reckoned the motor could be fixed in an hour or so and then the launch could be taken along with Gina and Tanni, back to shore and the boat locked away in the boathouse.

'Here's the key,' Zak said, thrusting it at her.

'Yes, but how do I get back home? With Tanni?'

Zak shrugged. 'In the Jeep of course. I'll go with Dmitri. His car is parked' - he indicated with a thumb over his shoulder - 'over there somewhere.' He raised a quizzical eyebrow to Dmitri who grunted, nodded and with his thumb, expertly flicked away yet another foul-smelling cheroot-like thing and walked towards the jetty where the rescue launch bobbed impatiently.

'Why can't we all go together?' Gina hated the way she sounded so plaintive but she was upset and needed to know what was really going on. She was sure there were other things afoot of which she knew nothing but could not bring herself to ask directly.

'There isn't room,' Zak responded flatly, and then more angrily 'as it is, we are breaking the rules by one person, but - it's a child, well, we'd get away with it.' His tone was harsh and edgy. He seemed nervous.

Gina's felt a bolt of fear run through her. She had come horribly close to losing one child and now it seemed that Zak was putting her two little boys in harm's way also. She found that she was trembling - a mixture of anger and fear.

'What's this all about Zak? You're leaving me here with Tanni - alone - you're just going off and you're leaving me here?' She was incredulous.

'You'll be fine - Dan seems very capable and he's a great sailor. He'll look after you. You've got to understand that the business,' he paused, adding more quietly, 'well, it's Dmitri - we just have to make this meeting, there's a lot riding on this. The loss financially, could be disastrous for us - for all of us,' he added darkly, 'you, me, the kids, we can't risk losing out on this. Trust me Gina.'

But she did not and said so. 'I don't trust you Zak, it's all sounding rather distasteful.'

'Oh stop that,' he said, losing patience and shouting. 'Let's not have that conversation - not in front of the boys - they don't want to know your opinions.'

'Well maybe they should...' She was indignant and very angry. She was shouting too.

'Why aren't my opinions of any interest or value?'

'Because you don't know anything about the business.' Zak's voice had taken on a powerful aggressive quality.

'I could do if I went to college - did a bit of studying. Maybe I could...'

'Don't start that again Gina, you know it's going nowhere, and this is not the time or place.' His tone had become harsh and bullying and he was clearly not about to enter into any kind of rational discussion.

Dmitri wandered over. 'You ready boss?' he said in his lazy-voiced way. 'Come. We need to move.' Yeshevsky was already at the coastguard's launch. The boys were waiting in the door of the hut.

'Come on boys - we're leaving - collect your things,' Zak shouted. He was abrupt. He would not be denied.

Han picked up the small ball they had been kicking around and then ambled after his father. Shafi followed. Gina stared at them as they boarded the little launch.

'You got the boathouse key? The car key?' Zak called. He was loud, cross, his voice barely softened. 'Make sure you lock up securely.'

'Yes, but...' Gina answered, and she ran forward to the jetty where Dmitri was already casting off.

'Boys, Han, Shaf, be good, be careful. Don't,' she stammered 'don't do anything silly. Do as daddy says, and be good for Rayna - she will collect you.'

She tried to sound positive, jolly, but she could not completely hide her misgivings. She noticed that her hands were shaking.

'You'll be OK - don't worry,' she said, in a tone that despite herself, indicated she was worried.

The little launch gave a sputter and then, with a confident throaty cough, burst into life and began whipping up the water at the rear. The boys had put on the lifejackets that James had given them and Zak and the Russians were now doing the same.

The sky was grey and low, the sea bouncy and the wind piling up the water into siseable waves. It had become rather cold. Gina was fearful but could do nothing. She reached up and touched Han's trainer, which rested over the sill of the boat.

'Go and sit down - don't get near the side, please keep an eye on Shaf, you know he can get over-excited,' she said anxiously. 'I'll see you later, when I get back.' And the little boat began turning, turning until it faced the mainland and with a sudden burst of speed rapidly pulled away so that within a few more seconds she could no longer hear their replies.

25

She slowly turned back to their boat from where she could still hear the tap, tap of a repairing hammer. Just then, she felt terribly alone and not a little afraid.

She decided that she would go and ask what the problem was and try to get an idea of the time it might take before they could leave.

'Hi,' she said as she neared the engine area, 'how's it going?'

'Oh, fine, I'll get the new part on soon, then we'll see if it functions.'

He struggled to his feet and turned towards Gina. He stared at her. She stared back.

Time had changed them, but not harshly. Indeed they were better looking than they had been 20 years before.

'Danny!' Gina said quietly 'Danny Moran. Fancy you being here.'

'Georgina Drummond - look at you!'

'Well. I'm Gina Sayeed now, and before that, Mackenzie.'

'And I'm Dan - I'm called Dan now.' They stared at each other for several moments.

'What brings you here? - Are you still living in Camberwell?'

Dan broke into laughter.

'I do not. Nearer to Camberley now,' he stressed the -ley, 'quite a change from where we used to be, when we were young.'

'God, do you remember?'

'...In the physics prep room...'

'Chemistry, it was.'

'Was it?'

'And your dad's van! What were we thinking of?'

'Oh, I know what we were thinking of,' Danny replied.

Gina felt the heat spread over her face and a familiar weakness came over her legs. She stepped back a pace. Quickly she asked,

'Would you like some tea?'

Danny grinned - a little too familiarly, Gina thought and she scrabbled in the cupboard to find tea and mugs.

'There, mmm, there is none - sorry - we-er - mm - Oh! There's some wine I think. Would that be OK? I'll check.'

Gina walked along the side of the little galley and reached up to where she thought she had seen a bottle of wine. Suddenly she became aware of the body warmth of Dan standing behind her. She stood quite still. His hand stretched above her head to the bottle, which, at the rear of the little cupboard happened to be just out of Gina's reach. His upper arm brushed Gina's hair, his lower hand found her waist. It rested there a few seconds and Gina felt the thrill of contact, her whole body weakening into a submission she had not felt in years. She leaned back into Dan's arms, the wine forgotten.

Within seconds, like the teenagers they once were, they kissed. A few moments more and they were in a lustful passionate embrace, when the world turned over for Gina and she released herself to Dan's caresses from his tongue, his fingers, his body. She did not resist. Dan fumbled with her shirt and his zip. Feebly Gina started to pull away, but her remonstration was short lived and soon they were trapped in an eager, gasping, grasping, panting and hotly emotional ten minutes until finally, Gina pulled Dan away from the tiny passageway, adjacent to the area where she hoped Tanni was sound asleep and into the space, aft of the helm where there was a double bed. They fell onto it with an unseemly haste and renewed their youthful desires in an almost desperate coupling.

Gina felt oddly moved and experienced emotions she had forgotten, as they relaxed.

'We, we don't know anything about each other,' she said quietly, 'are you married?'

'Unhappily, I am.'

'What do you mean, unhappily?'

'She left. A couple of years ago now, well, nearly. She took our son. I never see him.'

'What happened?'

'I was...Oh, you don't want to know.'

'I do. Tell me.'

And Dan explained that she had suspected him of having an affair with a work colleague, and left. As it happened, she went to live with a work colleague of her own.

'And were you?'

'What?'

'Having an affair?'

'Yes, well, no, not really, but it's true my wife, Karen and I weren't happy together, and I was spending more time, late evenings after work, with Lisa. A drink, a meal, you know. But it wasn't really an affair and I was willing to try and make a go of our marriage.'

'Even if it was failing?'

'Yes. Though I guess it was doomed.'

'And now?'

'As I said, she lives somewhere else and I don't know where she is.'

'Your son …how old?'

'Oh. Now? 13, no, 14.'

Dan's hand had moved to her breast. He was stroking gently and he moved closer. Gina breathed deeply and stopped asking questions. Dan moved his hand to her thigh and then higher. Gina closed her eyes and leaned to embrace him. She returned his caresses and they pulled more closely together. She could feel that he was aroused afresh and within seconds he had entered her again, this time, more slowly, and they climaxed again and lay together, not separating for several minutes.

When they did, Gina wriggled from beneath him and tiptoed to the bathroom. When she returned, she found him dressing and she too gathered her discarded garments and dressed hastily.

'How is the engine - the boat - is it fixed?'

'Well, I think so. I'm just going to put the part in place and give it a try.'

'What was the problem?'

'Sea water in the cylinder head - it had corroded. I've replaced it, well - nearly finished. I'll be a few minutes.'

Gina left him and walked to check on Tanni. She was still quite deeply asleep. Then she heard the welcome roar of the engine and noted a fresh smell of diesel.

'Oh, thank goodness,' she whispered as she came towards Dan.

'Yes. We're ready to go. Is your little girl still asleep?'

'Yes, she's fine. Can we leave?' Gina was anxious now.

'Have you got everything?'

Gina nodded and followed Dan's instructions. He left her at the helm, while he went to untie the boat from the jetty before they left. He came quickly back to steer them safely away from the island and back to the mainland shore.

They spoke little on the return journey. Gina was pleased to note that the sky had cleared, though darkness was falling, and now the sea was relatively calm. At the boathouse she tried to help to drop anchor and leave the boat in its place, though in truth Dan's expertise and ability in handling the boat allowed the task to be straightforward. He was very strong and made the heavy work seem easy. He dropped anchor and made the boat safe.

Gina lifted Tanni gently from her bunk and wrapped her in the duvet. Dan pushed the dinghy into the water and then gently took charge of Tanni. With care he helped Gina down, carefully handing the sleeping form of the little girl to her mother. When the dinghy reached the shore, he expertly leapt to the shingle and dragged the little boat to the safety of the boathouse.

Then he held Tanni again, while Gina locked the boathouse. Gina took Tanni and walked awkwardly to their jeep, Tanni over her shoulder. Dan carried all the rest of the bags including his own.

'Hope you can give me a lift,' he smiled. 'Or I could get a taxi.'

'No, of course I'll take you,' she said. 'You'll tell me where...'

'Yes, naturally, but Gina, give me your number. We can't just part like this.'

'No, Danny, Dan. I can't do that because...'

'Because what?'

'It wouldn't be right.'

'Oh, we've already done what's not right - we can't undo that.'

'No, but, I live so far away, and we couldn't, I mean, it wouldn't work.'

'I'd just want to talk with you, Gina. Please...'

He leaned across towards her, to take her mobile. She released it easily. He seemed to know how to find her number and he pulled his own phone from his pocket, and quickly put her number into his contacts.

Gina drove him back to his house unthinkingly following his directions. Where it was really, she had no idea, and he left her with the lightest of kisses, swinging his bag over his back and waving goodbye. Within a few moments, lights went on in his house, and she tapped 'Home' into the satnav, checked Tanni was still asleep and comfortable, and drove away.

It took her well over two hours to get home and was greeted by an anxious Rayna.

'What happened?' she asked

'I'll tell you later. Are the boys OK? Are they in bed?'

'Yes, but not asleep - they wait for you.'

Gina went up to see them both. They were sleepy and as soon as they had greeted Gina, were happy to settle down.

'Goodnight darlings,' she said.

How could anyone bear to lose their children, she thought.

26

Gina slept fitfully in the first part of that night, half waiting for Zak to return. She had a clear recollection of his arrival. The sky was already faintly lightening. She half woke when she heard him in the bathroom. Earlier, she had been troubled by disturbing dreams, waking briefly in mild terror before dropping off into a half-sleep, and at other times, sweating and suffering from what she might have described as an anxiety attack. Each time she struggled to get to sleep again, thinking thoughts that she had hoped would not perturb her consciousness - or perhaps her conscience - ever again.

On hearing Zak, she turned in half sleep to greet him, at least to say hello and was shocked by his reception. He took her almost viciously and with a desperate sexual hunger that he had rarely shown, indeed, he hurt her badly, with little regard for her body, as bruises the following day testified. He had clearly been drinking, but it didn't affect the vigour of his performance. Even though it seemed passionless to Gina, she offered little resistance while gaining no pleasure from what was a rather brutal act. On waking, neither of them made reference to this event, going to breakfast separately before even exchanging a greeting.

Briefly, she talked with Zak about the events of the previous afternoon, of course not mentioning Dan. Zak was fairly dismissive.

'You managed OK didn't you?' he said. His tone was not kind, more matter of fact and he shrugged. 'I'm glad that guy could fix the boat.'

'What would we have done if he couldn't?'

'Well, he did, so that's not an issue,' he said. The conversation was decisively ended.

On the Tuesday of the following week, Gina was due to meet with several of the women in the art group on a trip to the National Gallery in London. Yet another blockbuster beckoned and it just wouldn't do to have not seen it. She had called Marina, her Italian friend. She and Zak had dined a couple of times with her and her husband and another couple. Gina was grateful that these people were not all from the business circles that were Zak's territory and she felt a great deal more confident when she was with people she could count as her friends.

Marina was a slightly fatigued Italian beauty, but terribly thin, Gina suspected her of some eating disorder, which was never referred to. Her English was near perfect, with just enough of the Italian accent to be utterly charming. She worked in publishing, but Gina thought it was just something that kept her busy, since Tony, her surveyor husband was wealthy by everyone's account and their house was at least as grand as Gina's. Marina dressed elegantly and her short dark hair was always perfectly cut. Her deep voice betrayed an ex-smoker, and Gina imagined that she occasionally indulged even now, but she never saw evidence of that.

Marina was a woman with opinions. It was not easy to deny her, and yet often she wasn't accurate. If it ever became clear that she was in error, she would open her hands and wave her arms in a wonderfully Italianate manner and ask:
'What you want? I can't be right all the time,' as if to assure those listening that she was right most of the time. This wasn't so, but she had such a perfectly affable and attractive way of doing this, that her friends not only forgave her, but liked her anyway. And her husband was a great cook, though Marina herself was not, as she averred often.
'I'm lousy - don't expect good food from me! Tony is my chef.' And you'd believe from these remarks that she loved eating all Tony's food. In fact she barely picked at her meals and it was Tony's greatest sorrow that she didn't eat all the delightful dishes he prepared.
She had asked Marina for a lift - she lived quite close - and it was arranged that she would come over and take them both to the station. She discussed with Rayna the plans for the children for the evening and was happy that she would collect them from school and give them supper.
'It will all be fine - you go and enjoy the day.' Rayna was reassuring.

A short time before she was expecting Marina to arrive, and while she was waiting for her outside the front door, Gina's phone buzzed.

It was Dan.

She explained that she could not really speak as she was waiting for a friend and urged him to be quick, so with little preamble he asked her where she would be that day. She explained.

'And at the end of the day? Because I'm in London for a meeting.'

'Dan, we girls have a meal, and then I go home, we all get the train together.'

'You could miss eating with them and meet me - a drink?'

For a fatal minute she hesitated.

'The Duke of Windsor - drink and a quick bite?' He identified the location.

Gina paused. 'I do need to get home, not too late tonight, I'll have to call my girl - Rayna, and talk to the boys, and Tanni and I...'

Dan interrupted 'Let's meet early then, make an excuse and you could get a train back afterwards, you'll hardly be much later.'

'Sorry, Dan. Marina's here - must go.'

She just heard him say '5.30 then, in...' before she cut him off. She could ignore the whole thing if she chose. She hadn't promised anything.

The day was good, the exhibition spectacular and she had almost forgotten the phone call of earlier. However, at 4.30 she made a decision.

'Marina, Jo, Liz, I'm sorry but I'm going to have to leave you, please apologise to the others, but something has come up.' She was holding her phone, so it was reasonable for the others to assume that she had had a message and it meant she couldn't stay.

'I'm so sorry to miss the meal but I really have to go.'

They said goodbye warmly, expressing regret all round, and she walked into the breezy, early spring sunshine of Trafalgar Square. In St Martin's Lane, she waved down a cab and he slewed to a stop. Giving him the name and location of the pub, she climbed in and sat, tense and somewhat uncomfortably, as the taxi moved slowly through the beginning of the rush hour traffic. It took nearly 40 minutes to get there and she paid him mindlessly and nervously before alighting.

Anxiously she looked around. Dan was standing outside the pub and she waved hesitantly, still thinking she could make a dash for it, if he had not seen her. But he had spotted her, and came over, embraced her warmly and she slipped helplessly into his enfolding arms. They had a drink. They talked. She discovered that he had an engineering degree and then he'd started up a company, that he had made a lot of money following a venture involving prosthetic limbs, and now ran two successful companies. His work with the coastguards was part of his hobby which was sailing and boats, where his engineering skills were highly valued.

They had another drink. 'Are you hungry?' Dan asked.

'No. Yes. Well, I guess I could eat a snack.'

They ordered a sharing plate and as they talked more and ate, Gina looked at her watch.

'I can't be too long…'

'I know a hotel…'

'No Dan, I can't do that - you said a drink - a bite to eat, and we've done that.'

'Well, stay a bit longer then.' He took her hand, stroking it and looking into her eyes.

'Oh Dan,' she sighed deeply, 'I'm not sure about this.'

He continued to stroke her hand and leaned nearer to reach her face and began moving his fingers through her thick, dark hair. He pressed his hand on her cheek and drew closer. His mouth was close to her ear and then on her lips. They kissed lightly and then more fervently. In the gloom of the booth and with few people around, they were free to indulge in this activity for several minutes, until Gina drew away.

'Please Dan, Stop. I can't do this. Not now,' she added to make it sound kinder, and maybe offer promises for another time. She pulled back more firmly and searched for her coat and gloves.

'I'm going to go now - maybe you could get me a cab to the station?'

'Sure, I'll come with you.'

'No. No need for that Dan.' She was standing now, and Dan was throwing notes onto the table.

'I'm parked near Paddington - it made sense for my meeting,' he said.

She sighed again, then smiled weakly. 'OK fine. Come on.'

In the cab, they embraced again and he explored her body with obvious pleasure. She responded, unable to resist. The cab driver seemed unconcerned.

Gina was relieved that the taxi driver seemed to know a quick way through and they got to the station in twenty minutes. She fumbled for her purse, but Dan moved her hand away from her bag, though keeping hold of her wrist and pulling her back for a further passionate kiss. Eventually she did pull away and made her farewells, waving a quick goodbye.

She almost ran to the station and checked the departure time. It was ten minutes before her train was due to leave and she glanced around constantly, half expecting Dan to have followed her. But finally, on the train, she breathed out - it seemed for the first time in an hour - and sat back and relaxed a little, sipping water from the bottle in her bag. She called Rayna who was, as yet, unconcerned.

'I - we missed the early train, so I had to wait a while for a direct one.' Gina had no idea whether there was a stopping train at all, but then neither had Rayna, so she needed to give no further details.

'Is Zak home?'

'No, he called to say he would be a little bit late, maybe 8 o'clock, he will have eaten he says.'

'OK. I'll get a sandwich - I had a snack.'

She spoke to Shafiq and then to Hanif. She was aware that her voice was trembling a little, but the boys seemed not to notice. Tanni came on the phone.

'Mummy, where are you, I got a dolly - her legs bend and she's got shoes and she's got a sparkle jacket - can you come and see her?'

'Yes darling, I'll be home soon. Be good.'

And she rang off watching the dark countryside race by, realizing that the anxious face she saw was her own, lightly reflected in the window. She spent the journey thinking crazy thoughts, until she was back in New Street Station. She took a taxi and was considerably relieved to be back on her home patch.

Caught up in the business of dealing with the children, the day's events were to the back of her mind.

27

Zak returned. 'Good day out?'

'Great. You should try to get to see the exhibit - here.' She thrust him the little leaflet she'd collected. Zak glanced at it briefly and then pushed it to one side on the kitchen counter.

'And you've eaten?'

'Yep, but I'm going to make a sandwich, I didn't have much earlier - do we have some of that paté left Rayna?' And she moved on quickly to avoid the question of where and what. 'And that sourdough bread - could you pass it please? What did the children have?' She and Rayna discussed the children's supper. Zak, having lost interest, cut a slice of the bread, not bothering to cut any for Gina - helped himself to a large dab of paté and wandered into the sitting room and turned on the TV.

'Maybe you could use a plate,' she called, but Zak either did not hear or took no notice.

Her phone pinged and glancing at it, she declined the call. She turned her phone to silent. It vibrated, from the same caller, twice more that evening and each time she ignored it.

Gina made a decision. She was not going to get involved with Dan. The life she enjoyed was acceptable and she was trying to make the best of it. She understood that having unlimited money and all the help she could need, made it easier than it might have been. She could not contemplate compromising her relationship with the children. She could imagine Louise's response. 'Are two husbands not enough?'

The truth was that they were not. Zak treated her like a chattel. He was often verbally abusive to her, his interest in her was minimal, and his values were not hers. His chief concern was to make money - lots of it, and on the whole it seemed that he did. When they were in a social situation, he displayed an unpleasant complacency and an annoying arrogance. This was despite the fact that he expected Gina to look gorgeous and behave well in front of his friends. Many of these men and women Gina found difficult to relate to. Gina was often embarrassed and retreated into silence or went to the kitchen to slowly gather another course or get more drinks. She preferred it when there was no help, but Zak often insisted on caterers and always liked to have a maid, which meant that Gina had to be front of house for most of the time. She was beginning to hate it and hence came to cherish her group of art-loving friends more and more. Feeling miserable, and noting that Zak, sprawled in the armchair, was dozing, she went upstairs and called Maggie.

She told her of the events at the weekend describing the disaster with the boat and finally telling her the whole event with Dan, but not of her tryst today.

Maggie was appalled. 'Danny Moran - fancy it being him! But Gina, he's such a dweeb!'

'No, no he's not. He's interesting - we talked for ages ...'

'Doesn't sound like you had time for much talking!'

'Well. We did! And he has a good degree and he's set up a couple of really successful companies. He does the coastguard stuff as a hobby - loves sailing, boats and all that stuff.'

'But Gina, what are you thinking of? He was a teenage grope - what's going on?'

'Oh I'm not going to see him again. He's already rung me twice.'

'Are you sure you won't?'

'Yeah, it was just a silly fling really. I think I'm not very happy at the moment, but I expect I'll get over it. By the way, don't tell Issy, and especially not Amy, she's such a gossip. And anyway, as I say, it's over.'

'Well I hope so. I do think you are a bit nutty, you know.'

'Do you think it's nutty to despise Zak's behaviour - you know what he's like!'

And she did, but offered a measured response, suggesting that she and her husband Simon, should come to Birmingham and that they all go out to dinner together.

After she had rung off, it occurred to Gina that Maggie had suggested the visit so that she could keep an eye on her. Well, so. Let her, she thought, I plan to be the paradigm of a perfect wife.

And to her credit, she did try and managed to ignore all of the calls from Danny received in the week following her meeting with him.

Eventually, they became less frequent and when Maggie arrived, she was able to tell her that she hadn't heard from him 'recently' though she didn't offer details. Maggie seemed satisfied and they had a great time, getting back late from dinner out, and talking into the night. When she went to bed, Gina felt calmer and almost happy for the first time in months. Maggie noticed this and made the observation at breakfast.

'You seem in good form this morning Gina. Personally I feel somewhat hungover.'

'Well, drinking all that brandy late last night didn't help - did it?'

'Oh, you should talk!'

Simon interrupted 'Zak, you were very generous, we didn't expect you to pay - are you sure we can't offer...'

Zak waved an airy hand. 'My pleasure,' he said, 'and you must stay as long as you like, but please excuse me - I have a call to make,' and he left to disappear into his study for the rest of the morning.

At this, Gina found that she was again angry with him and felt he was not being a good host. She apologised for him, adding 'He is so busy just now.' But she didn't sound very convincing and Maggie noted that she became more morose.

The children came in, along with Maggie's two. Poor Rayna had her hands full and only the promise of a walk to the park accompanied by scooters, bikes and roller skates mollified the impatient kids. But because Zak was clearly not going to join them, Rayna had to come too. Even Maggie felt a bit resentful and taking a wide view, began to see why Gina was feeling so dissatisfied with her lot. Quietly, she said as much to Simon.

'All that money and she's still a sad lady.'

'Don't get ideas,' he said, 'good thing that even though we've got no money we're happy. We are aren't we?'

'We are,' she said. And she meant it.

28

Spring moved into early summer, but for a week or so after Maggie's visit, Gina remained low despite more sunshine and fun days out. She broached the subject of a holiday but Zak seemed reluctant. He claimed to have so much to do, and in truth, he had been away twice in the month already. It seems that he was in London on both occasions, but Gina noted that his passport was not in its usual place and although that didn't prove anything, it certainly pointed to a trip abroad.

The kids nagged for a boat trip but the memory of the last recent one remained unpleasant in Gina's memory and she did not encourage them with any enthusiasm. She offered them alternatives in the hope that they would act as ambassadors with Zak, and get him to consider her ideas. She wanted to go to Italy, or France - a big house in a country where she could indulge some of her new interests in art and architecture.

She wanted to take the kids to churches and palaces and look at paintings and statues that were a significant part of European history. She wanted them to grow up knowing about things, she wanted them to demand education, to take the chances she had had, but had not taken. She wanted them to see a cultural world as part of their growing up and to learn to love it with an artistic eye. When Shaf had his birthday treat, a few months before, eight of his pals (and Tanni) had gone to a pottery exhibit before going to a workshop, where they decorated dishes and bowls with their own designs and then had them fired to take away later. She had been very impressed with Han's efforts - he seemed to have a natural talent and even Tanni had produced a lovely design. Surely if her children had artistic skills, they should be encouraged?

She talked to Zak about this and her idea for a holiday. He was dismissive about the talent that she was claiming for the children.

'They just do daubs - all kids do that kind of stuff. They're not so special Gina, and what's all this cultural nonsense? Kids just want fun - swimming, biking, fairgrounds with rides - Disneyland would be better for them. We'd have fun too. We could go for a three day break.'

'Three days! I want a holiday, not a three day working trip trying to keep them out of trouble.'

'Oh, we'll take Mary Poppins with us.'

'I don't want to have Rayna with us. They're our kids, and I want you to be a dad to them for more than three days and in any case Rayna needs a break. She wants to go home - see her family.'

Gina felt she was getting nowhere.

A week later she tried again.

'I found some places online. Will you look?'

Zak gave the sites a desultory glance.

'This place - this one here,' he said stabbing a finger at the screen, 'it isn't even as nice as our house - we might as well stay at home.'

Of course, in a sense that was true, but if they stayed in Birmingham, Zak would never be there and it would not be the holiday that she dreamed of, a holiday which would reinforce the family structure that Gina felt was lacking in their marriage. She more or less said this to Zak and he exploded:

'What do you want from me?' he shouted. 'I work hard, I earn all our money, you have all you need, help in the house, you don't clean, the kids get cared for, you have all the clothes and jewellery you want and you can do what you like.'

'I don't. I would happily go to work... that's what I want. That's what I'd really like.'

'Never.'

'But I would like to, I'd like to study, I'd like to learn to be - well, something.'

'You don't need to.'

'But I do need to. I feel I'm wasting - wasted - my brain is going to mush.'

'Oh for god's sake Gina, you do talk nonsense.' Zak was really shouting loudly now. 'Just stop this crazy talk. You have children to care for - you can't start studying now - there was a time for that 20 years ago...' He moved towards her. She backed away, a little afraid. 'Don't let me hear any of this again,' he roared at her.

Gina was outraged. She couldn't believe that he was so controlling. She said so.

'You are a control freak Zak, do you know,' his face was very close to hers now, 'and you frighten me.' Zak jerked his head back and looked at her in amazement - 'You're mad Gina, do you know. Come to your senses.'

Hanif came down and asked what all the noise was about. Gina hastened to comfort him. He was quite upset and needed considerable reassurance before he would go back to bed and she encouraged him to read for a while before settling down to sleep. He was unwilling.

'I'm worried mum.'

'What about?'

'You and dad. Always yelling at each other.'

'I don't yell, Han…'

'No, but he does. I think he might hit you.'

'Oh. He wouldn't do that, darling. Now you just settle down and stop this fretting.'

In truth, Gina shared some of these anxieties. For a nine year old he was remarkably perceptive and impressively eloquent. And she was rather anxious about him too. She felt he was a sensitive child and would suffer as a result of his worries. Protecting her children was her main concern.

But Gina was aware that there were several pieces of calves liver on a plate on the kitchen counter waiting for her to cook. She went down and directly into the kitchen. She set a pan to warm, poured in a little oil, added a piece of butter, let it heat up, put in some sliced onions and turned down the heat. Returning to the sitting room, she found Zak on his phone. He did not see her.

'Well, let's not make a hasty decision, we need to discuss…we could meet - no, now? At Gimson's Bar? Yes OK, I'll be there. Oh, about forty minutes.'

He turned and saw Gina. She was standing in the doorway.

'I'm going out to eat,' he snapped. 'Don't wait up.' It was not the first time he had offered this injunction.

He slammed the heavy old door as he left the room.

'Wouldn't dream of it,' she responded quietly and bitterly.

Back in the kitchen, now uninterested in food, Gina recklessly and wastefully threw the liver in the bin.

Threw it in the bin! Even as she did it, she was shocked. She could imagine her mother's reaction. Lou had always been careful with money - she had needed to be and in any case had taught Gina, first, how to cook and always how to make best use of leftovers. 'What have I come to?' Gina thought. For a brief moment she wondered about retrieving it, but couldn't bring herself to do that.

Instead she poured a glass of wine and perched on a stool in the kitchen, and phoned Louise.

'Hi mum. How's it going?'

'Good. We're doing well.'

'Bet you wish you were back on the cruise! I can't believe you're 60 you barely look 40.'

'Good DNA Gina! But stop being ridiculous. Now listen Gina, it's good that you called, I was going to ring at the weekend but now...'

'Something bad?' Gina was a bit apprehensive.

'No. Not at all.' She took a breath.

'Come on then. Spill.'

'Well, I said it wasn't bad, but you might not like it.'

'Mum! Just tell me.' Gina was impatient.

'Jim and me - we - we've decided to get married.'

'Wow, Mum! That's fantastic.'

'You sure? Sure you don't mind?'

'Of course not - I'm delighted. Totally! Jim can really be 'Gramps' now - the kids will be absolutely thrilled.'

Louise expressed some doubt that the kids would care at all, except that there might be a party. Gina was all for this.

'Tanni can be a bridesmaid.'

'Well, maybe a little flower girl. I'm not going overboard with this Gina, we can't afford to spend much.'

It was on the tip of Gina's tongue to make a generous offer, but she bit back the words that she was excitedly composing.

'When?' She limited herself to practicalities.

'Probably August, maybe September.'

'And when's the Hen Night?'

'Haven't given that possibility a thought. Not even sure I know exactly what it is…'

'Would you let me organize one?'

'By all means, love, if you want to.'

'Can I ask Maggie, Issy and Amy as well as their mums?'

'Mmmm yes. Don't ask Amy's mum. Amy and she hardly speak anyway, they don't seem to get on these days and we aren't really great buddies now. But Sue, yes and Kathy too, and will you ask Jim's sister and …'

Gina interrupted. 'What about Lily?'

'Lily? Who she?'

'My cousin…'

There was a long pause. 'Do you know her?' Lou was surprised, cautious, wary.

'A bit. We met once.'

'No. No I don't think so. Not Lily.'

Gina began to make plans.

29

Zak was fairly perfunctory when Gina broke the news about Lou and Jim the following day. His anger had evaporated by the time he arrived home; Gina was thankful for that. He'd drunk a considerable amount it seemed and was lucky to have got back without being stopped and indeed without having an accident. Gina was already in bed, but he had crashed clumsily into the room - he would have woken her if she had been asleep. But she had been awake and was aware of his eager fumblings, pulling at her nightdress and grabbing at her thigh. He hauled himself crudely over her body and pressed his head into her neck groaning and calling as he did so. She felt him roughly penetrate and thrust hard; it seemed to be without feeling. Less than a minute later, barely pulling away, he sprawled at her side. Gina pushed him, with some effort and difficulty, off her body and to the other side of the bed. She slipped out of the bed and went to the bathroom. Zak snored.

He was not in the best of moods when he awoke the next day, and she left it a while before telling him.

'So there'll be a wedding - at least a decent party.'

Zak shrugged. He pressed his thumb and forefinger into his forehead. Gina suspected a hangover or at least a headache. 'Have we offered to pay for it?' he asked.

That was one thing that was certain about Zak, he never worried about the cost of anything and was seemingly very generous. He certainly wasn't very sensitive to other people, and it didn't seem to cross his mind that Louise and Jim might resent such an offer.

'No, Zak. I'm sure they'll want to do that for themselves. We could offer to supply champagne, but we shouldn't barge in with more.'

And meanwhile, Gina began to pull things together for a hen night, something her mother had never experienced. Even if there had been stag nights, back in the day, there certainly weren't hen nights and Gina was sure her mum did not know what to expect. Jim appeared more worldly about these sort of things.

'Don't embarrass her,' he begged, 'she wouldn't like that. She wouldn't cope.'

Gina knew that her normally robust mother would indeed be mortified if anything made her look silly in public, so she resolved to keep it relatively safe. But she encouraged her to have it sooner rather than later, as she still cherished the idea of a serious break and wanted to keep the summer holidays free.

She called Maggie and arranged to meet her in London to make plans.

Gina was surprised to see her friend. Apparently, in just a few weeks, Maggie had lost loads of weight, and Gina did not recognize her at first. Now tall, well, she'd always been tall, but also willowy, with a newly straightened hairstyle, she looked gorgeous. Her bright red hair was now a glorious dark red and quite stunning.

'Maggie,' Gina gasped. Maggie grinned self-consciously - and pirouetted for Gina, saying:

'You didn't notice that after I had Polly I'd lost over half a stone, and after the last time I saw you, I lost even more, so it's about a stone and a half now, new clothes make it more obvious - what do you think?'

'You look stunning.'

'I feel stunning.'

'How did you do it?'

'Hah! New baby...'

'No really, lots of people get bigger.'

'I know but I decided it was time to be different, so...'

'What?'

'Exercise, lots of swimming, and portion control - still doing it.'

'Well it's certainly worked and I'm really pleased for you. It really suits you.'

They went for lunch and chatted. They schemed a scheme and worked a plan.

The date was suggested as mid to late August and when they parted, Gina took the tube to her mother's where she revealed the arrangements and the approximate date.

Louise was a bit overwhelmed at first, but she accepted that Gina was the right person to make such plans and decided to put herself in her daughter's hands.

'I won't have to wear fishnet tights and do shocking things will I?' she asked nervously.

'Oh, you never know mum. Expect the unexpected!'

'Oh Gina. No!'

'Maybe police uniforms...' Gina said thoughtfully, chin lifted, staring into the middle distance. She had a pensive expression on her face, and her hands were pointed together beneath her lips, fingers lightly tapping together '...or nurses.'

Even now, Lou wasn't sure that Gina wasn't joking and looked sideways and warily at her daughter.

'You are a tease Gina,' she said more in hope than certainty.

'What, Mum?' she said as if hearing her for the first time.

'Oh stop it, Gina, you will tell me exactly what you are going to do, won't you?'

'Might do. But we'll all meet here on the afternoon of the event - OK? Then we'll have a cab to Mag's.'

'Oh, good idea. Jim,' she called 'Jim - come and hear the plans.'

When Jim came into the front room, he asked Gina what was to happen, and of course Lou hoped that Gina would reveal some of her secrets, but she did not. She placed a dramatic finger on her lips and looked wickedly from under her eyelids, smiling a small naughty smile and inclined her head negatively.

'I can tell you who will be invited,' she said. She named the usual suspects and Lou gave her approval.

'And now I need to get going,' Gina said. 'I don't want to be too late tonight.' Jim offered to take her to the station at Hitchin, and she accepted. She was home by 4.30.

30

Dan rang twice more in the week that followed but Gina answered neither call. It was almost a month since the incident on the boat and Gina was hoping it would fade into a distant memory. She had to admit that this wasn't actually happening and that she thought of Dan a great deal, but she tried to ignore him and her feelings for him. She told herself that it would soon be forgotten by both of them.

She met Marina for a seafood lunch at some fancy new restaurant in town, and when she came home, threw up, hearing, in her head, Issy's warnings about never eating seafood more than 40 miles from the sea. Despite feeling wretched, she laughed to herself, and went to lie down. Shafi came into the bedroom.

'Are you home already?' But she knew they were back, because she had heard the front door slam and Rayna calling the children to take off their shoes and not to drop their coats on the floor.

'Where've you been?' Shaf asked.

'I was at a restaurant with Marina. I had a bad mussel.'

'What's a mussel?'

'It's a small creature that lives in the sea, in a shell, like a snail...' she tailed off, as the image made her feel sick again.

'Yeucchh,' responded Shaf.

'Yes, well, it made me feel ill.' And she moved off the bed very quickly to the bathroom.

Returning she felt a bit better, and went down to crash into Tanni and Han as they raced up the stairs to find her.

'Have you had snacks?' she asked them gamely, attempting to keep up appearances.

'Yup! And juice and carrot sticks and crisps. Oh whoops, Rayna!' Han said, 'Sorry, wasn't supposed to tell you that,' he added, grinning at his mum. Gina shrugged unable to scold and resigned to the idea that her kids were probably normal. She bent to hug Tanni who was covered in crisp crumbs anyway, so there would have been no hiding it.

'I had salt and vinegar,' she confessed, 'and carrots and hummus.'

'Good, that's OK then.' Gina ushered them into the end of the kitchen where glass doors led onto the back patio.

'Want to go out?'

Shaf had already grabbed his jacket and his skateboard, and was out on the flagstones before the other two had got themselves ready too.

Gina had a small train and a doll and was aiming to give her a ride round the patio.

'You're in the way, Tan,' Shafi shouted as he crashed into her on his board. 'Move! Move!'

Gina reflected that he was rather like Zak in his approach and hoped she could help him find his more feminine side before too long. Han, much gentler, was in the mini hammock, reading. The sun was bright and warm and she would have liked to stay out with them for a while, but still feeling a bit out of sorts she returned to talk to Rayna about supper.

'I'm going to do a chicken dish,' she announced to Rayna, chucking a pack of chicken breasts on to the counter. She realised how little she fancied eating.

'What do you need?' Rayna asked, from the frig door.

'Onion, red pepper...' Gina continued somewhat listlessly with the list and took the items from Rayna, to begin preparing the vegetables for the dish.

Her phone rang. It was Zak. He would be home early, around 6, but then would have to go out again after dinner. She sighed. No change there then, she reflected.

'Better get a move on, hadn't I Rayna?' It was a rueful response. Rayna smiled and began chopping the pepper.

After supper, of which Gina ate very little because she still felt queasy, and when Zak had left, with no explanation, hours after Rayna had helped Tanni to bed and Gina had settled the boys in various activities, Shaf to some homework and Han to some piano practice, Gina called Maggie.

'Any further with the hen night plans?'

'I've booked a hotel, and - no, no, not a stripper, but some jokey karaoke which will be entertaining, and then cocktails and then a meal.'

'No costumes, then?'

'Don't think your mum would like that, let's just keep it fun and simple.'

'Have you talked to Lou?'

'Not yet, hey, Gina, are you all right? You sound odd.'

Gina paused. 'Zak just dashed out - no idea where he's gone - and I can't get him to agree to a holiday. He makes me cross.'

Gina spent a few more minutes unburdening herself to Maggie. As always, Maggie tried to be evenhanded in her response but she had to agree that Zak's behaviour and attitude was odd.

'I'm surprised he doesn't feel the need for a holiday.'

'Well, I certainly do, and the kids need to get some foreign travel - see some sights - and what's the use of all this money if we can't use it for fun.'

'You could go on your own...'

After the conversation with Maggie, Gina gave some thought to the possibility of going somewhere alone, but she would need Rayna to accompany her, and that wasn't the kind of holiday she wanted. Suddenly she felt tired. She spent some time with the boys and then shooed them to bed. Downstairs, Rayna had gone to her own room and Gina could hear her TV playing quietly. She poured a glass of wine set it down and then forgot it. She sat in an armchair staring at the black screen of the enormous TV on the wall. Her phone was in her hand and she toyed with the idea of calling Dan. Instead she turned on the TV and watched the news, although ten minutes later she could not have said what the main events of the day had been. She became reflective, considering her life and what she felt the future held for her.

Suddenly she felt sick again and she dived for the bathroom. She sat on the edge of the bath and stared at the tiles under her feet. After a few minutes, she was very sick indeed and then felt exhausted. She went to bed, realising as she clambered under the duvet and recognizing a familiar feeling in her body, that she was pregnant.

31

ZAK

And so the plan was made to take another trip to the coast - and of course it would indeed be a great opportunity to meet up with Yeshevsky and Dmitri. Of course he didn't tell Gina about the way Yeshevsky would arrive and meet them, as a matter of fact, he didn't know himself. Nor did he detail the somewhat nefarious dealings that Dmitri was part of but which were certainly material to their current business. In fact, Zak now recalled that it had probably been Gina who first mentioned the possibility of another trip, and Zak allowed her to think it was her idea. Indeed he had shown great enthusiasm and told her what a good idea it was.

As Gina's plans for the day out proceeded, Zak called Dmitri. They agreed that a meeting was needed very soon.

'Where are you?'

'On my way home, I think Gina is making dinner.'

'We need to meet - discuss getting to your boat. You know there is an island?'

'Yes. Didn't you tell me you used it when you borrowed the boat?'

'Yeah. You remember - got the early group in - took them to Bristol from there.'

'I do remember - that went well. How did you...?'

'A bigger boat - in the Channel - it was dark - middle of night. No problem - easy.'

'Are we planning to do that again?'

'Sure, but not with your family around - too risky. Some other time.'

'OK. But I need to meet with the finance guys - in Birmingham - we'll collect you and then go there in the evening.'

'How is your woman going to react to that?' Dmitri laughed. He was no fan of women who had opinions and his question clearly indicated that he didn't give a damn!

'Oh don't worry about Gina. She'll do as she's told. She can take the kids home; I'll come with you.'

'We need to discuss the details, call Yeshevsky.'

'I guess we do - can you get him to meet us?'

'Can you get to "The Site Office" for a drink? - opens at 10 - great bar? I'll sort Yeshevsky.'

'Sure, I'll humour Gina and have dinner with her, then I'll drive to town.'

'Let me call you later to check it's OK.'

'Sure. Speak soon.'

And Zak drove on, arriving in a slightly distracted mood to find Gina quietly preparing the meal. Of course he had to make his excuses and explain to her that he had to go out again. She was so full of questions. Why are women so curious, why can't they just accept that men make decisions and they should just be grateful that they don't have to - and that the money comes in anyway. Instead, she gets into a mood, bangs the plates down, and makes the meal a misery. Why do I have to put up with this? Zak asked himself. Time she realised who's the boss round here.

He spent longer then he'd intended, drinking coffee and making small talk - but fending off her curious inquiries, promising that he'd talk more at the weekend and finally leaving for the city. It took twenty minutes to get to the bar. Yeshevsky was waiting.

'Your little lady OK?' Yeshevsky asked.

'Oh, she's fine. Knows who's boss.'

'Good. What's the plan?'

32

GINA

Thirty-six certainly wasn't too old to have another child, but Gina was afraid. She did not know whose baby this was. Perhaps it was Dan's, it was barely a month since she had been with him on the boat. But how could she tell Zak? Of course, maybe it was Zak's, and in any event he would have to believe that. Of course he would not doubt it!

First, though she would tell her mum.

Lou was, of course, thrilled.

'You don't sound pleased,' Lou noted, 'why?'

'Oh, just a bit of a shock, I guess I'll get used to it.'

'Have you told Zak?'

Gina admitted she had told no-one.

'Why not?'

'Not sure I want a fourth child. I want to study - get a degree...'

'Oh Gina, what about the kids -?'

'Open University,' she interrupted, 'I can be at home most of the time, and I'll have Rayna.'

'So...'

'I'll have a termination.'

'You can't.'

'Of course I can - it's common - lots of women choose that route - God, mum, Zak practically raped me the last couple of times he came home. He was drunk and knew what he wanted, never mind what I wanted.'

'Didn't you use - I mean aren't you on the pill?'

'No,' Gina was glum. 'I stopped because my GP advised me to, and I - we - used condoms, but not every time.'

'Sounds a bit...'

'A bit what mum? What are you saying?' Gina was hotly indignant. 'I'm a grown up - I can decide what to do, and anyway, I hardly had time to think when he came back drunk and stupid.'

'I mean you didn't take precautions…'

'I know exactly what you mean, I'm talking about whether I terminate or not …'

'Gina, no!'

'Not your business, mum.'

'Well, it is…'

'It is not!' Gina almost shouted and became tearful. Her mother managed not to reply and after a few moments, Gina said,

'Let's not get cross mum, it doesn't help. I do respect your opinion, but let's just agree that we might disagree, and while I hear what you say I have to decide this for myself.'

Louise was sometimes amazed at how logical and sensible her daughter could be. She was filled with admiration for her strengths at that moment and although Louise had a lot in her mind that she wanted to say about this possible outcome, she said nothing and they quietly finished their conversation.

Gina spent many minutes thinking through her assertions - that she wanted to study, that she might not want a fourth child, and though of course she hadn't mentioned it to her mother, that it might not be Zak's child.

33

It was with great difficulty that Gina managed to hide her morning sickness from Rayna and the children in the next few days. Her mind was restless, constantly troubled. Zak was quite unaware of any such possibility. Indeed he was away for two days and when home, spent considerable time on the telephone, sometimes shouting sometimes just listening, nodding. One evening he walked into the kitchen, carried on to the outer room where coats hung, and grabbed his jacket, calling as he went, and barely before the door had slammed, 'I'll be late.' Gina shrugged, sighed, poured another large glass of wine and wandered into the sitting room.

She questioned the wisdom of drinking when she knew quite well she was pregnant. She had avoided it more or less completely when she had been carrying the other three, but she was still considering a termination. She had debated it quite seriously and there was barely an hour when she was not thinking and re-thinking through the issues and the moral concerns that were stuck in her brain.

She decided not to discuss it with Lou, but finally after an agonised day, she called Maggie and told her she was pregnant. Maggie was at least startled, but not terribly surprised. She was full of excitement and congratulation. After a few moments of thrilled response, she detected an odd silence from Gina.

'What is it Gina? Are you not excited?' And with considerable difficulty Gina was able to tell her closest friend that she might not want to proceed with the pregnancy. Maggie was shocked, but controlled. After a few initial questions, she decided wisely to stop, and asked Gina if she didn't think she needed a bit more time to consider.

'After all, it's bound to still be a bit of shock, I guess you didn't plan this,' she giggled, though the laugh dissolved in the space that was icy in their conversation.

'No.' Gina was brief.

'Look, I'll call you tomorrow. We can look at the issues then. Don't dwell too much, just, you know, relax into it.'

'I can't relax at all Maggie - It's driving me crazy - I feel I know what I want to do…'

Maggie interrupted her. 'OK, let's talk tomorrow, I need to go to Polly just now and I want to really talk properly with you about this, Gina.'

The following day, Gina told her that she thought the baby might be Dan's. She heard Maggie breathe in sharply, but she said nothing to condemn. Instead there was a long pause. Gina at once began to explain how she was planning to do a degree and had already approached the Open University, that she needed to do this for her mental health's sake, that she didn't think she could deal with another child especially one that was not Zak's. At every point Maggie offered no advice, but merely asked searching questions.

She spoke to Maggie at length, in the next day or so. Maggie was measured, not judgmental in response. Why don't you want to go through with it? What frightens you? Is it a moral issue? Do you think the others would judge you? Can't you afford it? (This certainly made them both snort with laughter - the only moment of light relief in hours of talk).

Gina's main focus was that she had decided to study, never mind what Zak wanted. That she was so bored, that her mind was wasting away, that she needed more mental stimulation. Wisely she didn't concentrate on the paternity issue. And wisely Maggie did not pursue this, but she did present the ethical concerns, not because she felt particularly strongly about them, but because she wanted to give her friend every opportunity to think through the kind of things that a clear-headed and sensible person would. Maggie was not entirely sure that Gina was quite rational at the moment. She realised that she needed to be her thinking self, her sensible friend, her devil's advocate.

But Gina was more and more adamant as the days went by and finally she asked Maggie to accompany her to a clinic.

She had already sent her preliminary enquiry, and had received a kind and courteous response, but would need to go for a consultation. She asked Maggie to go with her and one day as soon as the children were in school and nursery and she had warned Rayna that she might be late, she left for the station and met Maggie in Marylebone.

She and Maggie went to the very expensive clinic in Harley Street, where she was scanned, swabbed, blood tested and engaged in conversation with the doctor. She had plenty of chance for questions, and they were handled politely and with respect. She decided that she would have a vacuum termination and having signed some necessary forms, emerged into the shock of a cool bright day, dazed but determined.

'You can still change your mind, Gina.'

'Yes, I know.'

'Think you might?'

'No. Is it too early for lunch?'

34

Gina told Rayna and the children that she was going to spend a few days over the weekend with Maggie and Simon, that she would take Tanni with her, and that she would expect good behaviour from the boys. It gave her a particular pleasure to ensure that Zak would know where she was and that she was clearly leaving him with responsibility for the boys. Not that he would take it seriously - he'd leave the real care to Rayna, but at least he would need to be notionally on duty and answerable to Rayna for any plans he might make. That gave Gina a feeling of piquant pleasure. She felt no guilt at this spiteful emotion, merely satisfaction, and she packed a little case for Tanni and herself before climbing into the car and driving to London.

Naturally she had not told Zak ahead of time of these plans. He discovered where she was on Friday night, after calling her to say he would not be in as expected, but was eating out. Same old story, thought Gina as she clicked her phone and ignored the message. Later that night, she sent him a brief text to say where she was. She got no response.

On the following day, Gina left Tanni with Simon and Maggie's mum in the pretty, small house, in Borehamwood. Gina and Maggie went to the Harley Street clinic, where, preliminaries having already been carried out, they required only a little more paperwork of Gina. She knew she would be having a vacuum termination. This understood and the paperwork completed, she was accompanied to a charming room, and from there, she knew little of the course of events, except as she drowsily came to from the anaesthetic and sat recovering with Maggie, while they were served tea and biscuits in the pretty pale lavender and grey room and slowly came to terms with what she had done. She was astonished to note that barely 30 minutes had passed and that they had spent longer in recovery than she had having the procedure.

The doctor had explained that there might be considerable bleeding and Gina was prepared for that, and after some time and with an information pack and some surgical supplies, they were permitted to go. Gina had asked for a cab and on its arrival she walked slowly out of the clinic.

'This ride is going to cost the earth,' Maggie hissed

'Nothing compared with the bill for the clinic.'

'Are you sure it's OK?'

But Maggie knew that it was not a problem for Gina to pay either for the clinic or for the taxi, and that a discreet approach in all things including the payment, would mean that Zak would never discover the truth.

'Well, you've done it now girl.' But immediately Maggie was sorry for the flippant tone and Gina was sharp in response.

'It wasn't easy. I know you think it's only been a week or two, but I have thought of nothing else and what I did decide was that if it was to be, I should do it quickly.' Gina sounded tired, weary, sad.

'Yes, Lady Macbeth.'

And again Maggie regretted her irreverence, but Gina seemed unaware of the reference and did not reply.

Their journey back was quiet. Gina slept.

But she was glad to be back in Borehamwood and Tanni greeted her enthusiastically.

'Did you get me a present?'

'No, not this time darling,' she said and realised with a guilty pang that she had not given her children a thought in the last few hours.

'Mum and Maggie were busy,' Simon said kindly to Tanni. He raised an eyebrow. 'You need to lie down,' he said to Gina, 'I'll bring you some soup later.'

By Sunday, Gina felt a bit better. She felt up to the journey home. Tanni had enjoyed playing with Maggie's kids. Thomas, though much older, adored her and was her slave. Polly, the baby, however, had proved more of a challenge, which, since she was under six months was not surprising.

'Why doesn't she talk?'

'She's too little,' Maggie explained, 'give her a few more months.'

'Can we get a little baby mummy?' Tanni asked.

Gina pressed her lips together and looked away.

'Can we?' she persisted. Gina lifted her up and held her very close. Her eyes were full of tears.

35

Gina recovered well and any weakness was not observed and if so, certainly not remarked upon. Details and information came from the Open University and she decided on her options. She had no idea if she would qualify but intended to pursue her investigations and discover the possibilities.

Marina had advised her - her brother was a tutor - and Gina was thinking of fine art.

'But perhaps I would find history more rewarding...'

'You once said you were good at English in school.'

'Yes. Do I have the skills though?'

Marina thought she should do an access course - her brother had suggested it.

'It'll show whether you have any skills, boost your confidence - are you serious Gina, you didn't even do A-level?'

'No. You could leave early in those days. I wanted a job.'

'Are you sorry now?'

Gina mused on this for a few moments. She admitted to being ambivalent about it. 'I got a job. I liked it. I met my first husband.'

'Your first husband?'

Gina realised she had never mentioned Ed to Marina.

'What happened to him?'

'Oh,' Gina paused several seconds, and then shrugged and said 'he died.'

'How?' Marina couldn't help herself.

'Long time ago.' Gina's tone was dismissive. Quickly, she asked 'So, what's an access course?'

Gina signed up, paid up and waited.

Zak must have noticed the prospectus on the coffee table - or could he possibly have really not seen it? He never asked about it, never referred to her wish to study, which he certainly knew of, and never tried to engage her in the kind of conversation he had had with her a few weeks ago. Then he had shouted at her, derided her aspirations, in fact had apparently forbidden her to pursue any such line of thinking. His behaviour had served to anger Gina. She had felt alienated and disenfranchised, and her hopes for the future blighted. He had sought to control her entirely and she was resentful and dissatisfied.

Now, he seemed to be ignoring the whole issue, never referring to it, and leaving Gina in a frustrated state, with no idea what he now felt and she unsure how to proceed.

She felt sure that if she raised the matter again, he would scream at her, terrify her, and drive all her ambitions away. Fearful of these possibilities, she said nothing.

Then, on a subsequent warm spring weekend she announced that it would be a good idea if they made another trip to the coast - wouldn't another boat trip be fun? Surprisingly, Zak seemed to agree with this idea at once and she began to plan. The boys were delighted and even Tanni displayed interest.

'Don't ask your mother,' Zak ordered.

'Oh. Why not?' Gina asked indignantly.

'Too many in the boat for any kind of distance,' Zak claimed. 'No Rayna, either,' he added. Gina seemed to recall that there was some kind of restriction on numbers last time, so she did not argue. She and Rayna packed a lunch and the boys gathered toys, bats and balls, jackets and swimwear and Gina and the children piled into the 4x4. It would take them over two hours and Zak drove fast. By 11 they had arrived and were running along the back beach in ever-brightening warm sunshine, Gina already beginning to perspire as she carried a heavy basket and hauled Tanni along too. Zak strode on ahead with the picnic hamper and opened up the boathouse. The boys chased him and hurled the canvas bag into the gravel, balls, baseball bats and a cricket bat spilling and rolling away.

'Hey, hey!' Zak was angry. 'Collect the stuff. Come and help me get the dinghy out.'

For a few moments, Zak was regretting his decision not to have Jim along. Getting the dinghy into the water, when the boys were more hindrance than help, was not entirely easy, especially with Gina loudly exhorting him to take care. But eventually, they were dragging it down the slope to the water and somehow, with Gina and the children on board, Zak got it into the water. Suddenly, it seemed to Gina that organizing a trip on their boat certainly had its hazardous side and was both stressful and draining. Furthermore, Zak was no expert sailor and getting to the big boat was not without worry. Once they had climbed on board, Gina felt marginally better, but as she heard the engine throb into life, she became panicky and anxious.

'Zak - please don't go to the island - I don't want to - it's not safe, just go a little way, we can have lunch on the deck under the awning...please Zak - don't do this.'

'What do you mean it's not safe?' Zak was disparaging, dismissive.

Gina pleaded, 'It's too difficult, you need more people...crew. The boys, me, we can't do this. You can't do it on your own - you know you it's crazy - we'll all drown.'

'Hah!' Zak shouted, 'you're pathetic.' His tone was not kind.

Hearing this, Han scolded, 'Dad, don't call mum pathetic.' But Zak growled at him and continued to fiddle with the controls at the helm. Gina tugged Han away and with Tanni on her other arm, went to the deck, where they found Shafi playing with his new Mario Kart.

'Come on Shaf, help with the lunch,' Gina exhorted. Han led the way and reluctantly Shaf offered a half-hearted hand, still with an eye on his game console.

Gina set out the food with minimal help from the boys, and poured cloudy lemonade for everyone. 'Boys, Zak,' she called 'come on - please sit. I put some lunch out.' They gathered at the little fixed table on deck, under the shade, Zak dragging chairs and still cross. Gina fussed over Tanni and found a seat cushion for her. The sun was bright, and the day had become pleasant.

'Zak,' Gina said quietly, 'can we go back soon? I hadn't realised how difficult this would be - I'm nervous.' Zak just pouted his mouth and blew out his breath in a long-suffering manner, saying nothing, shaking his head slowly.

But in fact he was not without some worries about getting the boat back and safely moored, and he had decided that the trip would not be protracted. But for now, he dropped anchor and the boat bobbed in the sunshine, going nowhere. Sitting down, he took a couple of sandwiches and some cherry tomatoes. Pulling the stalk off with teeth and fingers he nodded approvingly. 'Good tomatoes - nice sandwiches.'

Gina supposed this was his attempt at appeasement and apology, not that he had actually taken a bite out of the sandwich, and not that Zak would ever really apologise. And he didn't, at that minute, say they would return to the shore soon. In fact it was almost two hours before they did.

Meanwhile, Gina put out fruit and cake. The children seemed happy, and eventually she managed to get them all playing a sort of mini deck quoits, which seemed to be part of the kit on board. This involved skimming rings along the deck, and although they were a bit fanciful about creating the rules, it seemed to work fine and even Zak joined in. Gina noted that he did seem to be enjoying it. The boys were prostrate across the deck floor, and they were all laughing. Tanni was scooting around and collecting rings, even when they didn't want her to, but they were indulgent with her. It pleased Gina - such occasions were rare.

Eventually the boys found the fishing kit and after many attempts and with some help from Zak, they managed to cast a couple of lines into the quiet sea. Gina was rather anxious about them as they seemed to be so close to the edge of the boat and they became impatient when they caught nothing. The sun sparkled on the water. Gina sat in a half doze leaning on the side, and watched the children. Tanni was snuggled up next to her, with her own rod and line draped over the side, dangling in the water.

Gina began to relax a bit and reflected how pleasant it was to share this time with her family. She longed for it to be the norm, for it to happen more often. She admitted to herself in those precious moments, that it was unusual. Zak was so often not there, and when he was, he was bad-tempered and paid her and the children scant attention. Furthermore, she had the abiding impression that he was involved in business that was dishonourable at least and yet she could not begin to think what it might be. He certainly had plenty of money and seemed to believe that he could keep Gina happy and uncomplaining, by allowing her free access to their main shared account. But Gina knew there were other accounts; that he was clearly up to something.

36

'Dad, can we start up again and make a bit more of a trip?' Shaf called out breaking into Gina's thoughts. She felt dismayed, but said nothing. Zak started up the engine, pulled up the anchor, and for twenty minutes after that, they mooched round the bay, until eventually, Zak steered for the beach again. The boys clamoured to have a go, and even Tanni had a turn at steering, held tight by Gina. They zig-zagged their way towards their goal, finally getting in close to the shore and Zak dropped anchor. He managed the dinghy with increasing expertise, and they got back to the beach relatively easily. There were shouts from everyone as they crunched hard on the beach and dragged the dinghy to the boathouse.

The boys threw themselves melodramatically onto the gravelly sand. Zak laughed - 'You pair of wussy weeds. Get up! I can't believe you're so easily exhausted. Shan't be bringing you again,' he threatened.

Gina was quiet walking back to the car. She was a bit disappointed. She realised that she hadn't thought through all the implications of making this sort of trip, and the practicalities had proved very difficult. Maybe she should learn how to crew and maybe they shouldn't have come without Jim and Lou, Jim being strong and able and, despite Zak's opinion, also familiar with boats.

But she realised too, that there was an issue about the number of people allowed on board or so Zak led her to believe. Now she couldn't remember if it was their boat or the rescue boat, but either way, she supposed there was some legal limit and knew that Zak would object loudly if she again started to question his knowledge and authority on this matter. Indeed she was sure that had she done so, he would have been even ruder to her than he was on the previous occasion. At that time she recalled being upset and distressed, remembered being scared and worried for both herself and Tanni. More calmly now she questioned Zak's motives. Why did he not want her to accompany him on that journey, why did he insist that she stayed with their own boat? These were questions that were troubling but which she could not answer. Of course on the previous occasion, she had been burdened by other events that were on her mind and of course, she had thought of little else at the time. This problem had been of far less consequence, so she had not really spent any time considering the possible inferences.

On the journey home Gina attempted to point out some of the drawbacks attached to the trip and to using the boat in general, but Zak was dismissive.

'We'll work something out.' He sucked on his teeth 'Maybe you and Lou can stay on the beach - Jim and I could take the boys.'

'Oh great,' Gina retorted rather crossly, 'so Tanni and me - we don't count?'

'No, no, we'd come back - give you a ride later if that's what you wanted.' His amused response sounded faintly patronizing. 'Don't worry about it Gina, we can make a plan. We'll all get a chance to enjoy the boat - though when that will be, who knows?' He barked a laugh. He seemed to know something that Gina did not.

Gina suddenly felt her head clear. Well, indeed who did know? She suddenly realised that she wanted nothing more to do with this boat, that she would never go on a trip again, that Zak would have to deal with the distress of the boys when it became clear that he would need to cope on his own. Of course he would be most unwilling to do this. Gina narrowed her eyes. 'And you can forget taking Rayna,' she thought.

They drove largely in silence for an hour. Tanni was asleep in the car seat; the boys seemed to be playing games. She passed them bottles of water and some biscuits, in which they showed scant interest, but they didn't need conversation either. Gina was still aware that neither she nor Zak was absolutely sure of the route, so she used the satnav, raised the volume of the voice, set it going and closed her eyes. She dozed for the last hour.

37

ZAK

Yeshevsky was in one of his bad moods when Zak met him at the bar. He grunted a hello and raised a lazy finger to the barman.
'You want?'
'I'll have a beer.'
Their earlier meeting on the island had gone as well as they could have expected. Dmitri had brought details of the next group of arrivals and they had met with their contacts at the meeting they had arranged in Birmingham. That night, Dmitri's arrival from the channel vessel had successfully been kept secret from Gina and the boys. Even Zak had no idea how they had managed it, but he had known better than to ask.
'You will need to collect on your own,' Yeshevsky grunted. 'You can do that?'
'What? Without help?' Zak was incredulous at the idea. 'You know I can't do that.'
'Try. Practise. Take the family again. See how you get on.'
Zak didn't answer. Instead he asked for the lists and looked over them closely. With a start, he looked up at Yeshevsky.
'What's this?' He tapped a finger on the page.
Yeshevsky shrugged and raised his eyebrows. 'So? Is a problem?'
'Sri Lanka? I thought we were sticking with Eastern Europe...'
'Is no problem. Is good for us - good money - don't complain.'
He threw back the last of his drink and signalled for more.
'How old? These girls?'
Yeshevsky snorted, 'Teens.'
'For what? Where?'
'Ach, they will be good wives. Men need wives. Women need husbands.'
'Keep your voice down.' Zak sounded nervous. In truth, there was little danger of being overheard in this bar. It was noisy and late

enough for many patrons to be the worse for drink, but Zak was edgy. 'Where are they headed?'

'I don't know. Dmitri knows - we don't have to bother with that - he covers it - London I guess, maybe Bradford,' he cackled. 'Maybe Birmingham - your Gina - she ready for new housegirl?' He continued to laugh unpleasantly.

'Shut up Yeshevsky. You're drunk. Cut it out. And you'll have to work out a way to get some help to me when we bring them in. No way I can do it alone. No way.'

'I told you - practise - maybe your Shafiq can help - he's strong - and not so bright - he won't ask any questions...' Yeshevsky sniggered.

'Enough of that - I'm going - I can take these?' he asked tersely, picking up the papers from the damp surface.

'Sure.' Yeshevsky waved an arm in a seemingly munificent gesture. 'They're yours.' He finished his drink. 'But keep safe - hmm - not for your lady - she can't know this, hmm - tell me what would she say if she knew?' His grin was not pleasant.

'Not your business.' Zak grabbed his coat. 'Keep my family out of your opinions.'

'Oh, I think is my business.' But Zak gulped down the last of his beer and walked out swiftly.

But Zak was well aware that it was important that Gina knew nothing. In the car, he carefully placed the papers he had received from Yeshevsky into a folder and placed it into a zipped case. That, in turn, went into his bag, and he threw it onto the back seat.

He drove home with a sexual desire that he had not felt for a while. Anger brought that about often enough with Zak. He hoped that Gina was still awake.

Some days later he managed to bring the conversation around to the boat - if somewhat tangentially but he was relieved and gratified to hear Gina ask why they hadn't been for a while. It was easy to get her to suggest a trip:

'Oh - good idea Gina,' he'd responded genially although she continued to whine a bit about family time and how he didn't pay them enough attention, and could they go to Europe for a cultural holiday? Culture! For god's sake, what did she want from him? He certainly had no time for culture but he managed to put her into a *better mood by saying positive things about going to the boat, where he hoped to see how he might cope alone.*

'Don't ask your mother,' he said.

But he didn't explain the reason for this. He had found that with Gina, it was best to ignore quite a lot of her silly stuff. Take this rubbish about going to University. Who does she think she is, he mused. All those brochures - just don't comment, say nothing and the whole idea will just fizzle out. Don't even think she's got brains enough, and certainly no sticking power. Anyway, she's a wife and mother and that's where her duty lies. She'll realise that as soon as she really starts to think about it. She's going to be all tied up with this hen night and then the wedding; soon enough, it'll just evaporate as an idea.

Satisfied with his analysis, he slammed the car door, locked it and walked into the dark house.

38

GINA

Lou called Gina. 'What's happening regarding the hen night?'

'Getting nervous mum?'

'Yes. No. Don't be daft, I know you wouldn't do anything embarrassing.'

'Well, I thought that was the whole point.'

'Gina, don't tease. I'm a bit too old for silly stuff. No crazy drinking - I can't really take it these days. I'm not a young bride after all, oh, and no costumes.'

'Oh mum! I can't send them all back now.'

'Oh Gina, stop! Just tell me what you've got planned.'

'Well. I've booked a hotel. Lots of rooms for all your mates - and my pals - thanks for saying that's OK mum.'

'Who's paying for…'

'It's my gift to you mum, so don't argue.'

'Gina, I really can't let you do that.'

'You really can. I want to and you know I can afford it - Zak's got pots of money.'

Gina paused, realising that her mother might object to being steam-rollered and maybe too late, she thought that she should have come on less powerfully, maybe should have been more circumspect about this. There was a gap in the conversation. Odd, how in a telephone chat, a silence is not easy to deal with. 'I can't really think of a good hen-night present,' Gina said, 'so I thought this was a good way to kill two birds…'

'Since when has it been traditional to give hen-night gifts? I thought the bride gave little gifts to - now who is it that gets a gift?'

'You're still thinking of bridesmaids mum, this is a different tradition.'

'Well, that's what I'm asking, a tradition since when?'

'Since just now.'

'Some tradition.'

'I just invented it. Tradition has to start somewhere.'

'Gina, you're just talking rubbish, but...'

'Oh mum, just let me do this, I haven't even told you about it yet.'

'Oh, go on then, and tell me what I have to do,' Lou sighed resignedly.

'It's just going to be a fun night. They have a pool and a spa. It's all about pampering.'

'Ah. Now that does sound good.'

'Yes.' Gina was relieved that her mother finally seemed to be acceding to her plan. 'So, you'll need your swimmies and a robe - no wait, they supply those - and a change of outfit for a nice meal for us all later on. I've got most of it in place - all in the hotel. And cars to take us from Maggie's - we're going to meet the rest of them there, earlier. Maggie'll do a bit of lunch at hers. Sue's bringing fizz.'

'Gina, we'll be drunk before we get there.'

'Well, I sincerely hope we will be merry, but isn't that the idea?'

Gina added, 'I'll look after you mum.' She was conciliatory. 'And you are a grown-up, you can just say no thanks.'

'But people spike your drinks.'

'What people?' Gina was indignant. 'Don't be silly, these are your friends.' She remained serious.

'As you just observed, we're not kids and we aren't going to behave in an irresponsible manner are we?'

Lou sounded anxious nevertheless. 'Have you got the list?' she asked. 'Who's coming? Did you say I had to give gifts?'

'No mum,' Gina sighed quietly 'I said, that's for bridesmaids. We treat *you* on a hen night. Can I read you the list?' Gina read out from her scribbled list of names.

'All people you know and like and Lizzie, who I don't know and,' reading carefully to check 'someone else here - Kate someone - can't remember her other name - got it on an email. She's said yes... You suggested her.'

'Oh, Kate Maynard - from the library- yes. Good, she's nice I like her.' Lou seemed to settle into a comfortable acceptance of the plan and even seemed to be looking forward to it.

'And mum, what about a honeymoon?'

'Gina, that would be a secret wouldn't it?' Lou asked rather coyly. 'Anyway, I would expect Jim to have that all in hand.'

'Well has he?' Gina wanted to know. But Louise was giving nothing away if indeed she knew anything at all!

Gina had checked with the hotel that all was in place. She and Maggie had made a visit there a short time ago. She had opted for the crazy sounding 'Water Karaoke' where, during the free swimming bit of the spa treatment programme, there was a sort of singfest led by a local chanteuse. Everyone would be encouraged to sing along with her, a tune of either choice or suggestion, in the hope that they were relaxed enough to eschew inhibition. Gina hoped it would be a jolly affair all round, and as Louise had a decent voice it would not be overly embarrassing to her. The supposedly amusing part of this feature, was that each singer would be asked to don a funny swimming cap. Some of these were apparently very funny indeed! Gina had been shown a selection. There was a duck's head, a panda, a dinosaur, a frog and some unidentifiable creatures, that Gina knew would be popular with several friends. She and Maggie had chatted through the menu choices and they felt they'd come up with something decent. Gina began to get quite excited about it.

A day or so later she did email Jim.
'What's the story on the honeymoon?'
Jim mailed back.
'Shhh. Italy'
Gina sent a one word reply.
'Jealous!!'

And she had not dropped her plans and ideas for finding a villa to rent. She really wanted them all to go to a gorgeous place in Umbria or Tuscany and see some culture as she thought of it, some history anyway, and she had checked the internet for suitable houses and villas that she could book for the summer.

There were of course, many places that were both attractive, and for Gina, affordable.

She got the kids together and they pushed their heads round her computer screen.

'What do you think of that one?'

'Wow, it's got a tennis court and a ping-pong table,' Shaf shouted.

'And it's got a pool...'

'With a slide...' Tanni was enchanted.

'Well, what about this one,' Gina moved onto the next screen, 'which do you prefer?'

'I like the first one.'

'But this has a swing...'

'And the pool is huge - it's got a diving board...'

'Are we going to get one mum?' Han asked.

'We won't buy one, but we can rent one for a couple of weeks.'

'Oh let's - let's get one.' Han was ecstatic. 'Please mum, can we?' he pleaded.

'We'll see. We'll have to ask dad.'

Han was thoughtful. 'Will he say yes?'

'He might.'

But of course she didn't dare bring the subject up, she almost knew what he would say. She wasn't ready for a row with him just now. He was becoming ever more preoccupied with business and quite often he was away for a couple of days or more. She felt a huge wave of melancholy surge through her head and her heart.

Only by writing down her thoughts, sad as they were, could she appease her feelings. These days she did this more and more often; maybe just a few phrases, sometimes carelessly angry, sometimes small secrets from her heart, and always in haste, and always pushing the book as deep under the shoeboxes as she could and to the back of her wardrobe.

And Gina had not given up her ideas for the Open University. She had registered and had been accepted for the access course, though she had needed to pay, which she had done and was ready to start in autumn on the arts and languages access module. She had said nothing of these intentions to Zak. She had briefly indicated to Rayna that she might want more time to herself during the day as she planned to do a study course. Maybe she could just press on with it and never need to mention it to Zak until she was well ahead in her studies.

Maybe she could even qualify, though exactly as what, she couldn't say. In the meantime, she always bought the catalogues from the exhibitions she visited, and had become remarkably knowledgeable, although she worried that it must be fairly superficial. On the other hand, how did anyone learn anything, she asked Marina, who agreed with her that reading was a pretty good first step. And since she also saw the paintings and the sculptures, at first hand, surely she was building an excellent information base. Furthermore, she had both the mature interest and a great desire to know more, which would surely give her the edge over many younger learners.

If only she could ask for some support from Zak. It was a vain hope and she sighed as she closed her notebook and pushed it deep into the closet.

39

Gina decided to immerse herself in the final planning of the hen night, which began with a shopping trip. The date was only a couple of weeks away. She didn't actually buy anything, but she ordered a cake to be delivered to the Hotel, some flowers, a congratulatory banner and quite a lot of party favours, all of which she asked to be delivered to Maggie's house on the day of the party.

She called Maggie to tell her. It was agreed that it was not wise for her to make a big lunch, and Kate, the lady from the library, would come over and help prepare some sandwiches. Sue would bring some champagne, and after lunch, they would all go off together to the hotel, in a minibus.

'We could order a stretch limo.'

'She'd have a fit.'

'No, surely she'd be totally charmed by it?'

'Not doing it Mags, there's a limit.'

'Bet you she'd love it.'

But they decided not to. Gina felt it just a step too far.

On the morning of the party, Gina had been to the patisserie in town and bought a cake and their favourite cloudy apple juice for the children and Zak, and indeed Rayna, to share.

She explained to the children why they weren't invited, though Tanni was cross and made a fuss. 'I *am* a girl,' she pointed out, and Gina had to explain that being over 16 was required, which made Tanni even crosser. 'It's not fair,' she cried, and stamped away.

Gina wished she could be sure that Zak would be around, but that was one thing she was unable to guarantee. She packed her case and went to the station.

At Borehamwood, Maggie picked her up in the car and they giggled their way back to her house. They spent some time erecting the banner: 'Lovely Lou, the blushing bride' and setting out the flowers and when Lou arrived, delivered promptly by Jim, everything was ready. Louise almost collapsed laughing at the banner and when Sue handed her a bottle of fizz, she opened it with great panache, saying that she had never opened a bottle of champagne in her life before.

As expected, they were all a bit tiddly by the time they left for the hotel, piling into the minibus and arriving in great high spirits 20 minutes later.

All went well. They had a wonderful time with the spa treatments, Lou and Gina had a facial, Lou asked if it would last 'til the wedding, and Gina told her that nothing could improve her beauty.

'Why am I spending money - your money,' she stressed 'on all this then?'

'Feels good - doesn't it?' And Lou had to allow that it really did!

'It feels as though all my pores have been opened, emptied out and then sewn up again,' Lou giggled.

'Yes, I know,' Gina laughed. They were all a bit relaxed by the champagne now, and were in the mood for anything.

The water karaoke went down particularly well. The singing was hilarious. There was something about the acoustic in the pool that encouraged them to sing with great confidence, and huge volume and Lou was a terrific success with a couple of Dusty Springfield numbers. Amy did Adele ('She even looks like her,' hissed Gina 'Not in that duck shower-cap,' Maggie replied) and Gina and Lou did Sonny and Cher as a duet:

"They say we're young and we don't know,

We won't find out until we grow…"

This had everyone collapsing and laughing, especially as Lou had to strain to see the words which flashed up on the screen in front of them, and she got quite carried away with the arm gestures, which unfortunately resulted in her slipping awkwardly on the steps and crashing into the marble side of the pool.

It all happened so suddenly and quickly. Gina grabbed her mother as she threatened to disappear under the water, shouting for help as Louise screamed in pain.

Kate was practical ('I'm a first aider') and Sue called for the management, who, in turn quickly summoned an ambulance. Within minutes, Lou was on her way to the hospital with everyone else in tow in the minibus, and it became clear that she had broken an ankle.

Gina realised that the dinner would need to be put on hold, at the very least, and poor Lou, equipped only in her spa robe and swim suit, had her triage completed with all her pals standing around, few of them very sober, and all of them inappropriately dressed.

It was decided to set the bone at once. Lou was rather sick because she did need an anaesthetic, and when she was all plastered up, and Jim had arrived, she was rather dopey and not really ready for her hen-dinner.

But her pals thought otherwise and they carted her back to the hotel several hours later, the management being very accommodating and helpful, and finally all were seated to enjoy at least part of the planned supper. Lou let Jim go home, everyone called their families and although the night was rather abbreviated, it was still very late when they took trains and buses back to their various homes, except Gina who decided to stay with Maggie, so that she could see her mother first thing the next day.

'I've brought you some cake, mum,' she sang out as she walked into her mother's living room. But Lou looked downcast.

'I do feel silly; I ruined the whole day.'

'Of course you didn't, it just prevented my star turn as Miley Cyrus doing "Jolene".'

'Aaah! Not all bad then,' Lou joked.

'Good! You can still laugh.'

'Well, you can do it now. Go on. Let's hear it.'

But Gina strongly resisted that request, protesting that she had 'no voice' which of course wasn't true, since she had a pleasant choir voice and once had a role in a school production when she was eleven.

'And anyway, I am totally hungover. I'm just sorry you couldn't get enough to drink - it was your big chance to get totally wrecked.'

'Well I'm sort of relieved I didn't. I've only ever been drunk once, Gina, and I didn't enjoy it.'

'Do you even remember it?'

'A bit.'

'Oh well you weren't completely done then!'

'If I had been really drunk, maybe I'd have just slipped and not broken my leg...'

'Or maybe you'd have drowned.'

'Nah, you'd have saved me.'

But it was clear that Louise would need to get married on crutches at best, and just possibly in a wheel chair.

'I'll push you down the aisle, mum,' Gina promised.

'As you know, I am not getting married in church, Gina. And for goodness sake, I've broken my ankle, my foot hasn't fallen off!'

But really, she was not happy. Fortunately, she had all of her outfit in place, so she was spared the agony of shopping on crutches, and as the day grew closer, she began to regain some of her sunny expectancy, although it was also clear that the honeymoon that Jim had planned (Venice, among other Italian cities) could not go ahead.

Gina, however, had a brainwave. She put it first to Rayna, and then to Maggie to get their opinions, and finally she spoke to Jim.

40

But then there was other bad news. Zak, who was to have given Louise away, announced that he had a very important engagement abroad and would not be able to perform this service. Gina was initially and outwardly furious. Certainly she was angry and disappointed with him for not putting family first, but actually it meant that she would be able to perform this special function for her mum, something she had secretly wanted to do all along.

When it had first been discussed, Zak had waved his arm airily 'Of course I'll do it - be honoured to, Lou.'

To Gina at least, it had not really rung true, but as with many of Zak's remarks and observations it was loaded with an arrogant assuredness, and he was difficult to argue with. At the time, she had been somewhat rueful and sorry that her mum had not actually asked her to take this responsibility but she supposed that her mum was a bit old-fashioned and had thought it more appropriate for a man to take this role.

But now, with this announcement from Zak, Gina felt awkward and she asked Marina on their way to a gallery, what she thought of it.

'As far as you tell me, it wouldn't be a huge loss.'

Gina was a little shocked. She hadn't realised she had revealed so much about her feelings for Zak.

'I-I feel my mother will be upset.'

'Try her - see what she says!'

'Well, I'm upset, I'm cross. He's always doing this.'

'Yes, you've said before - not entirely reliable.' Marina gave a short laugh.

Gina was quiet for while.

'Don't think too much about it - prepare a speech!'

'Oh goodness, hadn't considered that - will you help me?'

'Well, I'm no expert, but I'll do what I can.'

So now her chance had come, and there was very little discussion about it. Gina offered, Lou accepted; in fact she said she was very touched by Gina asking to do it. She admitted that the problem had not crossed her mind when she had heard that Zak was unavailable. Jim was easy, as always.

The boys were more outspoken about Zak not being there.

'Grandma will be sad,' Han said, and rather boldly, because in truth he was a little afraid of his father's bad temper, 'you should try to come.'

Zak ruffled his hair. 'Don't you worry about that - she'll be fine about it. Maybe I'll get to the evening bit - you'll still be partying later on.'

But now, Gina was working on her holiday plan.

Actually, Rayna thought it was a great idea, and made nothing difficult.

'I am pleased I can visit my mother - she is not so young now. It is a good chance - you are sure you don't need me?'

'Rayna, we'll be fine, and there's help in the villa - no cleaning, no cooking if we don't feel like - and we don't even need to shop, so really, it's silly for you not to go home for a bit. See your family. They must miss you. I haven't booked yet, but I'm pretty sure we will. Even so, you must take this time off.'

And of course, Gina gave Rayna the fare home and cash for the trip. She was a good employer!

Jim was more thoughtful. He considered the idea for a few moments and then asked:

'How is Zak going to react?'

'D'you know, I don't think he'll care at all - he's already told me that he has little interest in a European holiday.'

'Have you booked it?'

'No, I was on the verge of doing it, but I would have needed to confront him and I wasn't ready for another, you know, I mean, for a row.'

Jim looked at Gina sideways and frowned.

'Do you row a lot?'

'No. Well, we have our differences. Doesn't everyone?' Gina moved uncomfortably in her chair.

'But Gina, this is about a holiday, you'd discuss it, yes, but a row? A fight you're telling me you were afraid to engage in?'

'Oh, never mind Jim.' Gina tried to be dismissive. 'Let's think about this idea of mine.'

'You'd just present him with a *fait accompli*?'

'Ahhh. Maybe it was your idea - yours and Louise's?' Gina said archly.

'Bit complicit, hmm?'

'Oh go on Jim. Please!'

'You said it was your idea...'

'Jim, maybe talk to Louise? I'm going to have a chat with Maggie - see what she thinks.'

But Maggie was surprisingly in favour.

'It's a great idea,' she said, 'about time you had a really good break. If we weren't already booked, I'd suggest we all went to one place,' she laughed, then added, 'only joking.'

And within a day, and no reference to Zak, who was away anyway, Gina booked a superb-looking villa with far too many bedrooms and bathrooms, a come-with maid and chef on demand. The kids were thrilled. And impressed.

Lou was especially happy with arrangements, since Gina had made sure that there was a ground floor suite with total accessibility. Not that Lou was unable to get up the stairs, it was just difficult and slow.

Maggie whistled low when she saw the pictures that Gina emailed her.

'Look at this Si,' she said, 'that's what I call a villa. Look at that pool.'

Simon gave the photos a rather grudging glance.

'Bet they won't have as good a time as we will.'

'Simon, don't be mean, she needs a good break and I'm glad she's spending his money.'

'You don't much like Zak do you?'

'No comment,' Maggie replied 'I do like Gina though. Trying to be positive Si!'

41

The day of the wedding approached.

Obviously Louise and Jim wanted to keep it very low key. With Gina in the background, excitedly trying to make suggestions and throw ideas into the plan, it was not easy. Gina and Lou had a bit of a fight on one occasion when the question of flowers was raised.

Louise had phoned.

'Gina, can you get the nice girl who helps in your garden - what's she called - Mia? - to choose a whole load of mixed colour blooms? I could use them on the tables in my vases.'

'Mum, better to let Gary find you a colour matched boxful...'

'Oh no, Gina, he's such a full-on gardener - always getting it so perfect - I mean, look at your roses - d'you know he pulled out a shrub a few weeks ago, I watched him, because the pink was too dark... honestly!'

'He's a perfectionist, he's a professional gardener, one of the good things that Zak has done - found Gary.'

'Well I don't want that, and I do want...'

'Oh mum, I've already asked him to do Tanni's bouquet.'

'Bouquet! Oh for god's sake Gina, she's supposed to be a little flower girl and actually I want wild flowers for her. I don't want all this fuss.'

'But mum, I'd be so disappointed...'

'You'd be disappointed! Whose wedding is this? I'll do what I want, if you don't mind.'

And Lou rang off quickly. It took only ten minutes for Gina to phone her mother back. 'Sorry mum. I'm getting over-excited aren't I? I know it's your choice and of course I'll ask Mia to get you a big selection of allsorts. What shall I - I mean what do you want for Tanni?'

'Something resembling wildflowers?' Louise recognized that Gina had taken a big step down on this one. After all, Tanni was her only daughter and she did want her to look gorgeous, but Lou was sure that she'd look just charming with ordinary blooms and said so.

'It's mostly Love-in–a-mist and Marguerites.'

'Perfect! Add a bit of greenery, I'm sure Mia will know what to do, and it'll be fine. And by the way Gina, don't start on about a cake - it's sorted.'

Gina made no further reference to the wedding trimmings but she did make sure that Tanni's dress was gorgeous. Her mum's outfit was blue, and the boys and Tanni would wear blue also. Marina's friend Lynne knew a brilliant seamstress ('They're a dying breed Gina', Marina had said) towards the north of the city.

Gina had been to visit her - she worked near Erdington - and was pleased with the choices. The boys were not thrilled with silk shirts, but Tanni adored the dress. She had begged for a huge sash and a flower-trimmed alice-band and Gina gave in to that request. Eventually the boys came round and agreed to wear their shirts with navy bow-ties. Gina decided not to mention any of this to Louise. On the day she'd barely notice, but for sure she'd love that they would look great and that they would match her outfit.

The guest list was not huge, around sixty, and Lou had organized the venue and the catering. She showed Gina and Kate Maynard the menu one day when Gina was visiting her mother.

Kate thought it was brilliant. Gina thought it was OK but biting her tongue, she said she thought it was 'just fine' and then she fussed over her mother's foot and her general needs and did her hair for her.

'I think we could just run this colour through your hair, mum, see if you approve, it's not permanent, but if you like it, we can get you to the salon and have it done before the wedding.'

To Gina's surprise, Louise did not object, and rather admired the result. Jim was called in.

'That's not bad!' he said admiringly, 'not bad at all - I like it.'

On that he was absolutely clear. And it was also clear that Jim adored Louise and that this marriage was a really good idea.

A couple of weeks before the wedding, Gina drove to the dressmakers to collect the dresses, and also the very simple outfit that she'd had made for herself. Susie, the dressmaker had wanted to come to deliver the items, but Gina did not want that. She took all the children with her, and indeed the slightly intimidating circumstances and surroundings of the dressmaker's rather elegant, high-class studio had the children on their best behaviour. They tried on their clothes meekly, and waited quietly as Gina tried on her dress. There were one or two alterations that were needed but eventually Gina was able to take home both her dress and Tanni's, complete with sash! The shirts needed slight changes to accommodate the bow-ties better, and she promised to return in a few days time.

She clicked the satnav to 'go home' which simply reversed the route, but they went home via the gelateria, which was not far from the main road on the way home. This was so that the kids could sample the tastes they would be able to have regularly when in Italy. Gina stressed this.

'Italy is so fantastic,' she said.

'When did you go?' Shaf asked.

'I haven't but I've read all about it,' Gina replied. Shaf looked dubious as he licked his ice.

'Anyway, everyone says so, and what do you think of your ice cream?'

'Good. It's good,' he allowed.

'Wait 'til you try the real thing,' Gina promised, 'but please don't drip ice-cream on the car seat. Your father will be cross - you know how he feels about this car.'

'Stupid car, a Morgan,' Han said.

'You don't know anything about cars,' Shafiq returned 'it's a great car. I'm going to have one when I'm older.'

'Huh,' was all that Han had to say to that.

'Whatever,' Gina was impatient, 'just don't mess it up.'

42

ZAK

Dmitri called.

'We have new girls.'

'Where from?'

'Montenegro.'

'We never had girls from there before.'

'So. Is a problem?'

'I don't know,' Zak was dubious. 'How dangerous?'

Dmitri gave his hoarse, cracked laugh. 'Hah, you so worried! Is no worries. Is all fine. You just need to get here, soon.' He cackled some more.

'What, on the coast?'

'Yeah, we meet at Margate - discuss what we do with Kamal - he is agent - then we will leave to the guys in the Med.'

'Oh, not at the boat then?'

'Not yet. We go later.'

'When?'

'Leave to me. I arrange, you just do as I say. Did you make payment?'

'Yeah, but I need to know what's going on. My father, he needs to have something.'

'You just keep papa quiet - keep him happy.'

'Not easy, my father is demanding and wants to know where the money goes.'

'You're okay at telling him good story - no problem.'

Zak sighed. 'Right - I'll do what I can. When do you need me?'

When Dmitri mentioned the date, Zak exploded, 'Oh shit, that's the date of my mother-in-law's wedding, I can't do it.'

'You have to. Make excuse. You tell impossible to be there. Too bad. Business is business.' He was blunt. 'Too bad,' he repeated.

'Tell me a bit more, I need to know - where did these girls come from?'

'Here, there - mostly orphans. Nowhere to go.'

'Where are they supposed to be going?'

Dmitri barked his harsh laugh. 'Going to safe house. We don't have to know where.'

'Maybe we do - what will happen to them? Will they really be safe - I mean - who will take them?'

'Hah! They go where they have to go - we pay, they go.'

'But we don't pay them.'

'Zak, you crazy, less you know, better is for you.' There was a tone of finality in Dmitri's voice. 'You just say yes, OK? And you just pay as arranged. Later, you get return. You know. You said - "good value".'

'But...'

'Zak, no need for this. When they get place, money comes good - very good. Two are brides...'

'Well, not from Montenegro.'

'So - somewhere first, then, ach! You ask too much.'

Zak steeled himself and was forced to accept Dmitri's demands. When he went home, he told Gina that he was unable to fulfill his obligations.

'But Zak! You promised. Lou and Jim will be devastated.'

'They won't - you'll have to give her away - it's not so terrible.' He sounded more certain than he felt and became short and impatient. 'Don't fuss. No big deal. It's not the end of the world.'

Gina's anger flared and she had to be particularly controlled. Zak could see she was far from happy. He decided not to engage, simply walked away, pulled out his phone and made a call.

43

GINA

When Gina heard from Zak that he could not make the wedding, she was initially furious with him.

'Typical,' she muttered after she had been told, 'only considers his own needs. My family - not important to him.'

But as it turned out, Gina came to terms with the subsequent arrangements and was reasonably comfortable with her new role. She and Marina worked on a short speech.

'You don't need much help from me,' Marina asserted. Gina worked in a tribute to Jim, though his brother Ray was going to be at the wedding and would also be offering a 'few words' as he put it. 'I'm not too good at that sort of thing but Jim's a great bloke and I think I should do it. Your mum's been really good for him.' She did ask Janine, Jim's sister if she would like to say a few words, but she was very reluctant.

'I'd need to be a bit drunk to do that Gina,' she explained.

'Well,' Gina said archly, 'that might come to pass.'

Gina realised that she was very pleased with this match too. She regretted also, that sadly Lily could not be there. She toyed with the idea of getting in touch. She resisted.

Amy came to visit for a day, and first Gina showed her the speech.

'Brilliant, Gina. You do actually have a way with words!'

Gina was close to telling her about her university plans, but drew back. Amy was a gossipy chatterer and Gina didn't want it to be common knowledge. Instead, they talked about Amy's new man.

'Wedding bells?' Gina asked.

'Nah, waste of time, getting married. Oops - sorry Gina, just saying…'

'What's he like - can we meet him?'

'Maybe,' Amy smiled. But Gina was more interested in finding out why Amy and her mum were no longer in contact, and quizzed her on the subject.

'Oh, she's such a pain. She still treats me like a child. Hates all the men I meet - nobody good enough - you know what she's like.'

'Well, I really don't,' Gina interrupted.

'She can't bear my Lewis, doesn't like tattoos, doesn't like black men, etcetera.'

'You know, it's hard for your mum, different generation. She'll come round.'

'She won't. She's already told me not to come round to hers again. She practically called me a whore!'

'Oh Amy, I'm sorry. Generally, it's good to have your mum on board.'

'I know.' Amy gave a long sad sigh. She looked tearful, and looked up.

'You're lucky, Gina. Your mum's lovely.'

And Gina knew it was true. She also knew that she was indeed lucky in many ways, but did not mention her growing discontent with Zak's behaviour. In this she felt frustrated and miserable.

'Never mind Amy, you and Lewis should get yourself a place to be where you can find happiness, start a family.'

'We're trying. That's another thing, my mother gives me hell for - not having had a baby! Can you imagine? I mean, what's it to do with her?'

'Well, you're not getting any younger Amy!' Gina was laughing, and now, so was Amy.

'You're beginning to sound just like her, give me a break Gina. Oh, by the way, I met a friend of yours at work, well, in the same building.'

'Who?' Gina's heart skipped. She thought of Dan.

'Lily - don't know her other name. Says she knows you.'

'Where - where's she working?' Gina was thinking fast. As soon as Amy discovered her name was Drummond, she'd know at once they were related, so no lies now.

'She's on reception in the dentist's three mornings a week. Same building as my firm.'

'She's my cousin.' Gina stated this simply and waited to see what Amy would make of this. 'She's Lily Drummond.'

'No! You're kidding! I only found out that she knew you because I was talking about the hen, and the wedding and all that, and I told her who it was getting married, so…'

'Oh. You told her Lou was getting married?'

'Yeah. Was that bad?'

'Not great. She's not invited.' Careful now, thought Gina.

'Why not?' Best keep it simple, truthful, Gina decided.

'Lou doesn't see eye to eye, you know, family history - just, well, things.'

'Oh? What?' demanded Amy greedy for gossip. But Gina just clammed and said rather more firmly than she had intended:

'Sorry - can't really say. Please don't mention this to Lou, it would upset her. She's already pretty cross with me for having spoken to Lily at all. Promise me you won't say anything Amy - please?'

And Amy did promise, but Gina was troubled. More in the knowledge that Lily would feel hurt at not being invited to the wedding, although surely she would understand. She certainly hoped so.

And now she wondered about telling Amy the whole story, but realised she couldn't do that. Not even Maggie knew and if she found out that Miss Bigmouth had heard about something as significant as this, it could wreck a friendship, not something that Gina could contemplate. So she said nothing. Instead she suggested a walk to Edgbaston Pool - a couple of miles away, where the woods and trees bordering the lake were in full, glorious leaf, and looked quite spectacular.

There's something about walking that relaxes speech, loosens tongues, and Gina heard Amy tell her of her final months with the dreadful Josh.

'I can't believe you stayed with him so long.'

'No, me neither, but he was sort of mesmerizing. And bloody good-looking, if you remember.' They both giggled. 'But he was abusive. Verbally abusive. I didn't like that. And he was never faithful - whatever that is - men have such an unfair view of infidelity.'

'How do you mean?'

147

'He always said he was "just visiting" and he always expected to be able to come back to me.'

And Gina decided to tell Amy of her current feelings for Zak. As she began to open up abut his distant behaviour and his absences from the family home, she found herself also confessing that she no longer felt close to him.

'He can be verbally abusive too,' she said. 'He's really quite a bully, and for all I know he's playing away when he's not here. Maybe not as blatantly as Josh was, but anyway, I feel lonely, alone, a lot of the time.'

'Well, Josh certainly took every opportunity he could - whether it was welcome or not. D'you remember your party...?'

'Oh yes, I certainly do.' Gina spoke with feeling.

'You know, I never saw you at the end - what happened to you?'

Gina shrugged 'Can't remember,' she lied, 'long time ago.'

'You just said you really did remember it. Come on - were you snogging someone in a darkened room?'

'Amy, you're mad. My children were there, as indeed was my husband.'

'Makes no diff,' Amy said airily, 'never did with Josh, the bastard.' she added crossly.

'So when did you meet Lewis?'

'Oh, hold on, there was Dale first, he lasted four, no five weeks, then Kali, awesome guy, but too much religion, he was a Hindu - my god, you should have heard my mother on him...'

'I can imagine, from what you say.'

'Yeah, talk about not p.c.'

'And then Lewis?'

'Well no, before that I went out with my boss a few times.'

'I'm guessing - married?'

'Yeah. So not really going anywhere, so, then along came Lewis. Gorgeous. It's the real thing G, honest.'

'You sure Amy?'

Gina knew that with Amy nothing was certain, and she wondered if she'd ever settle with a partner.

Later, when Amy had left, Gina pulled out her journal. She wrote:

'Some people don't know how to get the best out of their lives, seem never satisfied, though they desperately want to be. I'm a bit that way. Is it my fault, or is it what's gone before in my life? Is it just up to me to create my own happiness, or does it depend on others also? Surely you can't do it alone. And who's in charge of me? Why can't I see Lily? I guess I know why mum doesn't want her at the wedding, but really - it seems a bit mean. Lily's real family.'

Then she snapped it closed and stuffed it into the back of the wardrobe.

44

Gina had pleaded with Zak to put off the business trip, to no avail.
'What is it that's so important?' she'd asked. But Zak was
dismissive.

'I have to meet with the Russians, also my father might have to
visit briefly, but it will be,' he paused, 'in London, so I have to be
there.'

'Why did you arrange it on that particular day?'

'Gina,' he sighed heavily and impatiently, 'you know nothing
about the business, so stop asking questions.'

'I could know about the business if you told me something about
it.' Gina spoke quietly, but there was anger and resentment in her
voice.

'Oh please!' he drawled, 'not this again. You just stick to looking
after the children and stop giving me a hard time.'

'Zak, I do resent the way you treat me, and talk to me.' Gina
knew it would anger him for her to speak in that way, so it was quite
courageous to try. As she suspected, he immediately became irate.

He raised his voice. 'Gina, just shut up. I don't want to hear
another word from you. Be quiet and leave me to my business. Do I
interfere in yours?'

'Don't shout, the children will hear.'

'I don't care if they do. They should know what a terrible nag you
are.' And Zak stamped out of the room slamming the door as he
went.

And the wedding day neared. Lou and Jim had everything in
hand; dresses, suits, shoes, food, drink, cakes and flowers were all in
place.

The hotel had been in touch with Gina, and she had given them a
running order, not that there was much to it, and on the day,
everyone duly assembled, Louise arrived in a big white Rolls, her
crutches decorated in blue and silver ribbons and little bunches of
flowers. She looked amazing. The hair colour was sensational and

the outfit quite perfect. The Sayeed family arrived, although without Zak. They came by train, with a great deal of luggage ready for their trip to Italy the following day.

The ceremony proceeded with no problems, Jim and Lou kissed in the approved manner at the end, the champagne flowed and the rather late lunch was excellent. Even Gina's speech was good, and Ray said his few words with dignity and confidence despite the fact that he claimed to be 'as nervous as hell'. He told a couple of youthful stories about Jim, so despite there being no best man (Jim's choice) Ray made everyone laugh. As the assembled crowd moved into the reception room beyond the dining room, there was a little shuffling disturbance at the door.

Heads turned, and Gina looked with astonishment as she saw Lily walking under the decorated arch at the entrance. There was a momentary silence. For the most part, no-one knew who it was, and to be fair, she was not really dressed for a wedding.

Gina rushed towards her. Of course Louise had seen her and of course she knew who she was. Gina stood in front of Lily and glanced sideways to where her mother was standing. For a moment, Louise was quite still. Then, with queenly grace, she approached Lily. She took her arm. Gina thought she might be about to escort her out of the door, but no, instead, she pulled her close and hugged her firmly. Within seconds they were both crying, but at the same time smiling, and the awkward moment had passed.

'Gina - did you ask her?' she asked a few moments later, when Lou had introduced Lily to Jim and Janine, who were standing near.

'No, it was because of a coincidence. Amy met her...' and she explained a little more.

'Are you cross?'

'No. I couldn't be cross today anyway, so I guess I'm glad she's here.'

'Me too, maybe we can all reconnect properly now?'

'We'll see,' Louise responded cautiously. As Lily came back to join them again, Lou limped away to other guests. Lily stayed with Gina, chatting to her.

'Where's Zak - I should say hello.'

'Not here - business calls.' Gina sounded awkward.

'Business! On a day like this.'

'Please Lily, don't let's go there - look here's Han - say hello to your Auntie Lily, Han.'

'Auntie?' Han sounded startled. 'Where?...I didn't know I had...' and he stopped, staring at Lily with his mouth open.

'Well, you do, once removed, anyway, and you've got some second cousins too! Go and get Shaf and Tanni and introduce them to Auntie Lily. Can you do that?'

'I guess,' Han responded, his eyes round and his jaw still loose.

When Gina turned back to her cousin she asked about Lou's foot and after Gina explained, she then wondered about a honeymoon.

'Ah, well, I've got that all planned!'

'*You* have?'

'Yes, we're all going to a fabulous place in Italy - deepest and most beautiful Umbria - Casalta - for a couple of weeks - well, we had to do that when Jim had to cancel the city tour - couldn't do that with a broken ankle!'

'Must have cost to cancel?'

'No, medical certificate covered that - and I've paid for the other place.'

'Gina, I get the impression you're quite well off.'

'Yep. Zak makes a very good living. I'm OK.'

'But you don't work yourself?'

'Don't actually need to, financially speaking, but I would like to qualify as something. That's why I am going to start an Open University course in October.'

'You are? That's fantastic Gina!' Lily was clearly impressed.

And Gina told her a little of her plans until they were interrupted when Jim tapped a glass and asked everyone to gather round as he and Lou cut the cake. Then the Hotel staff divided it up and passed it to the guests. More champagne was poured, there was much laughter as the evening faded into late summer light, and was filled with joy and suddenly, music.

45

ZAK

Zak arrived in Margate. Dmitri had already herded several young girls to a building that had once been a holiday home. How he had got hold of it, Zak had no idea. No doubt some of Zak's money had been used for this place and although it was somewhat run-down, it seemed good enough. At least the fabric was sound and there was glass in the windows.

'How did you get these girls?'

'They are orphans. They didn't like the children's home.' *He gave a barking laugh, and flicked a black cigarette into the hearth.* 'So we look after them.'

'What do you mean - "look after"?' *Zak frowned.* 'Where are we taking them?'

'Some London, some Glasgow, some to Cornwall...'

'Cornwall?'

'Yes, good money from them. And other places too - all good.'

'Who said we can have them?'

'Who says no?'

And Zak decided not to pursue this, asking instead only what the next step might be.

'There is big white van. Some go direct with driver. Kamal - good man - he takes them.'

'You spoke of brides...'

Dmitri sniggered 'Sure, they will be in South London, but they stay here for now in this house, then Kamal returns and delivers them. By then, boat is going to come here and collect. From other boats. Lots come. No worries.'

'Who is going to get the boat here?'

'You, my friend!' *Dmitri found this amusing and added* 'Not alone. There are others - will arrive on island. You just meet on coast, near boathouse.'

'When do I do this?'

'You will hear. No problem. You have cash?' Because the chief reason for Zak being there was to pay several shady characters for the children they were taking. And now he handed over a large wad of cash.

'Don't worry about money - we get good price from all peoples.'

'Will they have to work?'

'Sure they work - why people buy if not working?'

'And they pay well?'

'Oh yes, very well, we make big bucks. You see!'

Zak tightened his mouth and nodded thoughtfully and slowly.

'What kind of work?'

Dmitri gave an evil smile.

'Who knows? Many things - different things.'

And Zak knew better than to ask more. He also knew that he should not ask to see these girls. Whatever their fate, he was sure that he did not want to know. He told himself that he was simply the bank, that he had no moral responsibilities that in fact he was helping them to survive. 'Yes, without me, they would end up in a terrible orphanage. I'm doing the right thing.'

Kamal arrived with another couple of young men. One of them went into the inner room, carrying several large boxes and a cardboard tray of canned drinks.

'Pizza,' Kamal informed them. He threw himself into an old, stained armchair, snapped the ring off a beer, lit a cigarette and leaned back.

'Help yourself mate,' he said to Zak. But Zak was hungry rather than thirsty and said so to Dmitri.

'Anywhere we can get a meal?'

'Sure. We can go. These guys keep these girls safe inside here.'

And after a brief but important chat with Kamal, they walked into the evening air to find something to sustain them before going home, Zak back to North London, Dmitri to - who knew where?

When they had eaten a fairly dreadful pie and chips from a squalid café, neither speaking much, and Dmitri tapping his phone for much of the time, Zak stood to leave.

'Keep me posted,' Zak said. Dmitri grunted and waved a fat hand.

Zak pondered the postcode. 'Hotel somewhere near Hitchin,' he muttered. 'How the hell am I to find that - can't use the satnav,' he grumbled 'Bloody Gina, why didn't she set it for me?' He dragged out the old road atlas and decided he would get to the M25 then M1, follow it until he saw a sign that seemed helpful. He wished that he could just go home, but he had to collect the family and take them to Maggie's where they would stay overnight before flying off to Italy. Zak had shrugged when Gina had announced this. What did he want a holiday for anyway? He couldn't care less, and frankly it would leave the coast clear for him to press ahead with the business in hand.

More by chance than design, he came across the right main road, and stopping only once to check the road map, found the hotel, where the music announced the event as still in progress.

He found Gina. 'Tanni is asleep on the sofa in the cloakroom,' she said. And there she was, lying on a red velvet chaise, fast asleep. The boys were still racing around, guests were still dancing and Lou and Jim, looking happy but tired were sitting at a table as Zak approached. They exchanged pleasantries, Zak congratulated them and said he would take Gina and the children back to Maggie's now.

Once he had installed them all and unloaded the luggage to the front hall, he took his leave.

'Text me - send photos,' he called as he waved goodbye, climbed into the Jeep and drove back to Birmingham.

46

GINA

Gina sought out Issy.

'Where've you been all my life?' They hugged and Issy said indignantly,

'I saw you at the hen!'

'But we don't meet up regularly very much.'

'I've just started a masters degree - business analytics - sounds terrible, doesn't it? But it will keep me very busy. I need a masters just to sort out my time!'

'Wow, I didn't know. Where?'

'Bath - nice place, but I don't need to be there all the time, so I can see plenty of Finn. Still, it is going to be very demanding – and as you can see, we haven't had time for another child!'

'That really the reason?'

'Nah - just didn't happen, but we're fine, Finn is such a joy; funny little thing. We overindulge, of course but Twill's great with him and he's a happy kid.'

One day Gina would find out why everyone called her partner Twill, but it seemed to suit him. She looked around for him. He was dancing with Issy's mum and Tanni was doing her best to hamper that performance in every way she knew. Gina zig-zagged across the room and plucked Tanni from the floor. She laughed and bounced her head on Gina's shoulder in a vain attempt to stop herself from falling asleep. Gina stopped to have Tanni say hello to Issy, who she did not know well, and she responded very shyly. Anyway, in truth, her eyelids were closing and sleep overcame her before Gina got her into the sitting-out area, where coats and bags had been left. Here, she moved some coats and laid her onto the red-velvet chaise longue and tucked a jacket over her legs. She left her to sleep quietly.

Back in the main reception hall, some guests were leaving and Louise and Jim were surrounded by the crowd of well-wishers as they said goodbye. Lou stayed seated of course. Earlier, she had attempted a kind of hopping 'first waltz' but it was tiring and as she said, keeping up a smile and chatting all night is exhausting, so she was beginning to look a bit weary.

'Mum, I think you two are allowed to go if you want. I'm expecting Zak soon and I'm going to round the kids up. We'll go off to Mag's and we'll see you at Luton in the morning - are you all packed?'

'Oh, pretty well, love, Jim's done most of it.'

'Under strict direction,' he chimed from above her head where he had just been saying goodbye to Janine and her family. 'You don't think I was allowed any say in her clothes do you?'

'Well, why should you? What do you know about ladies' fashion?'

'True, my darling wife, nothing at all.' And he bent to kiss her newly blonded hair with such affection that as she walked away in search of the boys, Gina, felt a curdling emotion of real love and jealousy all at the same moment.

From across the room, she saw Zak arrive, who looked around quickly, then spotted her and came towards her. He greeted her briefly. He looked tired too.

'The boys are still racing around, doing silly dancing. Tanni's asleep.'

A glance at his daughter, then a quick 'congratulations' to Lou and Jim, and Zak was ready to leave. It took longer than he would have chosen - so many goodbyes! But finally, they piled into the Jeep and he drove them to Maggie's and although not far away, it still took over half an hour, and by the time they had off-loaded all their baggage for the holiday, it was quite late when they each got to their various beds.

And the holiday was such a great success!

Louise couldn't stop whooping at the villa, which was indeed altogether up to expectations and she loved the area, as they all did. The children were in the pool almost before the car had been emptied, and waiting to greet them was a delightful Italian Mama, who would cook supper and had left them some cold meats, cheese and salads for a very late lunch. Although the children had eaten their own bodyweight in snacks during the journey, the grown-ups had been more restrained and were really hungry. That first mouthful of cool, Pinot Grigio followed by some excellent local cheese, was bliss. The worries of the last couple of weeks melted away and they felt as if in heaven.

After two weeks of swimming and walking - even Lou did a bit - and playing table football and tennis, and various board games in the evening, and having visited several pretty towns, although Lou and Jim didn't always join them, they felt they had really seen a whole new world. The children seemed impressed by much of what they saw. Shaf asked, 'Did they really paint those pictures, with, like, real paints?'

'Yes, of course.'

'How many?'

'What do you mean?'

'Did they do a lot of them?'

'Never exactly the same.'

Shaf seemed puzzled. He asked:

'Why not?'

'Well, why should they? There were no cameras remember. These paintings recorded great historical events, some, especially the religious ones, were from the imagination of the artist, others told of battles and coronations.'

'What's a coronation?'

And Gina explained briefly what that meant. She even reminded Shaf of a huge picture of the Virgin.

'Botticelli - in Florence,' she said. 'All that gold...' Shaf frowned.

'Yeah, I remember, I think,' he added.

Han asked: 'What about that Leonardo de - what?'

'Da. Da Vinci. There aren't any of his near here, it's difficult to always know his work really, because he didn't sign it.'

'If it were me, I'd sign everything,' Shaf announced.

'Yes, well, people aren't sure why he didn't.' Gina was pleased with herself and proud of her knowledge. She was able to give them lots of information. Louise was impressed even if it didn't stay with the children very long. Gina added 'The famous one is in The Louvre in Paris. I'll take you sometime.'

'Mona Lisa,' said Jim, 'even I know that.'

They'd had days in Florence and Perugia - where again Gina was able to show off her knowledge of certain pictures. They went to Gubbio, Spello, Spoleto and even a tremendously hot and crowded day in Assisi, which was difficult to endure, and they were glad to get to the gelateria. Once home, the children were into the swimming pool before

Gina had even got into the big air-conditioned kitchen. Lou was sitting in a wicker armchair with a pinkish soda drink, looking cool, and she smiled.

'This is such bliss darling. Thank you so much. Do you wish Zak were here?'

Gina grabbed a can from the fridge and threw herself into the opposite chair.

'Truth? Not really. I'm just happy. Pleased you two have had a chance to chill.'

Lou waved her hand up and down in front of her face and said:

'Not much of that today - as you can see, Jim is in the pool and that's where he's been most of the day - he came in to get lunch for me, and I did sit out in the shade for a bit. But it's so hot, I had to get back inside. Just such a shame I can't get in the pool myself.'

As their time in Italy drew to a close, Gina became a bit reflective. The boys had checked in with Zak on Facetime, but he had never initiated a call. She had texted him four or five times and he had replied, rather perfunctorily. On one of the Facetime calls, he had obviously been in a bar and had walked outside, away from the noise to have a few minutes with them, but she had no idea where. She had actually asked him where he was but he just shrugged.

'Somewhere - some bar - I don't remember the name.'

But that was not what she had meant.

* * *

As they packed, they all agreed it had been amazing.

'We'll do this again.'

'Can dad come?'

'Of course, it's just that he was so busy this time, he couldn't get away.' Gina wondered if the children really believed this. She wondered if she really believed it!

47

Back home, they settled into their routines. Tanni was prepared for her first days at school, about which she appeared blasé and in truth, Gina was the one who was worried. She was concerned that Tanni would tire easily, and although she was scheduled for mornings only at first, Gina fretted for a long time before her little girl was due to start.

The boys were keen for a boat trip before term started and the weather was good enough to plan one. But Zak was oddly unwilling and showed little interest. Indeed he said that they needed proper crew and as Lou was still healing, and Jim therefore unable to join them, they would be short handed. When they protested about the inadequacy of that excuse, he found other reasons not to go. They all seemed feeble but he was dismissive. The boys especially seemed more than disappointed. Shaf was really angry with his father on one occasion.

'Why haven't we learned to crew and navigate properly yet?'

'You aren't old enough.'

'We are,' Shaf said, quite reasonably. Gina was puzzled too, what was going on?

'What's the problem Zak, why don't we send them to a residential school to do a week's course or something like that?' She showed him an item in a sailing magazine which advertised just such a course and reluctantly Zak agreed.

'But maybe next week,' he said therefore effectively putting it off for a while longer.

'Isn't it half-term or something?'

Gina was happy to get all the arrangements in place and after several phone calls and emails, a couple of places, at some huge cost, was secured on the course, a few weeks later, and Gina spent a morning driving with them to Southampton, to the marina training centre and checking them in.

It was really rather splendid, and the sleeping quarters, dining areas and leisure area were all good. She stayed an hour only and then rather slowly left, hoping the boys would rush to hug her before she went. But they were so engaged already, that they barely said goodbye. Gina was quite comfortable with what she had seen and the accommodation was all very satisfactory.

She and Tanni went home, Tanni complaining a little and Gina promising some treats as she wasn't able to join the boys on the course. Of course she didn't really want to go on the course, but she knew how to work a deal!

Zak was still unwilling to set a date for a visit to the boat. He made some excuse and then asked about the holiday.

'Show me the pictures Gina.'

'I told you, they're in Dropbox.'

'Not good with that - not sure how to, er, open it.'

'Oh for goodness sake Zak, you're such a technophobe! I have shown you how to do it before.'

And she accessed the pictures, which he then barely looked at. He made a few perfunctory remarks and commented on the weather:

'Looks like it was very hot.'

'It was, very. The sky is that deep, deep blue; you hardly ever get that in England.'

'How's the swimming coming along?'

But Gina could tell that he was barely engaged in this conversation and when she offered some vague reports of their abilities in the water, she added 'Tanni nearly drowned' which wasn't true, but she wanted to see his reaction. Sure enough, he merely said:

'OK, well look, I'm going to sort some paperwork,' and left the room. Obviously he was scarcely listening.

With the boys away, Gina and Tanni went to spend a few days with Jim and Louise. Lou was now hobbling about in one of those particularly unattractive boots and although Jim was with her most of the time, she was beginning to regain her independence. But Gina fussed over her and went shopping to get food and wine and various other treats. She walked slowly around the garden with her and they sat in the still-warm sunshine and watched Tanni playing with what she called her animal school. Dahlias flopped in the borders and even some late roses spilled petals onto the grass. A mass of asters bloomed bright in the little island bed that they'd created and Gina was relaxed. She always felt happy here, she reflected, and she said this to her mum.

'Aren't you happy at home then?' Lou was a bit snappy. 'You strike me as a bit gloomy when you're there.'

'Gloomy?' Gina protested, 'no, I'm fine - I just - you know I'm starting this course?'

It was an attempt to divert the conversation and Gina suddenly realised that she had told her mother nothing of these plans.

'What course is this?'

'It's the Open University. Just an art thing.' She tried to make it something and nothing.

'Is that like an evening course?'

'No, with Tanni in school, I'll be able to do some proper studying. I'll work at home, but in the day.' She decided to try to get her mum on side, 'Do you think it's a good idea mum?'

'Well, I suppose so, it'll keep you out of mischief.' Which was just the kind of platitude that Gina had hoped for; she certainly didn't want her mum to begin criticizing her plans. 'What kind of art?'

'Well. You know I go on these gallery visits - I see a lot of pictures, sculptures, you know stuff like that, so, the course is about the history of - er, of, so well, that, really…the, erm…' And Gina stumbled through a sort of explanation and realised that actually she herself didn't know much about it. She determined to spend a good deal more time searching out the detail of her course and becoming familiar with its requirements. There was certainly a book list and she planned to order up all the necessary texts. But she needed to get on with it, she knew that.

48

When she got home, Rayna gave her some disturbing information.

'Men have been here, they use the rooms, and there was child - two children - girls, I care for them. They need food and they tired, so tired.'

Gina approached Zak angrily.

'Who were these girls?' she shouted, 'what were they doing in our house?'

'Yeshevsky's cousin has girls, he wants them to get employment here. You can't say anything - it's a bit...illegal...' Zak flapped his hands dismissively.

'A bit illegal? It either is or it isn't! What are you playing at Zak? That man is a nasty piece of work - you should have nothing to do with him.'

'I said I'd help him, I mean, if they need, you know, asylum... he's been good to me about the boat.' He was offhand.

'Which reminds me - are you going to get the boys, or will I go?'

'You go, Gina. You drive so much better than me!' His sardonic tone was unpleasant, but Gina ignored him and tried to return to the subject of the illegals.

'What the hell are you getting involved with? Sounds as though you'll end up in gaol.'

'Gina, don't be ridiculous, you do exaggerate, and you know nothing about these circumstances, so stop offering your opinions, no-one wants to know, least of all me.' And he swiveled his foot and walked out.

Gina, hurt by his sharp response though not unused to such reactions, and concerned at the turn of events, was heated with annoyance. She walked quickly upstairs to Tanni's room and knelt by her bed. She was deeply asleep, and Gina stroked her dark curls, gaining some comfort from being close to her little girl. She whispered a few quiet words and was surprised when a teardrop fell on her forearm. She was certainly upset, troubled by what she had heard. She felt almost certain that Zak was lying, that there was something much more sinister going on. But what to do? If she informed the police, that would put herself and the children in danger or at best, it would put Gina herself in a difficult position. It might be argued that she had been complicit in some of Zak's plans, and she couldn't risk that. Goodness, it might even jeopardise her position as mother of her children. She had heard of children being taken into care for far less than this might seem to be.

She stood and went down again; there was no sign of Zak.

She tapped gently on the door of Rayna's room. They had a mutual understanding that unless by prior arrangement, they would never disturb each other in the evening and this was clearly breaking that rule, but she had to ask her certain questions.

'What nationality were these children?'

'I don't know, I suppose Russian?'

'How old were they do you think?'

'13, 14, so thin, can't tell for sure.'

'Did they seem afraid?'

Rayna pulled the corners of her mouth down in a thoughtful but non-committal way.

'Not really. Shy…quiet.'

'Did it bother you - when they came?'

'So. I am surprised. Yes. But…'

And Rayna gave a shrug as if to indicate that if she is asked to do something, well, she would do it.

'I don't complain.' She smiled sadly as she spoke, and though it was an odd way to put it, Gina understood.

'Right, I'm sorry I disturbed you Rayna.'

'No, is important, I know. Is OK.' And Gina left, and went back to the kitchen to try to pull something together for supper.

But she didn't feel hungry and with no sign of Zak, she could hardly be bothered, and instead made some sandwiches to take with her the following day, when she would go to collect the boys. Unconsciously, she bit into one…she hadn't even been thinking about what should go in the sandwiches, and cheese would have to do, though actually, the bread was a bit stale and the cheese not special. She sighed.

'They'll eat it if they're hungry,' she muttered and she wrapped them and put them in a box before storing them in the fridge.

When she had watched the news on the TV, and then recalled nothing of it, she went up to bed. To her surprise, Zak was already in bed, snoring softly, and she retreated to their dressing room. From the back of the big wardrobe, she pulled out her journal and began to write, sitting at the dressing table with a low light beaming on the page.

Tonight, she was distressed and wrote at length about the wedding, Lily's arrival, and some secret thoughts about Ed and then of her father. She wrote more fearfully of Zak's behaviour while she had been away, and in particular of his current involvement with these seemingly nefarious characters that appeared to be so much part of his life at present. It didn't cross her mind that such writing might in some way be incriminating. As far as she was concerned it was simply doing what her counsellor therapist had suggested all those years ago in Switzerland, even before she had met Zak. Just write things down. It helps to clarify. It helps to heal.

She wrote more on this occasion than she had for a long time. From the bedroom, she could hear no other sounds than that of Zak gently snoring. There was no danger of her disturbing him, he was always a sound sleeper. As for Gina, her sleep patterns were not so good, and she did not feel she could settle down to a good night until she had expatiated a bit more.

49

Gina collected her stuff in the morning and although she wanted to leave Tanni with Rayna, she made such a fuss about being left behind, that she took her along. And to be fair, she behaved herself pretty well, although she needed the toilet and Gina stopped at Chievely services. Here, she had a coffee and tried to call Zak.

When she had got out of bed, that morning, he was not there. Downstairs, unusually, he was at the breakfast bar talking to Tanni. It wasn't yet nine o'clock and Zak seemed ready to leave.

'Are you sure you don't want to come with me?' Gina was still fretting about taking Tanni alone.

'Nah, you'll be fine - you're good with the navigation thing aren't you?'

'Yes, but Tanni can be rather demanding and without another adult...'

But Zak just responded with a scornful laugh. Clearly nothing would persuade him to join her.

And, in the end it had taken her little over a couple of hours to get to the marina centre, and the boys were waiting, though not with huge enthusiasm, to return home.

They had enjoyed a splendid time, and while their instructor warned that they had some way to go, he was most complimentary especially about Shafiq's skills.

'He really picked up ideas quickly, and he's clearly got a real talent for navigation.'

'Hanif is more tentative,' he said, 'not quite as confident, but he'll get there.'

Gina was surprised to learn that they had done the course on a boat.

'No, we don't do classwork in that sense, it's all hands on, on board. So, it's fun for them all, and they certainly learn better in those circumstances.'

Gina helped to load the boys' rucksacks into the Jeep but she was invited to look around the centre and go on board one of the training boats before leaving. Tanni was keen to do this too and trotted off ahead of the others, Gina calling anxiously to her to take care, and warn her about the closeness of the water.

'Can we come again mummy?' This from Shaf.

'What do you think Han? Would you want to come again?' Gina asked.

'Yeah, sure.' Han was not hugely enthusiastic, but keen enough. Gina decided that they would get a second chance. She was a bit fed up with Zak's ineptitude and worried for their safety when they were on the boat.

'Who wants a sandwich,' she asked, 'cheese?'

'OK,' Shaf replied, but Han said he wasn't hungry.

'What was the food like?' Gina wasn't really worried that they hadn't eaten well, but she was curious.

'Brilliant. You could choose from a buffet - you can get chips and burgers and - '

But Han interrupted 'You can get salad and coleslaw and potato salad and stuff and ice cream, but it's not as good as Italian.'

'It's not like you ate salad all the time, you goody-goody,' Shaf said.

'I'm not a goody-goody,' Han protested, but he did like to sound superior to his elder brother, and Gina hugged them both, one with either arm, and towed them to the Jeep, Tanni skipping along obediently, slightly ahead.

But Gina noted, that when she offered the box of biscuits to the three in the back, they were all unrestrained in their indulgence.

At home, Gina asked Rayna if Zak was home.

'No, he is here with Russians at lunch, then they go.'

'Did they mention the girls?'

'No. I don't know. I don't listen - is not for me to know.' And Gina knew that she should not ask, should not put Rayna in that position, not make her complicit, but then, how else is she to discover what is going on and how can she be sure that she and her family will be safe.

When the children were in bed, or in any case upstairs, and Rayna had retired to her room, Gina texted Zak, 'where are u?' After ten minutes he had not replied. She tried again. 'Back at 10' he responded. She sighed and then turned to the Course folder she had barely hidden in the cupboard and looked at the details that the Open University had sent her. There was much to do and she resolved to get some of the reading material sorted while Zak wasn't around.

She searched the internet and found several books that were recommended, ordered them and then read some of the preliminary pamphlets and documents that she'd received. For an hour or so, she was completely absorbed in the task, in another world and happy. Indeed, it was only as she heard a car crunch up to the back door, and she knew Zak was home, that she began return to her former state of anxiety and dismay. She glanced at the time. 10.40. Well, he wasn't reliable in any way it seemed. She quickly gathered her papers and stacked them, put them back in the cupboard while she listened to Zak slamming into the sitting room, where she sat, shouting about Dmitri and someone called Kamal.

'No respect! No respect for each other. They just argue, fight, disagree, all the time, I'm driven crazy by these idiots.'

'Zak, you should not be driving when you've had so much to drink.'

He ignored these remonstrations. 'I am not drunk. I am perfectly capable of driving.'

'Zak, I can tell, you, you smell of booze.'

'Aach, Gina, give it a rest will you?'

'But Zak,' and even as she said it, she knew she should be quiet, but it was more than Zak could take and he interrupted her angrily, swinging round towards her, and striking her, even if unintentionally, hard on the head, with his flailing arm, shouting at the same time.

'Shut up and don't tell me what to do. Who do you think you are?'

As he hit her, she staggered, he paused and there was a moment's silence. They stared at each other. Tears started in Gina's eyes. Zak's anger did not abate, indeed he shook his head rapidly and crossly and stalked out of the room. Actually he had not really hurt Gina badly, and she was more in shock than in pain, but she sat down and waited for some moments before she moved at all. Then she stood and walked into the kitchen. He was not there. She turned on the cold tap and ran herself a glass of water, which she gulped down.

She went up to the bedroom and Zak was sitting on the bed his head down staring at his knees. He turned as she entered.

Rather gruffly he said, 'Sorry Gina. I've had a difficult day. Lost it. Sorry.'

Hearing this, Gina decided to make the best of it, and quietly prepared for bed. She recognized that Zak must have made quite an effort to say that, and she thought it best not to pursue it further, although she had been shocked and upset both by his actions and by his attitude. To be fair, this was little changed from the norm, especially recently and she was almost resigned to a submissive state of marriage.

But the following day she was more determined than ever that her studies should go ahead as she planned.

Jo and Marina came round, Jo's two children, 5 and 7, came too. Jo was a rather unkempt blonde, who spent longer on the needs of others than on her own requirements. Some might describe her as loud, but it was mostly her laugh that was noisy, and it was true that it could be a bit abrasive. And she did have the slightly annoying habit of interrupting with what she thought was to be the end of your sentence. Equally annoying was the fact that she was usually correct in her anticipation. Whether this was because she was being a sympathetic listener or because she was impatient, was hard to say.

She had been a landscape gardener and she observed that many years of digging around in soil, compost and heaps of dirt, had resulted in her nails and hair being irreparably damaged, something she just laughed about. The open air had, however, been brilliant for her skin and her rosy, pretty complexion shone wherever she went. The boys were remarkably good with Jo's two kids, showing them round the garden and letting them play with their toys. Oddly Tanni was less good, became clingy and seemed jealous of the attention that the boys were giving to Grace and Dexter, but a great array of snacks and drinks that Rayna brought out, seemed to please everyone. Marina, Jo and Gina were able to relax on the deck in the early autumn sunshine and chat about many things including Gina's plans.

'It's so exciting that you're going to do this,' Jo said, and Marina assured her that it would be fine despite her worries and reservations.

'You'll see, there'll be plenty of people that haven't half your knowledge…'

169

'Or half your brain!' Jo added.

She showed them some of the literature. Jo fluttered her eyelids in a dreamy way. 'You're lucky to get this chance. Wish I could.'

'It's not luck - it's more a rather reckless gamble. When Zak discovers that I'm in this for real, he'll go crazy.'

'Surely not?'

'He will. Doesn't believe in education for women.'

'Oh, don't be ridiculous - you're exaggerating Gina!'

'Not really - honestly - he does sort of realise that there are clever women helping to run the world, but he never seems to wonder how they got to be in their positions - I don't think it crosses his mind.'

'So what about Tanni?'

'Well. Who knows? She'll certainly get her chance if I have anything to do with it. Mind you, the way he behaves, he won't *let* me have anything to do with it.'

'You do paint a bleak picture of his views.'

'Oh, believe me - they're positively medieval.'

They laughed. But Gina did have serious concerns and wondered how she would ever express them when the time came.

She was sorry and a bit empty when they had left. She enjoyed the stimulus of pleasant conversation. They were not high intellectuals but they were interesting, her sort of people, whatever that meant, who shared her attraction to art and history, and they all had a lot of love for Italy. After Gina's recent visit she found she was able to contribute animatedly to conversations, with information about her time there. She showed them lots of pictures, and talked in an informed way about the places she had visited. She was somewhat astonished at how much they already knew about the towns and cities and how much of the country they had seen. Of course they had been many times as against her single visit and she felt a little foolish at her naiveté, felt a little embarrassed at displaying her innocent lack of sophistication, but was determined that she would change all that. Later that evening she called Issy.

She quizzed her about the things she felt she needed to know about mixing with scholarly types.

Issy was encouraging. 'They're not scholarly - they're just people. They want to learn. Lots of them are just like you.'

'But I'm old...'

'Oh, there are lots older than you - you'll see!'

'...and I don't know anything...'

'Well. It was you who left school early.' Issy couldn't resist a dig.

'...not even got A-levels,' Gina recalled.

'No, exactly, but it doesn't matter - it'll be fine. Stop fretting.' Issy sounded a bit impatient with the usually solid Gina. 'You're being a bit ditzy about this - not like you.'

Then she called Amy. She was much more airily dismissive of Gina's concerns.

'You can always give it up if you don't like it,' she pointed out.

Somehow, this approach suited Gina better and she felt some sense of solace hearing her say that.

'How's Lewis?'

'Toast!'

'No!' Gina was astonished. 'What happened?'

'Didn't seem committed.'

'What are you talking about? Who wasn't committed?'

'Oh, neither of us, I guess. Anyway, I met someone...'

'Who?' Gina wasn't that curious or interested, after all, Amy met someone new every six weeks it seemed.

'Actually he knows you.'

Gina started. 'Who?'

'We were at school with him.' And although Gina knew exactly who she was talking about she still said, as casually as she could:

'And who would that be?'

'Dan Moran. Said he met you recently. That you'd reconnected... He fixes boats or something.'

'Yeah,' Gina responded lazily and disinterestedly, 'we had a moment!'

'Sounded like more than a moment!' Amy sniggered with her lovely sexy laugh but showed no other emotion about his time with Gina, and certainly was not in any way censorious about what was obviously an extra-marital experience for Gina.

'Oh, men exaggerate what they think are conquests,' Gina was airily dismissive. 'but it was far from that I promise you. Well, good luck Amy - he's a decent sort of chap. You deserve a chance with a nice guy.'

And at that moment Gina meant every word.

50

ZAK

Another trip was in its planning stages. Darko, Lekso and Luka were key characters in the process, men Zak had met briefly in Margate. They were men of a certain age, affluent, all very sure of themselves, all experienced sailors.

Lekso owned a boat in the marina in his home town, a craft more elegant, even larger than the one Zak owned. He was clearly a wealthy man.

Zak talked with these business partners Darko and Luka - the Slavs, and Lekso their friend from Budva, as well as Yeshevsky and Dmitri.

'We have to make this trip again, soon,' Yeshevsky said.

Darko agreed, and added, rather patronizingly,

'We are very glad you have your boat.'

Zak seemed pleased.

'How's your lady feeling about your activity?'

'She doesn't know much about it. She's too busy with her kids and her girlfriends,' he said, rather dismissively.

'Do you tell her? How rich you gonna be?'

Zak laughed. 'She doesn't need to know any of those details. She has everything she wants.'

'When do we make the next trip, then?' Darko asked.

'Soon, before it gets too cold.'

He knew they were the thinking behind the negotiations and that they had choreographed the previous operations. They were in some ways easier to deal with than Yeshevsky or Dmitri, but he also recognized that they were tougher and more demanding. What they said, was what would happen.

Zak opened his diary of events. They had agreed that they would get the boat in September or October. That was good. The children would all be in school, so they couldn't complain about not going on a boat trip. Zak was still not certain that he would not, in the end, join Lekso and his pals. Somehow, he felt he should be there, but another part of him seemed to say it might be better if he was not. Nevertheless, he began to plan to make the effort to join them. He would have to rely on Yeshevsky and maybe Dmitri - not something he relished, but he felt he needed to do this, and furthermore, before the weather got too bad.

He was also quite sure that he would not tell Gina. The less she knew of this expedition, the better. She had too much to say about his business anyway and he could do without all that. He could easily fob her off with some business explanation.

Darko and Lekso were amused, and somewhat disdainful of Zak's knowledge of the water and of his boat, but they stopped short of laughing out loud and explained the plan. With sardonic looks and glances, they explained that they were to take his boat to Margate and from there they would pick up their 'cargo'.

'You mean in packing cases - how can you do...?' Zak stuttered. But Lekso interrupted his protestations.

'Please! You just leave this to Kamal and the others - they know what to do. It is all humane - Kamal is kindness itself.' He spoke remarkably good English and his turn of phrase was dignified, cultured.

Somehow, Zak was unable to see the implications of this arrangement as in any way humane, but he thought better than to quiz these three seemingly charming gentlemen any further.

'You give us keys and we will go to boathouse, do all that is necessary and then, when job is done, we return boat.'

'I thought I was to join you?' Zak said. He was more than a little anxious about giving over his beautiful boat to complete strangers for this seemingly repugnant piece of business. Even though he would have much preferred to have nothing to do with the whole undertaking, other than to rake in the profits, he was loathe to simply hand over the keys.

'I would like to be there,' he said.

The three men smiled inscrutably.

'What you worried for?' asked the bearded Darko, still with an amused grin on his swarthy, handsome face, 'you think we steal your boat?'

173

Zak said nothing, but shrugged lightly. The men countered with similar shrugs. 'No worries,' Luka responded laconically if rather ambiguously, 'whatever you like.'

I'll decide later, Zak thought. And he turned to the rest of the plans, which were very sketchy, but as they assured him, all he needed to know.

What they did need was Zak's signature on a particular document that would ensure the transfer of several hundreds of thousand Euros to complete the current transaction.

'Ten-fold, you'll get, for sure,' said Lekso, crunching his right eye in a conniving wink. Zak just nodded. He had already received large sums from the various dealings he had previously been involved with, so had no reason to doubt this. But this was on a different scale altogether.

'You'll see - no problem.' And Lekso continued to nod in a knowing and reassuring way. Zak signed with a shake of the wrist and a tight smile.

The following day, Zak went to his bank, or anyway, to one of several accounts in various banks, in his name.

He checked on the rather startlingly low residual amount therein, but supposed that this was all acceptable and he looked at some other transactions he had made recently all of them seemingly satisfactory. He spoke briefly also to his personal banker and was reassured on one or two issues. Then he returned home.

51

GINA

Gina was amazed by the preliminary meeting with her tutors and her fellow students. She had spent many days reading and preparing for the first get-together.

As nervous as she had ever been about anything, she haltingly approached the door, and when overtaken by a thickset blond chap who simply tapped on the door and opened it at once, she squeezed in also, and hesitatingly found a chair near the rear of the room, not easy, since the room was not very big.

After a few moments, the large woman who had been sorting through a file of papers and stacking up several piles in sets in front of her, looked up.

'Please could you all try to get round the tables - elbows on the desk please.'

She drew them all in, with arms gesturing an embrace. She was jolly and encouraging. Gina shuffled her chair forward, and moved into position near the corner of one of the three tables set in a rectangle in front of the smaller desk at which the woman, she presumed to be the tutor, was now seated. There were seven of them, four women and three men. Two of the women were younger than Gina, the other considerably older. The men were probably in their mid-twenties, though the blond might have been nearer forty. He looked unkempt and as if he had dressed in a hurry.

'Let's do names. I'm Dr. Oliver - tutor for this module. Please,' she said as she opened her hand flat to the first in the circle 'just your first name if that's OK?'

The names came and Gina tried hard to recall each as she heard them. Liv was the older woman, Warren was black, the girl in the hijab spoke softly and Gina thought she said Layla, but couldn't be sure. The stocky dishevelled chap was Ryan, then there was a Brandon and she couldn't catch the other woman's name.

'Fine.' Dr Oliver seemed to have checked their names off a list and was satisfied. 'Please! Pass these round,' she asked of Warren as she pushed the neatly counted piles towards him, and he distributed these dutifully to the rest of the group.

'I'm sure you did this in school, but I'm going to ask you to turn to the person next to you, Liv, you are to talk to Warren, and so on,' she continued, with an explanatory whirling of her fingers to indicate pairings.

'We'll work together,' she said as she zig-zagged a forefinger between herself and Brandon.

'Before you start, take a few moments to prepare a few words about yourself. It doesn't matter what you decide on, or how revealing, or not,' she smiled 'you are!'

'When you've thought that out, tell your partner, and by the way, partners, you don't need to be in a rush to move on, you might have a question or two to ask. That's perfectly OK, so do that if you like. Then reverse roles.'

She was precise and it was clear what was to be done.

'Start thinking.' She smiled again.

There was a comfortable quiet in the room. Someone started telling their neighbour a few details. Shortly, another began and soon the room was buzzing. Gina felt pleasantly at ease. She relaxed as she heard the woman next to her - the one whose name she had not caught - begin her account. She gave her age, 26, had been in the army, in Iraq, was keen to do something completely different in civilian life and was using her savings to achieve what she called "something worthwhile". Gina felt confident enough to be able to interrupt her and ask for her name.

'I'm so sorry, I missed hearing it,' she explained.

'I'm Jess. And you?'

'Gina.' And it was easy to go on chatting, each revealing a few more scraps until Dr. O. rapped on the desk.

'Yes, well, you all seem to be getting on pretty well. Please stand and find someone new to sit by, then repeat the exercise, both of you,' she said. 'then we'll do that once more. It might not be perfect, but most of us will get an idea of what we're like. Yes,' she said beckoning Gina to sit beside her, 'tell me why you're here.'

After about 20 minutes of this, it was certain that they all felt comfortable with various levels of respect and curiosity for their fellow students.

Dr.Oliver asked them all to take out the top sheet in their files, which had been distributed to them a short while before.

She explained that they would be asked to participate in a joint exercise wherein they could examine the words 'beauty' 'aesthetics' and 'art' and discover linkages in an ancient and modern philosophical sense; to decide if we look at art in ways that differ from the way we look at other things. They were not to be judged, merely to begin to use some words and terms that would allow them to go forward in their studies and development.

They read for a while and then began to respond to questions and ideas. No-one failed to contribute. They all seemed to have a view and all were generous in listening and observing.

Gina felt an inner glow that she had not experienced since she had won the English essay prize in year 10. It was exhilarating and she could hardly believe it when the session was over.

As they broke to leave, Gina said, rather boldly for her, 'Who fancies a coffee?'

She, Jess and Warren wandered off to the cafeteria where the conversation, though more wide ranging, continued for another half hour or more, until finally Jess said she had to go and Gina went to find her car in the parking lot and drove home. On the way, her heart was singing and her head abuzz. She could not go on, but stopped in a layby and called Issy.

'It's amazing,' she reported. 'Can't believe what it's like.'

'Told you it'd be fine,' Issy replied.

'There's this really scruffy journalist - some rubbish paper or other, but he's so smart and I had such a good chat with him - not really long enough - you learn such a lot from other people, don't you?'

Issy hooted with laughter. 'You're so funny Gina, honestly, of course you learn from others, and those tutorial sessions are indeed brilliant for that - you mustn't miss them.'

'I wouldn't - can't wait for the next.'

'Have you got an assignment?'

'Yes, can we meet up? I'll tell you, I mean, show you.'

Issy promised to check her diary and Gina agreed to work out a date for them to meet, always harder for Issy, before she rang off and restarted the car.

She put a hand to her cheek: she was burning with excitement!

52

When she got in, the children were home from school and could not fail to notice her high spirits. She did tell them that she had been to a class and that it been such fun. She showed them some of the papers and the pictures she had been given.

'Look!' Han shouted. 'There's that lady on the shell - that we saw in Italy.' And indeed he had spotted the birth of Venus and Gina was satisfied that if that had been the only event to emerge from the day - she would have been happy.

She met up with Issy a couple of weeks later.

'I've got this assignment where I need to look at something in a different way.'

'What?'

'Doesn't matter - the table, a sweater, a coffee cup...'

'...and then?'

'Describe it in a different way - like, you know, textures, the way it receives light, relative size, colour, all that stuff and I have to write it up properly, too.'

'Your forte, I'd say, Gina!'

'I'm hoping so. But the great thing is no-one was being competitive and people had different ideas, and different things to relate to and compare with - we all shared so well...'

'Well, that's adults for you...'

'...not like in school when the boys used to do a lot of shouting, and they tried to make the girls feel inadequate - didn't they?'

'Sometimes.'

'Is Finn like that?'

'A bit - thinks he's better than his little pal Cass. Only 'cos she's smaller, I think. But Twill's not like that - he's so kind... you should come over and meet him again. What about your boys?'

'Yes, Shaf is quite aggressive, bit like Zak. Han's OK - but then I think he's a bit too soft really - can't win can we?'

'We should meet more often, and not just to see if you're doing your assignments properly!'

Gina had seen relatively little of Zak in the weeks since she had begun the Open University course. He had been home on only about half of the evenings when to be fair, he had spent some time with the children, less time with her. She had spent time reading and writing, without Zak seeming to notice.

And she did not neglect her journal. She wrote of her pleasure and delight in her new role as student. She was still using it as a therapeutic tool and occasionally she would vent her anger on the page, over Zak and his general disinterest in her, except when it suited him to use her body for sex (that's how she saw it) and his minimal interest in the kids.

When he announced that he was going down to the coast and intended to pick up the boat and actually go somewhere in it, she was furious.

'Why can't we all go?'

'It's the middle of term time, you can't just take them out of school for a jaunt!'

'No! We can't! So why not wait until they've finished, or maybe the weekend?'

'Not appropriate.'

'What do you mean - appropriate - for what?'

'For us, for the trip.' Zak waved his arms in front of his face with a dismissive gesture. 'Gina, this is part of a business venture, I can't have three complaining, demanding kids on board as part of this event. I'm sorry, it'll have to wait until another time.'

'Zak, the weather is perfect for a little weekend cruise just now, so…'

But Zak interrupted impatiently, 'Yes, and it's perfect for me to do what I need to, and I don't need to turn it into a family jolly!'

Gina had been made so upset and angry by this exchange that she had feigned a hair appointment and immediately called Marina, who met her at Bonjour Café and Gina spent an hour complaining about Zak and plaintively asking Marina what to do.

'Don't ask me - I can't tell you what to do, you know that, but maybe you should be thinking about another sort of leisure activity for you and the children?'

'What! He spent a fortune on that boat and the boys especially just love it, even if I'm not overly thrilled by it. And the boys went on that course. They're dying to get hands-on experience. Anyway, what could I do? I can't take the kids to endless art galleries, even if it *is* my big interest.'

And eventually she had left the café and returned home, where Zak did not even notice that her hair seemed unchanged even though she had hastily combed it and swept it into what might have been called a different style.

Thus, Zak carried on with his plans until eventually he announced he was going to take off for a few days and packed a bag.

He asked Gina to put the boatyard address into the satnav.

'It's in there - you just have to search for it.'

'Come on Gina, you know I never use it - no idea how to find an address.' His tone suggested no sense of responsibility or shortcoming, rather he implied a failing on Gina's part for not immediately offering help.

Gina, somewhat moodily, found the location and left the device for Zak to collect. Then she marched out of the kitchen not offering herself for a farewell embrace and nor even bothering to say more than 'Bye' with a lazy wave.

53

ZAK

Zak had spent an hour on his phone some days before leaving, telling Darko of his plans.
'I'll meet with Yeshevsky, in the usual way, and we'll head to Margate, as arranged.'
'Bring some blankets,' Darko had instructed him.
'OK. Why?'
'Why! Why you think?'
'Oh. Yes OK.'
'How many you can carry?'
'Oh,' Zak bit his knuckle and frowned. 'No, I don't, I mean I don't know - what? erm, ten?'
Darko snorted 'Ha! 20, maybe 25 - small cargo! - will fit!'
'But,' Zak began. Darko interrupted him impatiently.
'Do you want to be in this or out?'
'Sure. In. Of course.'
'OK, get to the boat on the Friday - meet you Saturday morning in the Kingsgate Bay place - where you saw, when you were there - remember?'
'Yes, yes I do,' Zak responded, though he was not quite sure that he did. Nevertheless, he was grateful that Yeshevsky would be around, and not just to locate the meeting place. Truth told, Zak had to admit that he had very little idea of navigating and sailing in general. He knew the terms fore and aft and bow and stern, he knew about port and starboard, but once, with the sail up, when Yeshevsky had yelled -"We're heeling!" he was totally confused and Yeshevsky was furious with his lack of response. 'You just stand there - we need some action,' he'd bawled, but Zak just shrugged.
'You're in charge,' he'd responded irritatingly calmly.
When it transpired once in conversation that Zak's boys were going on a sailing course, Yeshevsky snorted:

'You join them - will help everyone!' And though Zak was indeed tempted, he did not accompany them.

Reflecting now, he thought maybe he ought to have done so, but although confident in all that he did in business, he was tentative when it came to approaching this new discipline, so he had to recognize his limitations in this area. It had a damaging effect on his level of confidence, however, and Yeshevsky had the annoying habit of making him feel particularly inadequate. Zak felt bullied and controlled by him and he frequently felt a rising anger that he struggled to control. There were times when he wanted to cry out angrily into Yeshevsky's face, and although he told himself that he was not afraid of the man, somehow, he did feel a certain anxiety and timidity in his presence.

But Zak pulled himself out of this self-doubt and shortly he connected with Yeshevsky and they agreed to meet at the boat house on Friday. Once there, they would organize blankets, some food supplies, and stay overnight, presumably on the boat, before setting off.

About 150 nautical miles for the trip, it would take them a considerable amount of time - maybe 10 hours and it was not without hazards. It was planned that they should drop anchor over night, fairly close to the coast, sleep for a bit longer and then push on through dawn, past the narrowest and most worrying bit of the channel before reaching Margate.

The plan was persuasively simple. Zak was somewhat tentative, but he was a compliant collaborator, and agreed to Yeshevsky's stratagem even with his misgivings. When he mentioned these concerns, Yeshevsky was dismissive.

'You have no faith. There is big money in this, Zak. We have to take small risk.'

'Hmmm. Who are, I mean, what are these girls, no, I mean, where are these girls going?'

'You care?' Yeshevsky snorted. 'They go to be wives, they work, go to massage places - maybe cleaning; some pick fruit. All get jobs, positions. All good for them.'

And Zak let it go. Perhaps he didn't really want to have detailed answers to these questions. Maybe it was better if he didn't know at all. In truth, he was well aware that his main function was to provide money for the whole enterprise. This he had done repeatedly over several months. But he was looking forward to huge rewards that had been promised. Indeed he had already banked considerable sums, although much of that had been drawn on for further spending.

'Venture capital,' Yeshevsky had said with a sneering grin, and Zak was in no position to argue with Yeshevsky, who seemed so full of confidence and quite sure of success. Zak did not yet feel as if he could even ask if it was all quite legal. Maybe he knew that it was not.

54

GINA

Gina was still angry with Zak. She did not hide it from the children.

'Dad's so mean,' Shafiq grumbled. Standing near him, Gina was in an easy position to defend Zak, and at another time and another part of her life, she might have done so, but on this occasion she said nothing.

'He is isn't he?' Shaf persisted. 'Why couldn't we go on the boat as well?'

'Don't ask me,' Gina said, rather spitefully, 'ask him.'

'Well we can't can we?' shouted Shaf, 'he's gone!'

'Where has he gone mum?' asked Han, 'how can he do it on his own - we could have helped. We did do the course,' he added reasonably and a trifle indignantly, 'so what was the point of that if we can't help?'

'Well,' Gina persisted, 'I've told you - he hasn't said anything to me either, so how do you expect me to know anything at all?'

'You should,' Shaf grumbled, 'he's your husband.'

'Hmmm,' was Gina's only response.

She decided to take the children to Louise and Jim's at the weekend.

'Hi Mum, can we come down on Friday night?'

'Yes, love, it'll be nice to see you all - is Zak home?'

'No, he's off on some jaunt and won't be back for several days. The boys are very grumpy because they can't go with, but, well,' she added rather more loyally than she meant, 'it is term time, they can hardly take time off.'

'No. S'pose not, and I've never really been happy about them on that boat, 'specially Shaf - he's quite wild isn't he Gina? I always think he'll fall in the drink.'

'Oh mum - don't be silly. Anyway, he always has to wear a life jacket and he's steadier than you think. If anyone is likely to fall in, it's Han. Head in the clouds mostly, that boy!'

'Gina, he's just imaginative and creative, and I bet he'd rather be reading or painting something than messing about on a boat.'

'Bet he wouldn't! They're both pretty mad with Zak and I wish I could do something about it.'

'Well, we'll try to make it a fun weekend love. Jim'll be thrilled they're coming. Shall we go to Woburn?'

'That's a good idea, we've never been there. Loads for them to do - even a railway - Tanni'll love that, and - oh, are there tigers? She's mad about tigers just now.

'Is she? Why? Er, yes, I think there are, Jeannie, my neighbour took her two grandchildren there last summer - they loved the tigers, and there's a sort of tree-top adventure thing too.'

'Shaf will go mad for that,' Gina agreed. 'I'll google it.'

And on Friday afternoon after school, having packed up all they needed, they piled into the car and drove off to Jim and Louise's place near Borehamwood. Louise was so happy for them to be there and although she was still limping and resorted to using her stick occasionally, she made a terrific supper for everyone. Just for once, no-one was arguing and no-one complained.

'This is delicious chicken,' Tanni announced in such a grown up way, that they all laughed and when offered seconds, responded rather grandly:

'I think I will.'

Gina drank too much wine, relaxed totally, and laughed a lot.

And they all slept well before their big day out.

Jim made what he called special pancakes for breakfast, but they all knew that he'd put too much flour in them, and then to make up for that had added another teaspoon of baking powder. So they were big, a bit heavy and what Tanni called fizzy, but there was a big pile of crispy bacon and sausages and a mass of scrambled eggs, and as Lou hissed: 'Bury the pancakes under the eggs....' they all giggled and then Shaf demanded ketchup. In fact everyone wanted ketchup, but Jim was completely good-natured about his lack of culinary expertise.

Breakfast over, Louise introduced the children to the new concept of clearing up and washing pans. True, plates and cutlery went into the dishwasher, but the boys had never before in their lives had to clear up after eating. Fulfilling all stereotypes, Shaf and Han managed to find a chair for Tanni and 'allowed' her to scrub the frying pan and the egg pan. When Tanni complained about the fact that the egg wouldn't come off, Gina took over. 'Oh dear,' she sighed quietly to herself, 'same old, same old...' but at least she was smiling.

Shaf was terrifically excited about the Safari Park and the various adventures on offer. He and Han were with Gina, Tanni had decided she wanted to go with Granny and Gramps, a decision that suited everyone. Tanni was always demanding and Lou adored her enough to give her total and undivided attention. Jim was happy in his role as driver.

Behind Gina, Shaf and Han were squabbling about the camera.

'I'm better than you at taking pictures,' Shaf said, 'anyway, I'm the oldest, so you've got to let me go first.'

'And I'm more careful than you - and mum says I'm artistic, so it should be me.'

'Of course you'll both get a chance,' Gina interrupted, 'stop bickering or I'll take the camera away altogether.' And then she asked - 'What are you looking forward to seeing?'

'I'm going on the zip wire and I'm going on that climbing thing - you said there was one - and is there a wall?'

'It's about animals, not adventure climbs and that stuff, it's about lions and tigers and giraffes and those kind of things...' Han said rather plaintively.

'Oh Han, you never really want to do the daring things, do you?'

And Han, who was indeed not particularly intrepid, just looked sulky and said nothing.

'Are we nearly there?' Shaf asked eagerly.

'Soon, not too far now,' Gina replied. She glanced in her mirror to check that Jim was following. She could see him two or three cars behind and in any case he knew the way.

Once arrived they inevitably needed to join slow-moving queues of other cars, but no-one minded as they could see the animals and were shouting with excitement.

187

They drove along in the prescribed manner, watching and pointing, calling out and whooping by turns, and the boys were totally engrossed in the experience. Indeed, Gina was enraptured herself, and astonished at the way the animals behaved. They especially loved the way the Squirrel Monkeys came up close and when the boys insisted on going round twice - she gave in. Second time round a tiger wandered by and the boys were thrilled. Gina took the boys on an 'on-foot' safari and a behind-the-scenes tour with a very knowledgeable guide. Gina was pleased with the way they seemed genuinely interested and asked lots of sensible questions.

Jim and Lou had taken off with Tanni to see the bird display and they followed that with a swan-boat ride.

Soon enough, it was time for lunch, followed by more decisions. Jim found the climbing wall with Shaf, and after that they went to the giraffe trail, Lou took Han to the outdoor play area, and later for a ride on the swan-boats, where they met Gina and Tanni after their ride on the train. Later they found ice cream and chattered loudly to each other about the awesome things they had done and finally piled back into the two cars for the ride home. They were grubby and tired. Tanni fell asleep at once, cradled in Lou's lap. Shaf and Han, for once, were amicable and interested in sharing notes and swapping experiences.

'I really nearly fell off,' Shaf yelled, 'I truly did,' he went on when he observed Han's dubious look.

'Well. I nearly drowned as well,' Han responded.

But they agreed that the swarming monkeys and even the sleepy lions were fantastic and when they got back to Grandma's they were in pleasant agreement that it had been a brilliant day.

55

When Gina had managed to get Tanni and the boys to bed, though she was clear that they were still too hyped to go to sleep, she joined Jim and Lou in the kitchen.

'Are they asleep?'

'Oh, heavens no, can't you hear them?'

'They've had a great day haven't they?'

'Well, so have we,' added Jim, 'it's been terrific.'

Lou asked Gina to open a bottle of white. 'Greasy hands,' she explained.

Gina twisted the cap, Jim fetched three glasses and they sat on the back patio hearing the childish yells from a still open window, as they were sipping sauvignon and crunching crisps.

'What's for supper?' Jim asked.

'Not too different from what the kids had - pasta - different sauce, a bit spicier. Oh, and there's cake.'

Lou baked well, so no-one was surprised.

'Gina, do you ever make a cake?' Lou asked cautiously.

'As a matter of fact, I have been known to, I don't let Rayna do everything.'

'Can she bake?'

'Er, not really. Mostly I buy puds, or anyway, she does.'

Jim poured a top-up, and asked, 'How's your course going?'

'Fabulous - I just love it. You know, it's like a new world for me. I can say what I think, I don't need to watch my step all the time.'

'Watch your step? You don't need to do that here.' Lou countered.

Gina bit her lip. 'Mmm, but I mean I do with Zak. I'm sure he does know that I'm doing more than just going to some local course. I write stuff and he sees me, but he doesn't ask. No, really,' and she shook her head at Lou who had looked sideways and raised her eyebrows, not really believing.

'He just doesn't ask me - either he deliberately ignores what he can see in front of him, or he has no interest. Or both!' she ended, laughing.

'Anyway, I don't care. He can think what he likes.'

'Gina, you sound so assertive, bit like your old self,' Lou began.

'What do you mean?' Gina asked her mother in a rather hurt tone, 'have I changed?'

Jim and Lou exchanged a brief glance. Gina could not fail to notice this. She frowned. 'How?'

'Gina - don't get cross with me,' Lou said, because she could see Gina's face betrayed that she was in the mood to be combative, 'it's just we…I've noticed that over the years you've become well, rather, erm, submissive.'

Lou held her breath, expecting Gina to explode. She didn't. She asked:

'And now?'

'Well, as I said, you seem to have more of your old confidence back.'

Gina was astonished. She had not really observed herself and had not noticed that she had been lacking in this area. She remained contemplative, quiet. She sipped her wine thoughtfully, as Jim passed her plates and cutlery and she set the table in silence.

Jim said 'Lou says you have an assignment - on what?'

'Alternative views of objects,' she responded. 'It's part of the assessment course.' And at once started on an explanation of what an access course was, what it meant and of the work it involved. She was thoroughly absorbed in this for quite some time, until Lou planted a steaming bowl of pasta and a pot of sauce on the table, and they turned to reminiscing about Italy.

Gina began to tell them of Han's observation about 'the lady on the shell' which brought smiles of admiration from both of them, and more chat about Gina's course.

'Listen!' Gina raised a finger, and looked up to the ceiling.

'Yes, asleep at last, they must be exhausted,' Lou observed.

'I'm sure they are,' Gina agreed.

After supper, they sat lazily and talked of this and that, a bit about the political situation, a bit about the transport issues that were besetting parts of Birmingham, about the high speed train link and its advisability, and several other more mundane and ordinary things, but which gave Gina a sense of family such as she did not normally have.

She went to sleep feeling contented and relaxed.

56

Gina was home for three days before Zak returned. He had sent her emails - at least he knew how to do that, and she had sent him phone messages. She had told him what fun they had had at the safari park and what a good weekend it had been. But as expected, he hardly engaged on the topic at all.

On his return, she asked him what he'd been up to. He was non-committal, vague, dismissive. She did not pursue it. She went to the room she now thought of as her study, and pulled out her notes. After twenty minutes, she had put Zak out of her mind and was engrossed.

When he called up to her asking what they would be eating, she was startled.

'There's cold salmon, salad - other stuff in the fridge - I'll be down soon.' And she hurried to finish the section she had begun.

Over supper, he did not enquire what she had been doing. They talked about the children in a perfunctory way. She ventured to say that she was going to visit Issy later the following week.

'Oh yeah, how is she - and - who is it she's married to?'

'Twill.'

'What kind of name is that?'

Gina didn't bother to answer, and Zak clearly wasn't that interested.

'Why're you going?'

'She's a friend of mine,' Gina's tone was ironic. 'I like her. We have lunch.'

'Ladies who lunch,' Zak said predictably and scraped his chair back from the table.

'Don't you want dessert?'

'What is it?'

'Crumble. I made it for the children.'

'You did?' His emphasis was on did, rather than you, and Gina ignored him, instead fetched it and served it, offering cream.

They finished in silence. It was so different from being at her mother's.

She recalled that visit with pleasure and wondered why Zak had barely asked her about the visit, the safari park, or anything else. He hadn't even enquired about the health of Louise and Jim in a routine way. He certainly had not asked about Louise's ankle - Gina found this rude at best and quite hurtful in fact.

Later when Zak had gone to bed, Gina went quietly to her study and returned to what she had been writing, but got so carried away that she stayed up another hour and finished her first draft.

In the morning she re-read it, made very few changes, was pleased with it, and printed it off. She put it in an envelope and slipped it into her very attractive briefcase which she had bought when she had started the course.

She texted Issy and reminded her of their plans to meet. She waited. Within seconds, Issy had replied, adding a picture of Finn - and agreeing on the time 'what a darling child' Gina replied and 'OK c u there'

But then sent another message 'can i bring essay will u read?'

'sure will hate if u don't'

'u may say crap'

'so?'

'nervous'

'don't be stupid'

Of course she had always planned to do so, but wanted to prepare her friend for this and also she did know that although Issy would be truthful, she would also be kind and understanding, and would help her to frame her thoughts in perhaps more appropriate ways.

The children all back at school after the half term break, Gina was free to read some of the set material. She took great pleasure in taking notes, sifting through information, and re-writing some earlier thoughts in an effort to make the ideas secure. She felt the joy that comes from learning and understanding. She knew she was making progress.

On Thursday, she went to meet Issy. She took the train and arrived at the appointed place for lunch. Gina had insisted on somewhere quiet and so they had ended up in the rather dull dining room of an even duller hotel, where the two of them brought down the average age of the lunch crowd by about 25 years.

But at least the table was a good size, covered in a smooth white cloth and Gina could lay out her papers without really getting in the way of their meal.

Issy picked up the menu and somewhat disingenuously, Gina thought, seemed suddenly surprised and said,

'Oh this is the wine list - sorry,' but Gina smiled and said: 'Well, choose something then!'

Issy grinned and said, 'Glass or bottle?'

'Oh, bottle - whatever.'

Lunch dishes selected, Gina passed her printed essay to Issy.

'Would you mind?' she asked coyly, 'I won't interrupt.'

Issy read and Gina looked at her phone, erasing trash and checking a couple of not very important messages. After several minutes, the waiter returned with a couple of starters, and taking in the situation, set them down quietly while Issy continued to read.

Finally, Issy turned the slim pile sideways, lifted up the sheaf and tapped it on the table and returned the straightened stack to Gina.

After a tauntingly quiet few seconds, and with great timing, she said:

'You are a dark horse Gina - that stuff is really good - 18 year-olds just don't write like that - they have neither the elegance, nor the inside knowledge that you obviously have - it's brilliant!'

Gina flushed and grinned.

'Oh Issy, that means a lot, thanks.'

And as she lifted her fork, she shook her head, as if in doubt, and explained to her friend how difficult it had become to believe in herself. She didn't really mention Zak, but it was clear that Issy had picked that up. She could tell from the nature of the questions she asked her about her relationship and the kind of conversations she had with him. When Gina had admitted that they were very rare, Issy snorted and said,

'Well, who the hell do you talk to then?' and, 'about time you started chatting to real grown ups with opinions that are stimulating.'

'I don't really like to disagree with Zak - he gets angry and shouts - I don't think it's good, especially not in front of the children. Not that he cares.'

'Well, time to find other people to talk to then,' Issy concluded, and certainly Gina was not going to argue with that.

Lunch was great, and they talked far longer than they'd planned, Gina rushing finally to get a later train and get to the kids before it made her feel too guilty. But she admitted to herself that she felt fine about it, that oddly she didn't feel guilty at all, and her time with Issy had been particularly therapeutic.

57

Gina suggested to Zak that they ask Marina and Jo and their husbands for a drink, possibly dinner. Zak was unenthusiastic.

'I don't even know them.'

'You do. You've met them, we've been to their houses - a dinner party just before Christmas - and to Jo's a few weeks later - in the spring, don't you remember? You talked to Maxwell, her partner.'

'No.'

'You did.'

'OK. I did. I don't remember.'

'Well?'

'Well what?'

'Can we? Ask them?'

'Why?'

Oh for god's sake Zak, why not, it's called being sociable, neighbourly.'

'You can if you get help with the preparation - I'm not planning to do anything.'

'Rayna will help.'

'No, I mean, get someone in to cater. Then you can ask them.'

And Zak had risen from his armchair and left the room in a bit of a sulk.

'Well,' Gina mused, 'I'm just going to do it,' and went directly to the phone.

As it turned out, she did get some cooking help, though she prepared the dessert herself, and planned and chose the rest of the meal. Both Jo and Maxwell and Marina and Tony accepted her invitation and she got on with the job of organizing the evening.

Gina was both excited and a bit nervous about their visit. She wasn't worried about the food, because much of it had been provided by the caterers, and Rayna was a star in that she helped to set up the table and get everything ready. Gina asked Zak for some wine from his store, and he plonked down several bottles before disappearing for the rest of the time that Gina was preparing. He appeared only when he had obviously heard Tony and Marina at the door.

When all the guests had arrived, the children made a brief appearance and were then waltzed away by Rayna and dinner started.

What Gina really enjoyed was the conversation. And it was great to have the help because she was able to relax and enter into debate and exchange, with no stress.

Zak said little, and she wondered what Luke and Tony thought of him. Not much, she supposed.

But she had had a great evening and realised that Issy had helped her to feel confident and bold, even cheeky and quite flirty with the men. As they left, Jo commented on this:

'You're very perky tonight Gina!'

'Yeah, well, you're all such good company.'

'No, but I think your course is good for you,' Jo laughed. And maybe she didn't quite understand that this was in fact the case.

But Gina did, and Marina too, who had emerged from the dining room, calling goodbye to Max and Jo who had more or less left.

'You've got attitude Gina!'

'Is that bad?'

'No - very good, and dinner was terrific.'

* * *

The response from her tutor was good. She was most encouraging and Gina found mental reserves she hadn't been aware of. Strengthened and emboldened, she turned her attention to the next assignment. She was clear that there was no danger of her being unsuccessful in this access course. She knew she would do well and that she would be able to start on the degree course at the next possible opportunity. She had more or less decided on the BA Honours Arts and Humanities course, commencing in February. She looked forward to it with such mental energy and enthusiasm that she could hardly wait. She bought books that were recommended for it, and even started reading some chapters, although she realised that really she should wait until after her final assessment.

58

And eventually, her results suggested that she had done particularly well, and she was finally ready to embark on the last stage of the course before starting her degree.

'Mags,' she shouted eagerly into the phone that night, 'I think I'm ready for my degree course - I did really well on the first two assignments on the access and I'm hot to go!'

'That is so good Gina - I'm very impressed by your determination - but I knew you'd do it,' there was a pause. Clearly the sentence was unfinished.

'I knew as soon as you made your mind up about - you know...' She stopped again.

'What?'

'You know when, when you had. When you...you know. The, the baby.'

'Yes,' Gina responded flatly but it was clear that she was not about to discuss this further. Maggie wished she had not begun this observation. Weakly, she said:

'Sorry. Not relevant?'

'No.'

'Shall we move on?'

'Yes.' Gina's tone was very firm, almost harsh.

And after an awkward few moments, they managed to regain ground and Gina returned to her excitement telling Maggie about the course and her various plans.

Ending the call and feeling good, Gina picked up a pencil and wandered over to the barely concealed pile of notes on the old wooden sideboard.

Gina skimmed a notebook and tried to organize some ideas, Zak had been prowling around in the hallway, phone clamped to his ear. The children were in their rooms, Tanni asleep, the boys mostly quiet, though an occasional shout and thump on the floor assured Gina that they were still awake and crashing around. She decided to leave them to it, and hoped they settle down eventually. Zak entered the room.

'It's dim in here,' he said rather crossly, and snapped on a light. Gina was working by a lamp and had not noticed the darkening room.

'Gina, sorry, but I'm going to see Yeshevsky and I'll be away for a few days. I've packed a bag and I'm going to go tonight. We'll be collecting the boat.'

Gina was neither surprised nor particularly moved. Of course she preferred it if he didn't just take off like that, with hardly any warning but she shrugged, resigned.

'What's it all about Zak? Why do you have to go off in the middle of the night on these strange assignments? And it's freezing out there - a frost is threatened.' But her tone simply indicated an acceptance of something rather undesirable, and she offered very little further resistance.

'I'll take the Jeep,' he announced. 'and I think it's got a heater,' he added sardonically.

'Why? What's wrong with the Morgan?'

'Yeshevsky,' Zak sighed in an irritated and bored way. 'He asked me...he said that, we needed extra stuff, so I need space to, to...Oh for God's sake Gina, what does it matter to you...' and he broke off in his stumbled explanations.

'You won't manage the satnav,' she replied, tauntingly.

'No, I think I know the way now, but you put the directions in didn't you?'

'Yeah,' she replied carelessly, 'I think so.'

She knew the full directions weren't in there. Too bad, she thought, let him work it out. It was only the last section she had not added, after the awkward climb down the cliff that they had not attempted to do.

59

What actually happened three days later, Gina never really knew. She only remembered as a blur that the police arrived at the door and a shocked Rayna shouted for her. As the policewoman helped her to sit, as she delivered her awful message, as she held Gina's hand, Gina said nothing. She breathed in ragged, shaggy gulps of air, and let out one long, deep, racking sob, and stared unfocussed at the rug. She called hoarsely, 'Shaf, Shaf, and Han, come. Come, and Tanni. Come here.' She dragged them into her arms and clung to them for many minutes.

'What happened to daddy?' Tanni asked, but someone took her away and the boys stared at Gina in shock. Shaf shouted:

'He's not, he's not - how can he?' And he threw himself down and just lay at Gina's feet sobbing.

Of course, there was a full investigation into the cause of death, which was difficult and distressing. Family and friends came, the children went to stay with Lou and Jim, in fact largely with Jim, since Lou spent a great deal of the time with Gina who did not speak more than the occasional word for days and when she finally began to question the course of events, became angry. Once or twice she shouted loudly at Lou, who was so distressed at the way this had happened, that she had to leave and she called Marina who came round and stayed for a few days, Tony bringing food for Gina and Marina, which Gina, with no appetite was unable to eat.

Jim had arranged, with Marina's help, that the children should spend time with Jo, and she was splendid in ensuring that they got to school and went to various classes, when Rayna came for them. At the weekend, Jim came over, collected the children from Marina's and they all stayed with Gina.

It seemed that the car had failed to respond to a particularly dangerous bend at the start of a steep hill. That was the point where on one of their early trips, Lou had got out and scrambled down the rocky path. They had stopped briefly in a stony, makeshift layby, more an escape route, and on subsequent journeys Gina had always complained that Zak was going too fast. This time, regardless of speed, he had apparently not seen the danger and the car had gone over the cliffs. The report said he had died on impact, but the car had burnt out and the flaming wreck had brought it to the attention of other passing cars. The verdict was accidental death.

Slowly, very slowly, over several weeks, Gina regained some of herself, and was able to talk to the children. Obviously they were all deeply troubled and Jo had arranged with the school for the children to see a counsellor. She also arranged for a private consultant to come to the house but she was not a great deal of help and in any case Gina was very dismissive of her.

'I don't need her help,' she had shouted at Jo, 'she's just making things worse.' After three or four visits, Gina somewhat sharply told her not to come again. The counsellor was quiet and kind in response explaining that she was there when needed and that Gina should contact her if she felt she needed to talk.

'Even just a brief conversation, or advice about something specific.'

Gina had shrugged and waved a dismissive hand but added,

'Yes. OK.'

'Maybe it needs to get worse before it can get any better,' Jo had said to her.

'How can it get worse?' Gina had responded in anger.

Marina and Maggie were discussing the situation.

'She just shouts at me when I try to make any suggestion.'

'Understandable. She trusts you to be there for her.'

'She gets cross with me too,' Maggie complained, 'but I think I get it. I just try to be patient. I'm going to get her to come and stay with me. I have broached the subject, but she seemed very resistant...'

'Maybe she should stay here anyway, it's going to be Christmas and...'

'She won't want to do anything at Christmas...'

'But maybe she should, at least for the kids...'

But Gina was mostly unresponsive to suggestions, indeed she was very quiet most of the time and seemed to talk only to the children, and even then only in a limited way.

Tanni was difficult and clingy and Jo often took the children to her house. But the boys especially became fretful and Shaf was often quite unpleasant in speaking to Jo, so much so, that on one occasion, Max had to reprimand him, following which incident, Shaf was in floods of tears and ran off, back to his house, pursued by Max, where Gina was surprised to see them, but hugged Shaf fiercely and they were both inconsolable for a long time.

Max, now joined by Jo, Han, Tanni and Rayna, who stood by watching helplessly, saw that no amount of soothing seemed to help. But it was the first time in months that they had all wept so ferociously. Even at the funeral, Gina had barely cried and the children had stood, solemn–faced and drawn.

But now, so many weeks later, their grief was huge and their distress alarming to witness. Rayna became especially perturbed and dismayed, but Jo tried to explain that it was no bad thing and that the anguish was part of the healing.

'Is good, is good,' Rayna whimpered, in an attempt to acknowledge Jo's wisdom, but she seemed quite distraught, and only when she went to prepare some supper did she regain some equanimity.

But for all that, Gina seemed slowly to come out of a fog, and gradually began to gather herself as the days passed. Always slim, she had become quite gaunt. Her hair had been neglected; too long and untidy. She did not consider her clothing, and never wore make-up.

However, one evening, she had eaten toast and soup and had changed a grubby top for something smarter. She insisted the children stayed with her and she had seen them to bed, in their own house, reading them their favourite stories and hugging them in a warm-hearted and attentive manner, something she had been neglectful of in recent months. She also called her tutor, who was fully apprised of the situation, and indicated that she might return to her studies quite soon.

Immediately after the funeral, she had announced first to Louise and later to Maggie that she would not continue with the course. Lou said it was probably a good decision, but Maggie urged her not to be precipitate.

'Wait a bit. Tell Dr Oliver - is that her name? - that you would like things to be put on hold, I'm sure if you tell her the circumstances, she'll be understanding.'

Actually, Gina did nothing, but eventually she had responded to a text, no doubt due to her continuing absence and explained briefly the nature of her situation. Dr Oliver had written her a reflective and kind note of condolence and assured her that she could take up her studies as and when. But at the time, Gina had been dismissive and had barely considered the issue at all.

60

Marina took her to lunch, then to Birmingham Art Gallery to see the Pre-Raphaelites, something Gina hadn't explored much. It turned out to be both uplifting and encouraging and later, Marina told Tony that she had seen Gina smile for the first time in weeks.

'She has seemed so despairing, I couldn't really do much to help her. You know, oddly, she didn't even show much affection for Zak, but anyway...'

'Yeah, but he was her husband, her kids' father - that's not easy, no matter how you feel about...'

'But she sometimes said things...'

'Makes no difference.'

As they came out of the Gallery, Gina announced she needed to visit the bathroom, and Marina suggested that the easiest thing would be for her to return to the gallery some way back from where they were now standing by the statue of Queen Victoria. She would collect the car from where it was parked, a little way off, and meet Gina in Waterloo Street. Marina hurried off, and several minutes later, Gina was crossing the square alone when she observed the familiar, annoying behaviour of someone approaching her in a direct line, head down, intent on checking his phone. She objected to the fact that this young man was about to walk into her if she did not take evasive action. She ducked left, but he, detecting her presence at the last moment, ducked to his right, and there followed that silly dance right and left as they decided which way each should go. Thus rather than simply passing each other by with no further word, they paused.

He looked at her and blinked.

'Gina? Gina Mackenzie?' he said.

'Yes. Oh, well, not now, but yes. But you, I'm afraid - you, yes...' and she faltered as she tried to recall where she had seen him before.

'Guess I've changed a bit - I'm Chris, Caroline's son - Ed's son. Remember? You came to stay after...'

'Oh, of course,' Gina said, 'I do remember - how is, how are your folks?'

'Fine - have you lost touch?'

'Well, I have rather.'

And they chatted for a few moments more, of mundane affairs, where she lived ('still in dad's old house?') and briefly, of her kids, his situation - not married, but working in Warwick, and then he asked:

'Why don't you call my mum?'

And suddenly, remembering Caro's kindness after Ed had died, she blurted out her news to Chris. He was clearly shocked and with renewed forcefulness, repeated his suggestion to be in touch and she tapped the number into her phone at his insistence, following which she hurried off to meet up with Marina, who, caught in traffic had only just reached the appointed meeting place.

'Sorry to be late,' she said.

'No, it's fine, I stopped, I met a friend, no, someone I knew years ago.'

'Who was that?'

'Oh,' Gina shook her head slowly and sighed, 'son of my first husband. His wife was very kind to me after...well, anyway, I went to stay with them - R&R I suppose. The boys were late teens then, maybe a bit older. I hardly recognized him - quite the grown-up now.'

'Well, he would be!' Marina reversed a few illegal yards and then drove on, quickly.

'So. Why is this significant?'

'Oh, it's not, just that he said I should get in touch with Caroline, that's his mother. Maybe I will.'

'Is she local?'

'Not really, near Northampton.'

'That's not so far.'

'It's Clipston, about an hour's drive.'

'Get in touch, Gina.'

They drove on in a comfortable silence, each with their thoughts.

Marina was keen for Gina to get back into a normal way of living. It was true that lately she had begun to regain some of her old self, but picking up with an old friend might be a good idea, and would surely be helpful. In any case, at present she was hugely reliant on Jo and Marina for support, and her mother was often with her. Marina wondered if it was a bit too much buffering and her mother had been exceptionally concerned and caring. Maggie had also come often although work and children were restraints on that and altogether, she was beginning to think it would be better if Gina had to do some thinking and fending for herself.

At once, Marina felt guilty. She knew that Jo would remonstrate with her, but then Jo was such a carer, and always put others first. Indeed, it was quite probable that she rather relished the role she had with Gina and perhaps, Marina wondered, was she a little bit jealous that her role as Gina's close friend had been somewhat usurped of late? Certainly Gina did call Jo more often these days, and no doubt that had something to do with Jo's natural generosity with her time and her home. Max too was kind and helpful with the boys, and when Tanni was being awkward, he would suggest to Gina that she concentrate attention on her and he would take Han and Shaf off to the park, or the pool. That's not something Tony would ever do, she reflected, and I ought to try harder, too, and then sighed deeply. She glanced to her left. Gina was dozing.

'Gina. We're here. Are you OK?'

'Oh. Yes, fine. That was quick.'

'You were asleep,' Marina laughed.

'Oh dear. Sorry.'

'No. It's fine. Look, would you and the children like to come over for Sunday lunch?' It was a gesture at least, and they could get some male attention if she could persuade Tony to unwind with them for a bit. She'd dig out those old games that her kids had, and were stowed in the attic. She'd do a big roast...or rather get Tony to do it!

'Thank you,' Gina sounded enthusiastic. 'I'd love that, so will the kids.'

61

A couple of weeks later, before Christmas, Gina called Caroline.

'I wish Christopher had got your number, I would have called you. What a terrible thing to have happened Gina - after all that had gone before that. How ever are you coping? I can't begin to imagine how you are dealing with this, and are there children?'

'Yes. Two boys and a girl. Not easy, no. No. It's been difficult. But I'm getting through it...and I remember how kind you were...and Dave - how is he?'

'He's in good shape. Come and spend some time. Would you like to? Bring the kids.'

'I might leave the kids with mum. I feel I need some time on my own. I can't really talk when they're around. Still get upset, you see. We all do.'

'Yes, of course! A few days after Christmas? Or New Year?'

'Not sure what's best - can I think about it a bit?'

'Yes, do, and would you drive?'

'Yes, It's not so far. And have you still got your dogs?'

'Yes! You remembered - well, there's three of them now. The old one died and we got two puppies a few years ago. They eat us out of house and home! Yes, it isn't far, I know. I get into Birmingham now and then for a shopping trip. Do plan to come Gina.'

And just after New Year, she arrived in Clipston, met by three delighted dogs, a smiling, jolly Caro and Dave, much fatter than she recalled him being, wearing wellies and looking exactly like a country squire. Their house was warm and welcoming, with a big log fire burning fiercely in the grate, and they encouraged Gina to talk as much as she needed which, under the influence of a terrific meal and excellent wine, some of which she had brought with her from Zak's wine store, was easy for her to do.

On the second night, their two boys arrived, both now living away from home, but back with their parents for their winter break. On the previous night, they had been at the younger son, Ben's Coventry home for a party and had stayed over. Gina wondered if that had been a tactful move on their part, but in any case they entered with frost on their shoes, the garage being a partly converted garden building across a small paddock, stamping on the doormat, puffing steamy breath and calling out greetings. Chris gave her a friendly hug and asked if she remembered Ben.

'I met Gina in Birmingham - imagine seeing her there,' he told his brother.

Ben frowned slightly. He thought that Chris sounded a bit proprietorial, but he smiled warmly at Gina and though he didn't embrace her, he clasped her hand in his two and asked after her, in a concerned way.

'We heard what happened,' he said

'Oh, goodness,' she swerved verbally, 'oooh, you're cold.'

'I think it's below freezing now. Only takes a few minutes to get chilled,' and he rubbed his hands. From a small bag he pulled out a bottle of malt whisky.

'Here, dad, mum, small offering. After dinner?'

They all sat down to another hearty meal; Gina did not wonder at Dave's girth! It had been quite a time since Gina had eaten so heartily. During the Christmas holiday, she had done her best to make it as fun for the kids as she could, but it had been difficult. There was always the inevitable feeling that someone wasn't there.

Tanni sometimes asked, 'When is daddy coming back?'

Lou and Jim had stayed for several days, Gina prepared something approaching festive meals, and she and Rayna bought in a huge amount of food, cake, mince pies, but much was not eaten and she had sent Lou and Jim home with bags full of stuff, even a whole ham.

And Jim had also dealt with some rather unpleasant phone calls from the police.

Jim explained to Gina, as gently as he could that Zak had been up to some difficult and dodgy business, that his two pals Yeshevsky and Dmitri had been pulled in by the Home Office and the UK Border Agency. He told her that he believed that they had been deported and that several others had been taken into custody, accused of transporting immigrants with a view to employing them in unpleasant and illegal situations. The words slavery and prostitution were used, and Gina, while shocked to hear such things, refused to believe that Zak had anything to do with this. However, it had preyed on her mind and in addition to her general distress, weighed heavily on her heart and was a source of serious torment. Her appetite had certainly suffered and she had been careless of her personal appearance.

Jim, however, knew more, and it was clear that Zak had indeed funded a large part of the operation, while at the same time, had been receiving huge payouts during the last few years. Seeing Gina looking so battered and shabby, he decided to spare her the worst of what he knew, and indeed, she asked for little more. But he did tell her that a great deal of Zak's fortune had been seriously depleted. At that time, Gina was dismissive of this, whether because she felt it was untrue, or because she genuinely didn't care, knowing that she had lots of money of her own. Either way, she merely shrugged.

'Good thing I spent a lot of it already, then,' she said rather bitterly. Jim was rather shocked to hear her say that, but he put it down to distress and anger, and chose to ignore it.

Some of this went through her mind now, as she accepted seconds of the perfectly cooked roast pork that Caro had prepared - She noticed that Dave and Chris ate huge platefuls and did not hold back when the pudding came. They drank large amounts of wine and later sampled the malt without much caution, either. She was not surprised that Dave had grown so large, but she noticed a similar expansion in girth in Christopher too. Caroline and Ben seemed to be much more restrained. How different we all are, Gina mused, and thought of Shafiq and Hanif and how Shaf was so like Zak - fiery, snappy, aggressive, but Han much calmer. Not even really just like herself, either, and she almost smiled at that thought. Zak used to call Han a wuss, and Gina had objected, but there was some truth in his observations. Oh dear, her poor boys; they missed him so much and Tanni did too, when she could get to grips with the idea that he really was never coming back.

Jolted from her musings by Caroline asking if she'd like more apple tart, she patted her tum and said:

'So full! Thank you, but no. It's been so good. You're a marvellous cook Caro!'

Slumped in huge chairs, later on, Gina found herself agreeing to Chris 'dropping in' on her at some time in the near future.

'I have business in Birmingham, so I'll call in and see how you're doing.' And despite herself, Gina gave him her address and he promised to call before he came.

'Don't want to just arrive - I might interrupt something,' he said, in what she later recalled as a rather lewd manner. There was certainly a smirk and she was somewhat troubled by what seemed to be an inappropriate time to make such an inappropriate remark. But of course she did not respond.

Driving home on a frosty, sunny afternoon, she reflected on his comment. It came as a shock for her to realise that he was coming on to her.

62

Less than a week later, back from a brief visit to Jo's, her phone rang. It was not a number she recognized, and because she had been getting several scam calls, she was not keen to answer but it looked like a regular mobile number so she picked up.

'Hi. I said I'd drop in, I'm not half a mile away - OK if I come over?' It was Chris.

He sounded friendly enough if rather cocky. Gina felt it would be churlish to say no, and anyway she didn't have an easy excuse, so she agreed and darted about the kitchen looking for biscuits, and set up the coffee machine.

He drove rather too fast up the drive, parked and strode to the door. Gina was welcoming and polite.

'Do come in. I've made coffee - or do you prefer -?'

'Oh, no,' he interrupted, 'coffee's great - thanks.' And he shook off his coat, which Gina hung up, and he perched, somewhat proprietorially, at the breakfast bar.

They chatted. During the conversation he referred again to the course she had paused with the Open University. She'd mentioned this during conversations at his parents' house.

'I'm thinking I might re-start,' Gina disclosed.

'Good idea. Tell me a bit more about it.'

Gina did. There was no doubting that Chris's understanding was excellent, and he clearly showed a fine appreciation of art. Of course his job as an associate architectural designer was no surprise. Somewhat self-interestedly, Gina wondered if he might be helpful or useful to her.

'I have my notes, my course-work - and stuff that I've been doing,' she began.

He wasn't quite as eager to tell her that he'd like to see her work as she had hoped, but after a moment or two, he said:

'Why don't you show me sometime - though I don't really have time just now.'

'Oh,' Gina was disappointed and yet she said:

'Thanks, yes, sometime, that would be helpful.' She tried to sound grateful.

And Christopher changed tack and asked in a vague sort of way about her family.

'How are the kids dealing with things?'

'Not brilliantly, my mother is a great comfort and my friends here help out. They deal with quite a lot of the emotional difficulties. To be honest, I'm not so good at that myself.'

'No, I don't suppose you can be - do you get out, see friends, take your mind off things?'

'No, not really.'

'Do you fancy a movie? Or we could go for a meal?'

'Maybe.' Gina felt cautious and also anxious, she could feel his interest and it made her feel quite uncomfortable. He was hitting on her, she knew that, but felt inadequate to deal with it. At the same time she craved company and also felt he could help her. She stalled.

'Well, you could call. You have my number. Perhaps,' she put a finger on her lip, 'no, er, no not next week,' she prevaricated, 'but the one after - maybe?'

And Chris said he would do that.

'Do you good,' he assured her, 'no point stressing.'

And Gina, though not happy with his approach supposed he was right, and they chatted a bit more in a desultory way, she responding off-handedly to his questions, and not really asking much about him. He had come rather too close for her comfort and she felt quite uneasy about his proximity, edging away when she could, trying not to give offence.

Finally he tapped his watch and he made ready to go, giving her an unwelcome hug, a damp kiss on the cheek and promising to call.

'Hey, Gina,' he said familiarly, as he shrugged on his coat, 'good to see you, I'll be in touch. Sorry to rush off - and thanks for coffee.'

He moved towards the door, Gina following and saying goodbye. Once in his car, he reversed and then rather messily came forward again before grinding through wet gravel and out to the road.

63

ZAK Redux

('Right. I'm not letting those guys just take my boat. I'm damned if I will. I'll go down there and I'm going to be part of the gig. Friday, need to let Gina know I guess. I'll collect a few blankets from the chest and just go. Gotta phone Yeshevsky - damn, need a better signal - as usual - best in the boot room.')

He parked the car carelessly, mud and stones spattering up from the flower bed, and he crashed into the room at the back of the house. He tapped his phone.

'Yeah, it's me. Yeah, I am. I'm going to leave soon. You all gotta wait for me. Yes, I have keys - you guys have one of the spare sets - but I'm...No! I'm not drunk - what do you mean I sound it?...I'm fine...No. No. I'll just tell her I'm going away for...she doesn't need to know where I'm...Oh, for fuck's sake Yeshevsky, stop making such a goddamned fuss, it's my boat and I'll do what I want. Yeah, yeah, I said I'd get blankets, sure, yes, the 4X4 - well she can just manage without - not my problem. Look I'm going into the living room, can't talk now. See you later.'

('Christ, it's dark in here - what is she doing? Writing her secrets again - what in hell has she got to write about, she does nothing!')

'Gina, it's dim in here,' he said. He switched on a light. Gina started.

'What? Oh yes.'

'Gina, sorry, but I'm going to see Yeshevsky and I'll be away for a few days, I'm going to pack a bag and I'm going to go tonight. We'll be collecting the boat.'

('Now we'll get the questions...yes, here we go - try to be patient with her...')

'I'll take the Jeep - it's got a heater.'*('Ha ha! She thinks it's going to be freezing. So what? Oh, and now she wants to know about Yeshevsky and I can't be bothered, what does it matter to her anyway? And now she's going on about the satnav, as if I need that - I know the way now.')*

'Gina - it's OK. I'll see you in a few days.'

('Wait for it...she's going to start telling me I should say goodbye to the kids - but no, seems to have lost interest - thank god for that. Right. Must get going - get the bag and the other stuff. Now, where does she keep the blankets?...Spare room - Ah, yes, here we are. OK, done. Toilet bag, yeah, couple of shirts, sweater, yep, those shoes, no, better take those; socks, pants. Enough. Better move. Car key, boathouse keys, yeah, all good. Bottle of vodka - yeah - that'll work, goes down well! Ha!

Right, seems to be enough petrol in there. Now, how do you work this thing? "Where to?" Yeah, there it is, "boat"! That's it. Take well over 2 hours even if I put my foot down. Better move fast.')

64

GINA

Chris was in his office, his sketches pushed to one side. He took up a well-sharpened pencil, and started sketching aimlessly - shaded circles, and then circles inside circles. He didn't even think about what he was doing, just continued scribbling and shading.

And then, on the instant, he picked up his phone. He turned it over and around in his hand. Maybe a text? Yes, that would be easier for her to deal with. She could think about his suggestion and reply at leisure. Now, what to ask?

Finally he came up with:

'free for dinner Thursday? call for u at 7-30? do u like Italian?'

Gina was somewhat surprised to get a text from Chris. Before replying she called Maggie.

Maggie's conclusion was that it seemed a bit weird

'Your first husband's son...I mean - Gina!'

'He's not related to me...'

'No, I know, but even so, isn't it a bit odd?'

'It's a date - you know - might be OK?'

'Isn't he a lot younger than you?'

'Oh, no, a couple of years, maybe three.'

'Really? But you said he was a bit creepy...'

'Oh, yeah, I know but maybe I wasn't used to - you know - that kind of thing.'

'What? Had you and Zak given up sex?' Maggie laughed.

'Well, not entirely, but it was when he fancied it, not when I did. To be honest, Mags, it was pretty horrible - I mean brutal, and rather random, I mean infrequent, so I wasn't exactly enjoying it. In fact I felt as though I was being...you know...'

'What?'

Gina held back from saying raped, he had been her husband after all, but she did pause.

'Oh, you know - used.' It was a lame finish, but she felt she couldn't say more.

'Why didn't you tell me any of this?'

'I did, didn't I?'

'No, you didn't, and I'm very upset to hear about it Gina, very! What was going on, what was he thinking?'

'Don't think he thought anything of it, don't think he thought about me at all.'

'Now, this sounds like a weepy - am I supposed to be listening like an agony aunt, or, in the light of events, is this all behind you now?'

'I still remember, Maggie - can't forget that sort of thing, not a great relationship if I'm honest.' Gina began to feel tears spill. She was glad Maggie couldn't see.

'I'm still not in a great place...'

'Sorry G. I can hear you're upset - didn't mean to...'

'No. It's OK Mags, I get a bit weepy now and then.'

'Well of course, and I shouldn't have...'

'No, it was me, I was asking about Chris and what to do. Still not sure if I should say yes.'

'So are you asking my advice?'

'Guess so.'

'Well, it can't hurt can it? You're a grown up, you can look after yourself can't you?'

'Guess so.'

'You don't sound sure. Do you want to meet him or not?'

'Oh, I guess so...'

'You're beginning to sound boring! Oh, god, give it a go, Gina, don't make any promises to yourself, or him, just have a fun night out - you probably need it.'

'Guess so.' She responded, predictably, and they both burst out laughing.

And Gina texted back to Chris to say that it would be nice, and yes, 7.30 was good, and Italian was great.

Chris was on time and Gina, who had dressed carefully - not provocatively, very modestly, in dark colours, slid into the passenger seat. He drove fast and, Gina thought, rather recklessly, to a well-known restaurant where they had a table reserved in a relatively quiet area. Truth to tell it was all rather noisy, but perhaps that was better than dull and quiet. Once they had ordered and had broached a bottle of wine, they loosened up a bit and began to chat.

'Tell me a bit about Zak - can you? Is it still very painful?'

'Oh, not really, well, yes it is a bit, but what can I tell you?'

'What did he do?'

'Oh. Jewellery trade, and gold and silver - stuff like that - he was in business with his father.'

'But hobbies? What did he like to do?'

'He'd bought a boat...'

'Really?'

'Yeah. Not that he was that good at handling it, but he had friends who...' and Gina paused remembering the horrible Yeshevsky and the unpleasant Dmitri.

'I think they just used him. His money. You know.'

'Ah. And what happened to the boat?'

'Well, that's a problem, because I don't know what to do with it. I know nothing about boats, I used to worry about...'

'Oh,' interrupted Chris, 'but I do. My grandfather lived on the Broads, and we spent loads of time on the water and in boats - It became second nature - maybe I can help? Where is it?'

And Gina told him, 'On the South coast, a little way from Southampton, takes about two hours to get there.'

'Can we go?'

'Oh, I don't know - it's, it's near where - you know, his accident...'

Chris nodded slowly and sympathetically, but said nothing. There was a somewhat awkward silence, broken by Gina saying:

'I'll think about it. Hmmm, maybe, not yet, but perhaps. I don't know. Not yet.'

'No, I understand. But if you want me to give you a hand with anything, let me know.'

And as the food arrived, they changed the subject and talked of other things.

Oddly, and to Gina's surprise, they actually got on rather well. He was, after all, something of an artist and certainly he had studied much of what Gina was now intent on studying for herself. He was surprisingly unpretentious in explaining some of the theories about colour and form that Gina found fascinating. He flicked his phone and showed her a picture by Hans Hoffman, and talked her through the colours he'd used.

'Never heard of him.' Gina admitted, and Chris went on to tell her about some of Hoffman's contemporaries and where their work might be seen. He even suggested that they might take a trip to look at some of his work, but since most of these locations were all in America, Gina was a bit disdainful of this idea, and laughed at Chris, saying that she couldn't contemplate such a thing.

'Well where would you contemplate?'

Gina looked startled. She was surprised that he should assume that she'd go anywhere with him. How had she managed to convey that impression? Or maybe he was just being overly presumptuous? In either case, she was twitchy with the idea and it was only when Chris again referred to visiting the boat, that she felt more at ease and able to discuss such a possibility, more calmly.

'Why don't you check your diary?' Chris asked. 'We could make it a pleasant little trip.'

'Oh, I don't know. Though it's true I do have to do something about it and probably sooner rather than later,' she ended lamely.

'Well, we could meet up again - another meal maybe?'

'Look, why don't you come over again and we can have a chat. I'll sort out some times, for maybe when it's a bit warmer. Come and have supper - I can cook a bit.' She giggled modestly.

'Great, I'll leave it to you to suggest a date,' Chris said, checking the menu. 'Fancy a pud?'

65

It took more than two weeks for Gina to find the emotional energy to resolve her decision. She had thanked him for the meal very soon after, but had made no mention of a new date.

At the start of the third week, however, she felt that it was churlish to ignore what had, after all, been a generous offer, and certainly she needed some advice and help with the disposal of the boat. She sent him a note to ask him to come a week later, a Friday night, and he very quickly responded positively, thanking her for asking.

Jo had just brought the boys back and she told her of this plan. Naturally, Jo was aware of all that had passed between them.

'But he's never shown any impropriety, has he?' Jo asked. Gina laughed,

'Do you mean is he hitting on me? Well, I guess that's in there somewhere - bound to be, hey?'

'Can you handle him?'

'Think so - though he's a bit smug - arrogant. Bit of a know-all, but mind you, he's good on the art - been quite helpful. I'm going to get him to look at some of my stuff.'

'Well, watch yourself!' Was Jo's advice and Gina smiled. Actually she didn't feel too threatened by Christopher Wilson, and in an odd sort of way began to plan for the dinner with some pleasure. She did toy with the idea of asking someone else, another couple, but decided not to. Maybe she felt it would be rude to Chris or maybe the cooking challenge was a bit too great, but either way, she planned for just the two of them. She remembered Jo's warning words - watch yourself - and she hooted - perhaps a bit of sex was just what she needed!

On the Thursday before his visit, she prepared a soup and a simple pie for dessert, buying ready-made pastry not wanting to risk a disaster, and she also bought two excellent steaks, with Rayna's help. Tony suggested some wine, she bought salad, and Marina came with a table decoration. Tony offered to make a salad dressing 'My speciality,' he averred! She accepted. She tasted. It was excellent.

'Have you got candles?' Marina asked. This resulted in some scrabbling around in cupboards, but a couple were located and all was made ready; she was rather nervous as Friday arrived.

* * *

Gina assumed that it was because it was so long since she had had anything like a real date that she was so anxious, so apprehensive and tense. The cooking was not, now, a worry. She would enlist Chris to help in the preparation of the meat - he could decide when it was ready, and no blame could then be apportioned to her for cooking it too much or too little. She had vegetables ready to go, and she had set the table with care. It looked lovely. She worried only that it looked a bit too romantic and that he would misread this, but then she shrugged and decided better to have it look pleasant rather than unattractive and careless. She recalled how much Caroline had tried to make her welcome, and she just felt she should do the same for one of her family.

It turned out to be a very pleasant evening. Their conversation ranged from global issues to local politics, from the cult of celebrity to the role of reality shows on TV, from natural disasters to the way aid and help is operated for refugees. When Gina heard some of Chris's indignation at the treatment of certain asylum seekers, she was reminded of the incident at her own home when Zak permitted Yeshevsky's cousin to let his daughters stay in their house. Or that's who he said they were. She had no idea if it had been true and she felt dismal and sad that she had not followed it up at the time. Truth to tell, she had been significantly afraid both of what appeared to be going on and also of the possible knock-on effect on her and the children. She spoke of none of this to Chris.

Towards the end of the evening, after she had made coffee and they were comfortable in the armchairs, she decided to bring up the subject of her work. More relaxed together now, she felt relatively comfortable in asking him for help.

'Would you mind? Giving it a read?'

'Sure, let's have a look.'

Rather nervously, Gina stood and walked to the big sideboard where she had left her work. She could not see the heap of papers she had left. But then she recalled that Rayna had been tidying and she searched around, and found the pile. She brought it over and set it on the coffee table.

Chris stood up and walked towards her, he picked up the top pamphlet, set it down, reached for the next, read a bit of it, but Gina said 'There's a piece here,' and pulled out an item she had written with which she'd been quite pleased. 'Look at this.'

He shuffled round and was now slightly too close for Gina to feel quite at ease. He breathed heavily; she could hear him and even felt his breath on her neck. Too close, she thought and squirmed a little. She really felt somewhat awkward and wasn't sure how to deal with the situation. He was her guest, she had asked for some opinions, some ideas from him, so to react brusquely would be ungracious. Rather than simply retreat, she moved, if a little abruptly, saying:

'Must go to the bathroom - would you mind having a read? Back in a tic.'

Gina decided to go upstairs in order to buy a little more time to compose herself and think through her next move, which would probably need to be evasive. She certainly had not liked the proximity of Chris and his large, somewhat sweaty body, and felt it was rather presumptuous of him to assume that his behaviour was acceptable. She was not in any doubt that he was making a move, and she really didn't like it, especially not given the inherent relationship that they had. She stood pondering in the bathroom, rubbing an idle finger at a smear on the bathtub.

Christopher sat down and glanced casually at Gina's draft. It seemed fine; well written so far as he could tell, from a brief read of the first two sentences, which moved into the subject quickly and with immediate relevance. He skimmed through a page or two, nodded, and decided he didn't really need to read much more than that - obviously a smart woman - no worries there. Somewhat lazy by nature, Chris left the paper on the table and quite disinterestedly, leafed through the rest of the pile. A battered journal caught his eye. He tugged it from the pile, opened it randomly and began to read. Within a few seconds he was riveted to the page and could hardly believe what he was seeing. Despite the somewhat insinuating language that was used and rather cryptic allusions, it was not difficult to discern what was going on here and he breathed out a ragged breath. To be fair, nothing was explicit, but Chris thought he could see exactly what must have happened on that night when his father went to the meat plant and then called Gina... And if this wasn't a confession, well, what was it?

He heard Gina's footsteps approaching, and he briskly stuffed the journal into the lower part of the pile.

When she came into the room he was already on his feet.

'Gina, I've just seen the time and I really should go.'

'What did you think?' Gina asked, 'of the draft, I mean.'

'Yeah. Good. You've got it! - Right on the money,' he said, and Gina smiled.

'Thanks.' She was pleased, and relieved that he seemed to be no longer flirting with her or maybe it was just that he realised he was late, either way, she was able to relax with him a bit and added:

'That's kind of you, I appreciate you looking at it. You must know plenty about the subject.'

'Er, yeah, yes, but hey, er, I'll be in touch. Sorry to rush off - and thanks for dinner.'

He went to get his coat and then moved towards the door, Gina following and saying goodbye. He offered her a brief peck on each cheek, and once in his car, he reversed and then rather messily came forward again before struggling through the gravel and out of the gates.

Gina went slowly back into the sitting room, sorry that she had not had a chance to make some plans with him regarding the issue with the boat. She had hoped to set up a trip, but that hadn't happened and she wondered now if he ever would.

She scooped all her papers together and pushed them all into the big file box, which in turn went into the lower part of the sideboard. She sighed, stacked the dishes into the dishwasher, cleared away the rest of the dinner paraphernalia, and scraped the unfinished leftovers into the bin. What had she expected from tonight? She had been fearful of having to fend him off, and here she was, alone early, with no suggestion of any impropriety and she realised that her jokey thoughts about sex earlier in the week, had been real.

66

It was two weeks before Chris got to contacting Gina again. In the meantime, Gina had begun to wonder if he ever would. He had texted her:

'Still thinking about the trip to boat?'

'Can we take kids?'

'Better not.'

She had wondered at this. Was he still interested in her, and thus needed to be alone with her? Or was it something else?

They made plans. He would call for her and they would drive down one weekday, when Chris could combine it with a stop in Winchester, where he had a client.

'We can have lunch there; I know a good place. And you might want to bring a swimsuit.'

'No thanks - it's still too cold to swim, and I'm not that good in the water, but lunch in Winchester sounds great, and that - that's the way we, I, went - A34... we never stopped - took a packed lunch.'

'I'd need to leave you in the town for a bit...'

'No problem, I'll be fine. So, I'll bring a bite for coming back, shall I?'

'Can do, sure.'

It was a pleasant, bright day when they left, spring was in the air, and daffodils bloomed on the roadside. They talked on a variety of subjects. Chris had opinions that often brooked no challenge, and on the whole, Gina was happy to let him chat on, offering an occasional affirming remark, or a very modest challenge, along the lines of

'Oh do you think so?' and more often than not, Chris would point out why he was so sure and certain of his ideas. He didn't ask much about her or what she had done with her life and for this she was grateful. But she wished he could show a little more interest in the children, her family or her course.

She asked him about his time in Norfolk. He told a long rambling tale of life with Grandpa, which kept him content for a while, and

Gina was amused to notice how pleased with the sound of his own voice he really was. But the journey therefore passed comfortably enough and they arrived in Winchester for lunch, and before that for his business meeting, in good time.

Gina wandered around the shops for an hour or so, starting in the Brooks shopping area close to where Chris had parked and near to where he was meeting with his client, but moving to Parchment Street, where the shopping was more to her taste. Here, she spent most of her time investigating jewellery, and making one or two purchases. She met up with Chris at 1.00, in his chosen restaurant, where they selected lunch and shortly after continued to the shore.

In little under another hour they had reached the road at the back of the beach. At the point close to the accident, Gina had gestured and muttered something with the word accident in it, and Chris had understood, driving on with no other comment and reaching the shore soon after.

'What...?' he began at that point, but Gina flapped a hand, pursed her lips and shook her head. Instead she turned and pointed to the boat moored a little offshore.

'There. That's our boat,' she said.

Chris nodded. He liked it, Gina could tell.

'Stern drive,' he nodded approvingly, 'why is it called "Rosemarie"?'

'I actually don't know - nobody said.'

'Is there a dinghy?'

'Oh, yeah, here's the keys.'

And they crunched together to the boathouse from where the little rubber boat was deployed in getting them to the larger boat in the deep water.

Once on board, Chris trundled about looking at its features, opening boxes and seat covers that Gina had never bothered to do. She was surprised by some of the contents.

'Deck quoits, or something approximating to...' he announced.

'Oh, yes, well, we've played that - made up the rules a bit, I think - but it's good fun.'

Chris was scrabbling in one box seat, when it seemed that he had found what he'd been looking for.

'Look! Fishing rods. And lines.'

'The kids wanted to, but I think it got squally, so I'm not sure we ever got around to it, maybe once.'

'Shame, there are plenty of fish in this area.'

'Really?'

'Sure, very good location, always mackerel, and probably bass too. Want to try?'

'Oh, no, I don't think I'd be any good. I don't know how.'

'Gina, you bait a hook, drop a line and wait...'

'Surely not just as simple as that?'

'Can be. Shall I show you how?'

'Well...'

'Actually, since we don't have any live bait, we'll make do with this bread from our home-going snack - is that OK? And there's a tin of crab...'

Gina burst out laughing. 'Never,' she said 'that can't work.'

'Who knows?' Chris responded. 'But you need to know a bit about how to do it anyway, so it doesn't matter if you catch anything or not.'

He got a rod and line ready and attached a bit of bread to the end. He didn't so much cast it into the water as just sling it over the side of the boat and let it land in the water. He reeled it back in and handed it to Gina.

'You do it.'

'OK,' Gina said, and actually quite dexterously hurled it back into the sea.

'I've got a bite,' she squealed at once.

'No you haven't. It's just snagged on the weed.' And it was with some difficulty that Chris disentangled her line and pulled it back.

'We could be in a better place,' he explained, 'we could move from here and not get into a tangle.'

'Can you start the boat?'

'Don't see why not - let's go see.'

And to be fair to Chris, he certainly seemed to have the skill and expertise to get it going at second try and within a few moments they were gently chugging away from the coast. The little island came into view, and Gina became agitated.

'Don't!' She sounded distressed. 'Please don't go there - had a bad experience there.' And he was happy to steer away and move towards the horizon.

'This all right?'

'Yeah, yes, that's fine, I just - there was - you know - it was, oh - a while back - can we not - you know- discuss?'

And Chris obligingly moved beyond and ahead, until it was almost out of sight.

Gina continued to fling the line over the side of the boat, when Chris suggested that she might do better if she stood towards the stern.

'Know what the stern is?'

Gina affected offence and said:

'Course I do,' and moved there. She tried the fishing line again.

'Just leave it sitting there for a bit.'

'OK.'

'Keep an eye - if it stretches, you might have a bite.'

'OK.' Gina seemed intent on the task.

After a few minutes, Chris announced that he was going below.

'Little bit worried about a bit of a leak I spotted. I'll investigate,' he announced. 'I don't think it'll be a problem, but I might need to start the engine. Don't be alarmed.'

And he pottered down, leaving Gina practising her casting, or rather her throwing, and he sat thoughtfully by the wheel, watching the rippling sea, the occasional wave breaking with a splash, far off and not seen.

As if on an impulse he twiddled something and then started the engine. There was a great roar, and the boat leapt forward with jolt.

He heard a scream. A splash. He did not stop the now racing engine, but pulled the boat round fast and hard to observe splashing in the otherwise calm water. He hopped up to the deck. Gina was not there. He returned to the wheel and swung the boat again. It seemed that he was looking for her in the water, but he did not see her. He saw a bright red flash - she had been wearing a red woollen sweater - maybe her? He took off his jacket and folded it on the deck, then climbed over the side and dropped into the water. He saw nothing. A strong swimmer, he circled and searched, still nothing. After a further minute or two, he returned to the side of the boat and hauled himself back on board, and again set the boat in rapid motion, circling and searching and seeing nothing.

It took a few more minutes for Chris to find his phone and call for the emergency services, and almost as quickly, he heard the noisy yellow Westlands of the air-sea rescue team arrive in response to his urgent call. Seeing no sign of a body, the team dropped two rescue swimmers into the water and a further search ensued.

During this period, Chris was being attended by paramedics and wrapped in blankets to guard against hypothermia. He was given warm drinks and eventually he was escorted back to shore and to the local hospital.

It was his father and his brother Ben, who came the following day to collect him, and for his father to drive Chris's car back to Clipston. It was assumed that Chris was in shock and the family, solicitously concerned, was helpful and supportive in the next few weeks.

Of course there was an inquest, where Chris told the court of the events preceding her fall. He supposed that she had been over-ambitious in casting the line. He explained that he had not been there when she fell, but he'd heard a scream, and had raced up to see what had happened. Realising that she had gone overboard, he dashed back to the helm and set the boat in motion, slowly turning the craft and searching for her. He then had dived into the water in an attempt to find her, but failing to locate her he climbed back on board and immediately alerted the emergency services.

A postmortem determined that the cause of death was drowning. The coroner returned a verdict of death by misadventure, describing it as a very tragic incident, and after initial excited attention from the national and local media, the affair faded from interest.

* * *

And for Christopher Wilson?
He felt he had found some closure.

26093366R00131

Printed in Great Britain
by Amazon